A BETTER WAY TO KILL

RICK BUSH

INVERTED PUBLISHING

For Natalie

A BETTER WAY TO KILL

ABOUT THE AUTHOR

1

DEAD MEN DON'T PAY

The addition of bullet holes had irreparably transformed the sleek curves of the rented Audi i5, which caused the car to whistle as it sped past the Imperial Business and Estate Park in Gravesend, Kent. With one flat tyre and another deflating fast, Jason Blaine had to find somewhere to stop. His agent had rented the car under a false identity, and though Blaine loathed leaving any tracks behind, this one was a necessity.

When the brakes pressed against the wheels, and the exhausted vehicle came to a halt, the left tyre fell apart, leaving a trail of melted rubber in its tracks.

Quickly, Blaine stepped out of the car and looked at the surrounding empty buildings next to the river. His dark-blue eyes and defined features gave Blaine an immediate sense of authority. His dark hair lay gelled back over his head, and the long single-breasted cashmere coat he wore hinted at a background of private school education.

His years in the SAS had kept his mind sharp, and within moments, a plan had formed. At this time of night, there wouldn't be a soul for miles; he could hole up in the factory opposite, bottleneck his assailants, and take them down one by one. This all hinged on there being only one way into the building, however, but this risk, he had to take.

'Get out of the car.' Blaine slammed his door shut and made his way around to the passenger side, where the client eased open his door and tried to exit the smoking vehicle in haste. He got caught on his still-fastened seatbelt. With his right hand, which featured a small silver ring on his little finger, Blaine held the door wide for him, as the client fiddled with the release button.

Blaine looked up past the roof of the car when the sound of screeching tyres drew closer. They must have seen him turn onto this road; in only a matter of seconds, they would be in line of sight. He pulled the Sig P229 out of his hip holster and held it in his hand, pointing down to the ground. His trigger finger rested alongside the trigger guard.

The client stumbled his way out of his seat, and Blaine grabbed his arm and hurried him toward the large factory. The client's name was Peterson, though Blaine preferred to avoid using names whenever possible. In his mid-fifties, he wore glasses that pinched his nose, leaving red marks around the bridge whenever he took them off. He had a single sports bag with him, which clashed with his expensive business suit and coat. It had never left his grasp from the moment Blaine had picked him up at Gatwick airport.

Blaine had been working on a bigger job for the past few weeks already; a contract on an investment banker's life. A straight-up hit meant more cash in his pocket and detailed research. Blaine's agent, Tommy, had sold him this contract as a simple armed escort job; not to expect any kind of trouble.

'An easy ten grand in your pocket, Blaine,' he had told

4

him, beaming that smile that seemed to repeat in the wrinkles of his face. Blaine had grown used to Tommy stretching the truth, but whenever his life was on the line, Tommy always spoke straight and made sure every piece of intel got double checked.

The gun-toting hit-squad that had started following them as soon as they passed the M25 had made for a worrying surprise for both him and the client. Blaine had to outmanoeuvre the chasing car while listening to him explain that he *didn't think they'd go this far.*

'In here,' Blaine said and kicked in a back door. Outside, a car screeched to a halt, and bright headlights filled the wall next to them. Blaine shoved the client inside and moved into the shadows. He could smell the sweat on the client's face. Though sheepish and jumpy, he seemed happy to take any orders.

'Absolute silence,' Blaine said. 'Don't move.' He moved away from the client until he couldn't hear his whimpering. Only the lowered voice of one of the two men making their way to the back door could be noticed while he spoke on his phone quietly, giving the building's address. It meant more of them were on the way.

Two men in black jackets inched inside the doorway with their suppressed semi-automatics drawn. Professionally, they covered each other as they moved past the machinery and stacks of cardboard sheets.

Blaine prepared himself while the two men made their way toward the edge of the large stack of cardboard he hid behind. As soon as the end of the suppressor poked around the corner, Blaine grabbed it, pushing it up, and shoved the mercenary in front into the man behind.

Blaine still had hold of the weapon as he brought his knee

up into the merc's chest as hard as he could, knocking the wind out of him. Then he aimed the suppressed gun at the man on the floor and pushed his finger onto the trigger. With two loud pops, the man's chest burst with plumes of blood. The smell of cordite hung in the air. Blaine grappled with the remaining merc and knocked the gun from his hands. It slid across the cold, hard factory floor, and Blaine got a punch to the face, which took him by surprise. The merc scrambled across the ground after his weapon. Blaine drew his pistol from his hip holster once more and put two bullets into the man's shoulder. Involuntarily, the man dropped the gun and cried out in pain. Blaine had hoped to avoid any gunfire at all, but with the car chase through Kent and the gunfire through Gravesend, the police couldn't be far away. He stamped on the man's bleeding shoulder, pushing him against the cold factory floor. The man let out another cry of pain while Blaine rustled through his jacket and pulled out his phone. Hastily, he went through his last calls and contact list.

'Who hired you?' Blaine stared at him. 'Who's your client?' Apart from a little whimpering, the man remained silent. Outside, headlights approached. No sirens. He unloaded another bullet into the man's left leg.

'Uuugh ... Parker! His name's Parker.' Blaine found the name in his phone and showed the screen to him.

'This Parker?'

'Yes.'

Blaine put a bullet in his head, pressed his thumb to the de-cocking lever on the side of his gun, and holstered it.

Two vehicles pulled up outside, and several men made their way to the back door.

Blaine grabbed the client and led him further into the

building and through a door, which led to a staircase. While they climbed the steps, Blaine could hear the men entering the factory.

At the end of the hall, Blaine opened the door to the office and pushed the client inside. Then, with care, he closed the door, ensuring not to make any sound. The office was, obviously, used by a manager of some kind. Decked out in nice carpet, it held a desk that looked expensive.

'I think I'm going to be sick,' the client said.

'Use the bathroom.' Blaine pointed at the en suite at the back of the room. The client held his hand to his mouth and shut himself inside the lavatory.

Blaine took out his phone and speed dialled a contact. After a single ring, the call answered.

'Tommy? It's Blaine,' he said, keeping his voice down. 'There's no way I can get him to the location. I've got a squad closing in and estimate we have about three minutes until we're both dead. I'm sending you the name and number of their client.' Blaine forwarded the contact details from the dead man's phone. 'See if you can get the contract.'

'You're sure about this?' came the reply from Tommy. The usual wit remained noticeably absent from his tone.

'Dead men don't pay,' Blaine said. 'Unless you're paid to kill them.'

'Stay on the line,' Tommy replied, and Blaine could hear him dialling a number frantically on another phone. Outside the office, sounds of footsteps and doors opening reached him, and a single voice gave commands. The door to the stairs opened, and the voice ordered a few men to follow him. Blaine unholstered his gun and held it in his hand, ready.

'I'm going to need an answer now,' he whispered into the phone. On the other line, Tommy tried to make the deal.

'Mr Parker, this is a one-time only deal,' Tommy said. 'If you need this man dead, this is the only way it will happen.' Footsteps crept along the hallway, and the first office door at the top of the stairs slammed after someone kicked it in during the search.

'Tommy?' Blaine said, still waiting for a response. The footsteps exited the searched office, headed back into the hallway, and collected outside the next door along. Blaine waited for the sound of the door getting kicked in.

The flush of the toilet stopped every footstep outside, and Blaine watched as the client walked out of the en suite, calmly wiping his hands on a sheet of rough, blue paper. He froze as soon as he saw Blaine staring at him, phone pressed against his ear. Blaine couldn't quite believe the man could be so stupid. Did he forget about the crew of armed men trying to kill him? Or did he welcome the inevitable? Either way, the client had sealed his fate.

'Got it,' Blaine said. While the footsteps gathered around the door, only meters from him, Blaine raised his gun at the client and put two bullets through his chest and one in his head.

The door burst open, and the squad commander and his men stepped inside, brandishing their weapons. Blaine stood over the dead body of the client. His gun holstered, he took a picture with his phone and sent the image to Tommy.

The squad commander lowered his gun, and a smile fell on his face when Blaine looked over at him. He recognised him from his time in Kosovo; Matt Cable, known in the freelance mercenary world as a hot head. A blunt instrument used if you wanted to send a point. All he knew was killing and guns without a thought of consequences.

'Son of bitch,' Cable said.

Blaine, nice and calm, pocketed the phone, unsure if Cable had recognised him too, and walked past the armed mercenaries. They wouldn't engage him in gunplay. The only reason they'd come here was for the money. And now Blaine had taken that away from them, their main objective became to vacate the area before the police arrived. Even Cable with his temper could see that. Police sirens wailed in the distance. Blaine walked along the docks next to the river. The water looked black, even under the moonlight, as Blaine pulled the battery out of his cheap phone and threw both parts into the cold, dark depths.

Alone, Blaine walked toward Gravesend station and caught the eleven-eighteen train to Woolwich, where he hailed a passing cab. While the vehicle crossed London Bridge, he watched out of his window. The lights of London city filled his view. He guessed most people out there would be in bed by now, watching TV, snuggled up to their partners, readying themselves for another day at work. Blaine had never felt comfortable in the daytime; he believed it a place for the rest of the world. Blaine felt at home stood on a rooftop at three in the morning, looking out over the city, surrounded by silence, and with only himself for company. He had always felt distant from everyone else; never able to figure out what they were thinking or feeling. He thought them quite odd.

That night's contract lay heavy on his mind. He had noticed a change in his attitude toward the job. It had been quite a while since he'd had to engage in combat like that. Usually, he preferred to avoid any unnecessary violence, as it brought attention to him. Anonymity was his friend, and he had just let a room full of mercenaries see his face. Maybe, after this next job, it would be time for a change of scenery.

2

DATE WITH DEATH

Blaine had awoken later than expected; most days, he would set an alarm and head out for an early morning jog, but after last night's activities, he had allowed himself a lie in. His body needed it too. His muscles ached, and his face felt swollen. The punch from the mercenary had landed hard and, although his skin hadn't gone black or blue, it had definite redness. A bruised face tends to stand out in a crowd, and Blaine couldn't afford that. Not tonight.

The apartment, one of twelve, sat within a converted church on Junction Road in North London. With the area not particularly upmarket, when he walked to the local shop for cigarettes or milk he would often pass a homeless man wandering around or a strange woman with worn out shoes, who had a glossed-over look on her face and absolutely stank of B.O. The apartment itself felt sublime. The church windows proved huge, and he liked to recline on the wide window sills, blowing out smoke into the night air.

He rented, of course. In his line of work, he had to be prepared to drop everything at a moment's notice and leave the country as a wanted man. However, he had been cautious with his job and considered himself the best in the business. The apartment, though practical for work and presented immaculately, had begun to feel small. He had often thought about investing his money in some property in the country; an estate, with open fields and a pool house. Maybe he would even start a family? In his early twenties, he'd wanted that, but now he'd reached his thirties, the idea had drifted from his priorities. Girlfriends had come and gone, and in all honesty, he never took any of his relationships that seriously. No-one ever seemed good enough. Blaine wouldn't settle down truly until he got out of this industry. He couldn't have it both ways.

By midday, Blaine sat on his large corner sofa with the TV on, watching a superhero show. One of the few programs he watched to help switch off his brain. His phone had messages from Tommy and one from Kelly, a girl he chatted with on an online dating website. He replied to both parties in quite different tones. Tommy had told him that he'd managed to get the kill contract for Peterson at a greatly reduced price and that he would put the money along with Blaine's other investments that Tommy looked after.

Kelly would meet him that night in Leicester Square, and Blaine had planned out the first pub to which they would head. She had left a message asking if he remained okay to meet. He smiled when he read it; the text meant she felt nervous and needed him to take charge of the evening; just how he needed it. For the past month, Blaine had researched this job, gaining his target's weekly routine and daily habits. After last night's debacle and Tommy's messages this morning, Blaine had to make sure that tonight happened as planned.

Blaine sat at a table in the middle of The Two Brewers pub just off the Five Dials near Covent Garden. He nursed his pint of Peroni, which clinked against his ring on his smallest finger. Opposite him sat Kelly with her bright red drink in front of her, which had a curled strand of lime peel bobbing about in the liquid. The cocktail list had impressed him, and their expansive collections of spirits. Also, it gave him a pleasant surprise to find how better looking Kelly proved than her pictures had suggested. He put it down to bad lighting in the photos, or maybe she had gone the extra effort with her makeup tonight. Either way, it amused him that he had tried to dress down with the black spectacles covering his eyes and his hair put into a conservative side parting. He wanted to blend into the crowd as much as possible. Kelly's hair, a light brown with blonde highlights, she had spent a while curling until her locks cascaded over her shoulders with a slight bounce every time she turned her head. The slight wrinkles around her dark-green eyes gave away a truthfulness to her smile, and Blaine could only assume that his looks pleased her as well. The bruise on his face, he had covered up with some minor makeup and, in the dim lighting of the pub, he felt sure that no-one would notice. The spectacles also helped cover any sign of a recent fight.

The place ended up rather busy; full of city workers, still in their business suits, laughing and joking. The background hum of the other patrons didn't overpower their conversation. Kelly took another tiny sip of her florescent drink.

'It's so good,' she said, smiling. 'It kinda tastes like ...

well, sort of fruity. Not alcoholic at all. Give it a try.' She pushed the cocktail glass across the table toward Blaine, who smiled back at her and took it in his hand.

'I don't want to take all your drink. It's only small compared to my pint.'

'Oh, I drink slowly. Two drinks and I'm stumbling down the road. What a cheap date!'

Blaine smiled once more and took a small amount into his mouth. He knew just what to expect, of course, as he'd drunk every kind of cocktail there was and even invented a few. Blaine, cautious, took care not to drink too much before he made his move.

'Well, it tastes good.' Blaine handed her drink back. 'Secretly, I love girly drinks.'

'Oh, really?'

'I don't think beer would have been invented if they'd discovered cosmopolitans first.'

Kelly chuckled and fingered her glass. 'So, how long have you been on the website?'

'Oh ... about four months or so,' Blaine said. His stock answer if asked that question. 'How about you?'

'About a year and a half on and off.'

She seemed almost embarrassed, and Blaine wondered why she would bring up the subject if it would only make her feel awkward about it.

'Any luck?' he asked.

'Obviously not. I dated one guy for a while, but it turns out, he was a bit of a dick. Most guys on there are just looking for a fuck.'

Her choice of words startled him, as she seemed so clean cut and sheepish.

'Sorry, I swear like a trooper. I try not to.'

Blaine smiled, pleasantly surprised at her candidacy. 'Honestly, it's fine,' he said. 'We can both swear. We're grown-ups, in a grown-up place, and we'll fucking swear if we cunting well want to.'

Kelly let out a yelp of a laugh, and several other customers turned to look at them. Stupid. This date was supposed to be low key. Blaine couldn't afford anyone keeping an eye on him. He hid his disgruntled demeanour behind a false smile and another sip of his expensive beer. Briefly, he gazed over at the group of five men stood at the back of the bar. Blaine singled out the one in the snazzy tie and could just about hear him boasting to his colleagues about money.

Blaine had watched his target come to this specific pub after work every Thursday evening. Always, he would buy the first round of drinks, openly displaying the wads of twenties in his wallet. Did one of the very men in his company right now want him dead so badly they'd pay for it? Unlikely; whoever the client was, they had offered a ten percent bonus if it looked unsuspicious.

'So, what does a business consultant do?' Kelly said.

Blaine had put that down as his profession on the dating website and, as far as the tax man knew, that *was* his job. A strictly on-line business with no offices or assets, Rogue Fire Consulting provided a front that allowed him to seem like a legitimate business consultant with money and taxes, all above board.

'Well ...' Blaine said. 'A company will hire me to help them with a problem they have. I look at their business and give them solutions.' The reply he gave didn't fall far from the truth. Rarely did he get paid to kill someone; perhaps once a year. The rest of the work entailed intimidation, high-risk debt collection, and a few more militant jobs overseas. The requests had lessened over the past couple of years, and contracts like this had become few and far between. Tommy had put it down to a flooded market and that the never-ending war on terror didn't have the same job opportunities as an actual war had for mercenaries like himself.

'You sound like a dull Sherlock Holmes,' Kelly said, holding back a giggle and taking another tiny sip of her drink.

Already, Blaine had drunk half of his pint. 'Yes,' he said. 'I am. You're right.' His target finished his drink, and one of his colleagues pulled out his wallet.

'Same again, guys?' the businessman said. 'Steve?'

The target said, 'Yeah, another pint of mild, please, pal.' And his colleague headed to the bar.

Blaine downed the rest of his Peroni and looked over at Kelly's two-thirds-full glass of cosmopolitan. 'Another?' he said. 'There's this great cocktail I invented a few years ago; I'd love for you to try it.'

'Oh, yeah ... okay,' Kelly said, a little shocked that she had been rushed to finish her first drink.

Blaine took his empty glass to the bar and stood next to the businessman, who ordered five drinks. After a few moments of waiting, the other barman asked Blaine for his order.

'One part Midori, one part Triple Sec, juice of one lemon, and two tablespoons of cherry syrup,' Blaine said.

'Triple Sec? Okay, let me just see if we have that,' the barman said.

Blaine looked over at the businessman's drinks. Two sat on the bar, and the mild ale for the target was on its way.

'Yeah, okay, we've got that,' the barman said. 'Never

heard of that cocktail.'

'I recommend it,' Blaine said with a smirk.

'Anything else?'

Blaine watched the pint of mild get set down just to the right of him. He pretended to look over the choice of beers they had on tap and raised his right hand so that it hovered above the dark, foamy pint. Then he pointed at a beer tap while pressing his thumb hard into the back of the ring on his little finger. A quick shot of liquid squirted out of the metal band and into the top of the ale.

'And a pint of Peroni, please,' Blaine said. He brought his hand back into his pocket and wiped off any excess liquid against the fabric of his trousers. Straight-faced, he watched the barman pour the bright green liquid of the Midori into a measuring cup and then into the shaker, quickly followed by the clear liquid of the orange liqueur. Next to him, the businessman had received all his drinks and handed over his cash. He picked up a couple of lagers and took them over to his colleagues while the barman handed Blaine his unique cocktail.

Kelly looked rather impressed with her new drink when Blaine set it down in front of her along with his pint of Peroni. He glanced at the businessman, taking another pint of lager and the ale over to the men. He tripped over a bag on the floor and managed to spill the top two centimetres of alcohol from the target's pint onto the patterned carpet.

'Oh, you div,' the target said and took the pint glass from him. Blaine had two options. He could hope the poison hadn't settled in the head of the beer and let it all play out as planned. The concentrated liquid he used was designed to rest in the target's system for 72 hours before activating and killing the victim as he slept. Too little a dose would cause a severe stomach upset and an explosive case of what would seem like food poisoning.

Alternatively, he could administer another shot of poison, using the same method. This would double his risk of getting caught in the act, and also, he could give the target a double dose by accident, causing him to die in the middle of the pub that evening. Neither seemed ideal, and Blaine couldn't quite believe the amount of trouble that could come from a simple spilled pint. Blaine realised Kelly had seen him staring, though she remained unaware of how serious that simple spillage could have been.

She turned to see what all the fuss was about. The men laughed about the spilt drink. Kelly turned back to Blaine with a smirk. 'Some people just can't hold their drink.'

The orgasm came long and intense, and Kelly's leg twitched while she arched her back, and Jason pushed against her. As he lay next to her sweating body, which still tingled with pleasure, he dealt with the condom, tying a knot in the end. It always amused her when guys did that—as though they were putting a lock on their sperm and eliminating the chance of anyone getting their hands on their precious baby-making fluid.

'Oh, that was good.' Kelly stretched every one of her limbs. 'My legs are shaking.'

Jason leant over and picked up the ashtray that they had knocked onto the floor. She didn't care about the mess it had made. In fact, she remembered laughing out loud when her bedside lamp nearly followed it, and Jason had managed to catch it before it hit the ground. He rummaged around in his jacket on the floor, which she hoped hadn't gotten covered in too much ash, and pulled out a packet of cigarettes. With a silver Zippo, he lit one and laid back, looking relaxed.

Kelly glanced over at him, expecting him to offer her a cigarette, but as he lay there, blowing smoke up to the ceiling, a feeling of discomfort washed over her. She didn't know this man at all, and here he was, lying next to her in bed, in her home. Kelly ignored the feeling and sat up.

'Ooh, I need a wee,' she said and got up to leave the room. Jason kept staring at the ceiling.

Kelly sat on the toilet, pulled a few sheets of toilet paper from the roll, wiped, and flushed. While she washed her hands, she looked at her messy hair in the mirror. Then she grabbed the mouthwash, which sat on the side of the basin, took a quick swig, and spat out the blue liquid. She gave her hair a quick tidy and left the bathroom.

With a sly smile on her face, and naked confidence, Kelly walked back into the bedroom. Her bed stood empty, and Jason's clothes had gone. His cigarette still smouldered away on the edge of her ashtray, on the bedside table.

3

FAMILY VALUES

Julie watched Nick aim his metal replica BB gun at the cereal packet he had placed above the fireplace and fire. The 6mm plastic yellow ball hit the cute cartoon monkey right in the face and tore a hole through the back of the cardboard. The ball ricocheted off the wall behind it and landed somewhere on the ground near Julie and their eight-year-old daughter, Jessica.

'Would you stop shooting that thing inside the house,' Julie said. 'I find those little balls every day.'

'All right, all right,' he said. Nick threw his toy on the sofa and ran his fingers through his perfect hair. Why did he bother combing it in the mornings? He could towel it dry, and it would, automatically, get into the shape he wanted. Not exactly curly. Not exactly straight. Just immaculate. Perfect brown hair. Side parted and pulled back to one side, it complimented the suit he had to wear for work.

'Okay, I'm dropping her off, right?' he said.

'Yep,' Julie said, still brushing Jessica's hair. 'Can you find her shoes, please?'

'We're going to be late,' Nick said.

'Then, don't play with your toys in the mornings.' Julie pulled the brush through Jessica's hair.

'Oww, Mummy, you're hurting me,' Jessica said.

'Well, do you want to do it?'

'No, you do it, just gently.'

'Where are they?' Nick said.

'In her room, probably.'

'Oww, it really hurts,' Jessica said. Tears formed in her eyes, and she gave another yelp of pain when Julie pulled the hairbrush through the unending tangled mane that fell from her little head.

'Jessica, this is ridiculous. We need to get your hair cut.'

'No, I don't want it cut.'

'But it won't hurt to brush it if it's shorter.'

'No, Mummy. I like it long.'

Julie held her hand on her scalp and ran the brush through the hair once more, knowing what was about to come.

'I can't find them,' Nick said.

Jessica wailed a high-pitched scream in pain while Julie kept brushing. 'Nearly done,' Julie said.

'Oww, how much longer, Mummy?' Tears streamed down her face, and she stamped her feet.

Nick walked in, holding a single, tiny black shoe. 'Found one,' he said.

He looked uncomfortable with his daughter crying. Just crocodile tears, though. The sooner it got done, the sooner she would forget about it. One thing for sure, she was getting a hair cut.

'All done,' Julie said. 'Now, where did you take off your shoes yesterday?'

The tears stopped, and Jessica seemed perfectly fine as if nothing had hurt her at all.

'I don't know.'

'Well, look, please.'

Julie searched under the sofas and moved all the clothes, which lay on the dining table, waiting to get ironed.

'There it is,' Nick said. He pointed at the window sill. Jessica's shoe lay on its end, leaning against the window.

'Jessica? How did it get there?' Julie said.

'I don't know. These things happen, Mummy.'

'Right, I'm off to work,' Julie said. 'I'll pick her up after —what is it after school today?'

'Lego club,' Jessica said.

'Of course.'

Jessica finished putting on her shoe and bounced over to Nick, who walked her to the front door.

'All ready?' he asked.

Julie grabbed her handbag. 'Nearly,' she said. 'You go; I'll see you tonight.'

'Don't forget the chocolates, Mummy.'

Nick waved and closed the door. Julie took a breath and sighed. Then she took a seat on the sofa and lay back.

Silence. It had always been a rarity in her life. She looked at Nick's BB gun next to her. It had annoyed her when he'd bought it. She didn't want Jessica exposed to such things. She knew, first hand, what damage it could do. But still, Nick insisted on playing with it around the house. Boys playing with toys. Was it just hardwired into every male to kill each other? Maybe, if they did, she would manage to get a moment's peace.

Julie picked up the replica weapon. A Beretta 92F. Standard American Army issue. Not that Nick knew that. He had seen Chow Yun Fat use two of them in some Jon Woo movie.

The cereal packet that Nick had shot at remained placed on the coffee table. It had a hole where Coco the monkey's nose had been. A lucky shot.

Julie held the gun in her right hand, brought her left hand up, and clasped the butt of the gun underneath, folding her fingers around her right hand. Slowly, she put her finger on the trigger and pulled seven times.

Coco's nose hole now got joined by two eyes and a smile. Boys' toys. None of them had a clue.

Julie put the Beretta away in the bedroom, picked up her handbag, and pulled out her keys. She caught her reflection in the long mirror next to the door, and then pushed her fingers into her highlighted blonde hair, giving it an extra boost of buoyancy. Thank God it was Friday. The office became a lot more relaxed on a Friday.

Julie pulled the black BMW X6 up to the curb outside the school and waited for a black van to pass her before opening her door and stepping out.

While she walked through the forecourt of the school, she noticed a couple of mums picking up their daughters wearing onesies. She couldn't quite believe they could afford to send their offspring to a place like Churchwood House. The small private school only had about forty students. It proved near impossible not to notice the parents who struggled to send their kids there. Why didn't they make more of an effort to fit in? Though silly, she worried that Jessica would soon start dropping her Ts and saying free instead of three.

Jessica waited in the classroom, putting the last of her Lego bricks together. She had fashioned an impressive zoo, containing figures of a zebra and monkeys. Her work in the after school Lego club surpassed all the other eight-year-olds in the class, and Julie felt quite proud.

'Jessica,' Julie said. 'Hello, monkey; ready to go?'

'Yeah,' Jessica said.

'*Yes*. There's a *suh* on the end.'

'Yes, Mummy. I'm ready. Is that better?'

Julie smiled while her daughter raced past her and toward the front door.

'Where's your coat?'

'On the hook,' Jessica said.

'Well, go and get it.'

Jessica ran to the row of coat hooks and pulled off her school blazer and hat.

Julie walked her out of the school and over to the car.

'Mummy, did you bring me the chocolates?'

Julie strapped her into the booster seat in the back of the car. 'What chocolates?' She closed the door, walked round to the driver's side, and got in.

'Mummy.'

'What, Jessica?'

'Did you bring me the chocolates?'

'Which chocolates?'

'The ones you said you'd bring because you ate mine yesterday.'

'Oh, monkey. I forgot.'

'You ate them, didn't you?'

Julie started the car and pulled out into traffic.

'I didn't eat them. We can stop at a shop on the way

home.'

'And I can eat one in the car?'

'Yeah.'

'Yes, Mummy. There's a suh at the end.'

Julie gave a look into the rear-view mirror. Her daughter beamed a smile back at her. Proud that she had managed to catch out her mummy.

It would be a fifteen-minute drive back to the house, and Julie had turned up Jessica's music in the car, hoping she would forget about the chocolates.

She pulled onto the main road and increased her speed. The nice thing about picking up Jessica that little bit later was that she missed all the other school traffic in Hertford. Julie had the whole road to herself, apart from the black van behind.

Julie's heart-rate increased. It looked like the same black van that had passed her at the school. Not many black vans around. It drew closer, too. Julie pushed her foot further down to get some distance between her car and the van. It matched her speed, and then overtook her.

Julie glanced out of her window when it came past. Tinted windows. She put her foot on the brake slightly. Again, to create distance between her and the van, but as the black vehicle moved in front, it also slowed to almost a crawl. Julie had to slam on her brakes to avoid driving into the back. Julie braced herself by clutching onto the steering wheel, and Jessica jerked forward in her car seat. The singing stopped abruptly, but the music continued while Julie tried to swerve around the van.

'Mummy, what are you doing?' Jessica said.

The black vehicle cut her off and came to a complete stop, blocking the road ahead. Once again, Julie's car jerked to a stop. Two armed men stepped out of the back of the van. They wore black fatigues and black tactical vests. Both gunmen carried Glock 17s. A semi-automatic pistol currently favoured by British Armed Forces.

The two men held up their guns at Julie. One of them said, 'Keep your hands on the wheel. Hands on the wheel.'

Julie kept her hands put, as Jessica started crying.

'Mummy,' she said.

Julie kept calm. One of the men stood by her window. The other walked to Jessica's and tried the door handle. The car locked automatically after a minute of not moving with the engine on. Never had Julie felt gladder of that.

'Unlock the doors,' the man said. 'Do it.'

Slowly, Julie took her hands off the wheel and reached down to the unlock button on the door. She pushed it. The man near Jessica lowered his gun from the window and pulled the handle, opening the door. Jessica screamed with fear, asking her to do something, screaming for her mummy.

The man next to Julie lowered his gun and looked over the top of the car. Quickly, she put the vehicle into reverse and pushed her foot as hard as she could onto the accelerator.

The car jolted backward, and the man next to Jessica's door got pulled to the ground, as his fingers remained in the door handle.

The other man fired his weapon. One of the BMW's front tyres exploded, and she yanked the steering wheel to the left, forcing the car to skid around to the right, facing away from the gunmen.

Julie pushed the gear stick into drive and slammed once more on the accelerator, trying to ignore the piercing screams from her daughter.

With a look in the mirror, she saw the black van coming

up fast behind. She couldn't get her speed up with the loose rubber flapping around her wheel. The van rammed into her backend, and Julie struggled to keep control of the vehicle. The van pulled up alongside and shunted into her. The BMW careened off the road and skidded into the ditch, which ran alongside the tarmac.

Julie's head hit the driver's side window hard, and a sharp ringing started in her head. The sun, low in the sky, beamed through the windscreen, directly into her eyes. She held up her hand to block it. The two gunmen ran past the van and directly toward her.

They pulled open Jessica's door and fiddled with the seatbelt while she thrashed around, still screaming for her mummy. Julie unfastened her seatbelt and lunged into the back, holding onto Jessica's body with one hand.

One of the men put a gun in her face. Through the ringing in her head, came the threat, telling her to let go. She ignored it—nothing would make her let go of her daughter. Nothing. The man brought the gun down onto her head. More ringing. She clasped Jessica's clothes tighter and climbed into the back fully.

More hands fell upon her, pulling from the front of the car. Julie lashed out, kicking someone in the head. Hands on her face. Pulling. Prying her hands off Jessica. An arm around her throat. She put every amount of strength she had into her grip, but suddenly, the clothing she held came loose. The arm around her let go and, before she could work out what had happened, she sat alone in the car, holding onto a jumper.

The armed man shouted at her when she tried to leave the vehicle. He grabbed her by the throat and forced her to the ground.

'Listen to me, you bitch,' he said. 'Go home. Wait by

your phone. We'll be in touch. You call the police, you never see her again.' He held her face and forced her to look at him. 'Do you understand?'

Julie nodded. He let go of her face and released his weight from her body. Then he ran to the black van. Her daughter's screams came from inside. Julie picked herself up, hurting all over. The pain seemed like nothing, though. Not compared to what was happening. Panicked and distraught, she ran for the van. It pulled away just as she reached it, screeching off toward the setting sun.

Julie raced back to the BMW and dropped into the driver's seat. Then she pushed the start button, and the engine roared to life. The wheels spun against the grass and dirt in the small ditch. The car didn't move. Julie yelled out at the top of her lungs. Her face turned red, she slammed her hands down on the steering wheel, and pushed her foot down harder on the pedal.

The wheels spun faster and faster. The car didn't move.

4

RANSOM

Julie watched her husband's frustrated face as he spoke on the phone. Nick's thin features only accentuated his anger further, and the scowl on his face looked as though it had set hard. He was still wearing his suit from Friday. She remembered feeling hurt when she walked into the living room last night at past 3:00 am and found him snoring on the sofa. How could he fall asleep when their daughter had been taken from them earlier that day? She herself hadn't been able even to sit still for two minutes, let alone shut her eyes. Every time she did, all she saw was Jessica's innocent face, bawling her eyes out for her mummy, who couldn't come save her. They had waited an entire day to call.

Nick spoke into the phone, saying he understood and placed the phone back in its stand.

Julie tried to mask the quiver in her voice by deepening her tone. 'What do they want?'

'Five million.'

'When?'

'Three days. They're gonna call again on Monday night

to tell us where to go.'

'Okay,' Julie said. 'We just give them the money.'

'We don't have that money. The house is only worth a tenth of that.'

'I wasn't going to suggest selling the house, Nick. I'll just get the money from work.'

'Julie, it's not that simple. If you take money out of your clients' accounts, they're going to notice.'

'Who cares if they notice. I don't fucking care about consequences. I don't even know why you have to think about it; we're getting her back, and I don't fucking care how we do it, but we're going to do it.' Her brow now mirrored Nick's. And her temperature rose along with her frustration.

'What about your dad?' Nick said. 'I mean ... the way you spoke about him ... he knows people, right?'

'I don't think we should involve him.' Them running to her dad wasn't an option. She hadn't spoken to him in two years, and even then, only for Jessica's sixth birthday, and he had insisted on coming over. Julie had known about her father's less-than-legal activities for a good few years before Jessica's birth, and by the time she and Nick got married, she had made the decision to cut him out of her life completely.

'I just thought he seemed like an option,' Nick said. 'It's a lot of money that I don't think you can afford to lose. Yeah, we get Jessica back, but you'll be in prison. There has to be another way.'

'I'd rather just get it done and deal with the consequences later.'

'I never told you this,' Nick said. 'But when your dad was here, just before he left, he set me aside and told me if there was ever anything he could do to help, to let him know.'

'Of course, he did, that's just like him. He manipulates —wants to be in control. Nick, we're better off without him. Let's just do this ourselves. Jessica's the priority, right?'

Nick agreed and nodded. He approached Julie with a comforting look; his expression said *everything's going to be okay,* but Julie could see through it, through to the fear behind his eyes. She loved him for his honesty and practicality. This kind and good person couldn't have been more different from her father. Probably the reason she'd fallen for him. Right at that moment, however, she didn't need him being practical and rational. Julie walked away to the study to look up details of her employer's most successful accounts and left Nick looking defeated.

5
TOMMY

Blaine stood at the doorway to Tommy's offices on Charlotte Street and pressed the buzzer, glancing up at the camera mounted on the top right of the door frame, which Tommy was—no doubt—looking through. He imagined Tommy would take a moment before letting him in; Blaine preferred email and text rather than meeting face-to-face, and him turning up unannounced may give Tommy pause for thought.

The buzzer sounded, and Blaine pushed open the door and walked up to the first-floor offices.

The two large gentlemen that greeted Blaine were a new addition since he'd last come, some nine months ago. While they frisked him, Blaine felt curious about just how many people Tommy expected to bring firearms into the middle of London. It seemed a little paranoid, and Blaine tried to shrug it off. Tommy opened his door, waving his hand as if calling off his boys.

'That's fine, guys,' Tommy said. His voice sounded commanding, but the Essex accent always grated. 'Jason, come on in.'

Tommy's office made Blaine uncomfortable. Large, towering shelving units covered the walls, each packed with books, files, and general trinkets that Tommy loved to collect. A far cry from Blaine's well ordered, structured way of living. He couldn't understand how Tommy could work surrounded by such chaos.

Tommy greeted Blaine and offered him a seat in front of his old-fashioned leather-topped desk. 'I've gotta say, I'm surprised to see you. It's been a while.' He wandered over to his drinks table as Blaine sat down. 'Drink?'

'Just water, thanks.'

'I'm not sure you've ever just popped in for a chat. Something wrong with the Millican job? It should be done by now.' Tommy fixed himself a scotch and soda and handed Blaine his glass of water.

'He's due to drop dead at 10:00 pm tonight.' Blaine placed his glass on the desk without drinking.

'You want to talk about Peterson?' Tommy reclined in his office chair and took a sip of his drink. 'It's all taken care of. Cost a bit to deal with the car, but since we got more cash for the hit, I'm not too bothered. Plus, we gained another client. Not such a bad outcome overall.'

'We haven't had a high-profile job in a while.'

'Sign of the times. No more gangsters. Just a bunch of kids willing to do your job for a fraction of the price. The days of clandestine hit-men living the high life in a penthouse suite and holiday homes in Majorca are gone.' He paused to take another sip of his whisky and soda. 'You complained about me giving you work in the middle of another job, and now you're telling me you want more?'

'You made me the bodyguard of the most hunted man

in the UK.'

'I remember a time when you would have held your ground against an entire hit squad like that.'

'It was different back then,' Blaine said.

'Yeah, we were having fun. You, the young soldier, thirsty for some secretive work and the money that came with it, and me, the connected, mysterious man with promises of riches. I reckon it worked out for both of us.'

'The work shouldn't be fun.'

'I suppose not. So, what can I do for you?'

Blaine took his glass from the desk. Though he didn't feel the need to drink, he would rather have something in his hands and didn't want to seem nervous. He was about to make this man, who had made his entire adult occupation possible, furious and needed his hands doing something.

'I made a decision,' Blaine said, slowly turning the glass between thumb and forefinger. 'I'm leaving the UK.'

'Really? Where you headed?' Tommy looked perplexed. 'What are you talking about?'

'Thought I'd meet some contacts in South Africa. A change of scenery.'

'You're after military work? Private security?' Tommy seemed like he had to reach for a reason for Blaine to stay. 'I can get you that.'

'I want the money you invested for me.' Blaine took a sip of the water.

Tommy hesitated. 'You know it's making money, right? You don't need to take it out; it's paying that allowance you get every month.'

'I'll take my money. It's time.'

'Retirement? What are you gonna do? Buy a house? Raise kids?'

'Maybe.'

Tommy grew rather agitated. 'Once you've done what we have, you don't get to go back to living a normal life, Jason.'

Blaine didn't reply. He knew the power of silence.

'Hey,' Tommy said. 'Whatever you want. I've gotta say, though, I don't think you're making the right decision.'

Blaine put his glass of water back on Tommy's desk, no longer feeling the need for it.

Tommy stood and looked down on Blaine. 'See, it's gonna take a few weeks to sort out. It's a lot of money.'

'Sure. I'll get you a bank account number.' Blaine got up from the chair. 'I'll talk to you soon.'

'Take care,' Tommy said and watched him leave the office.

6

HOME INVASION

As the light Sunday evening rain eased, Blaine continued to watch his target's house from the bottom of the garden. He had waited until nightfall and planted himself, firmly, among the overgrown hedges and remained out of sight. The black coat and gloves he wore made him blend into the dark shadows, and only his face stood out, but he wouldn't get seen unless someone looked for him specifically.

The large house had sizeable grounds, and Blaine had found it no bother making his way, unnoticed, down the back road, which ran alongside the garden wall. He had scaled it effortlessly, and using a small pair of binoculars, watched and waited for his target to drop dead at 10:00 pm. That would happen if the poison ingested correctly. Blaine had brought along a shoulder bag that contained a balaclava and lock-picking tools in case he had to enter the building and finish the job. He wanted to make any kind of break-in look like a burglary.

The time neared 9:45 pm, and Blaine could see into the kitchen on the ground floor. The living-room curtains, though drawn, still allowed the light to glow through them. On the top floor, only the bathroom showed a light, and Blaine had seen his target's young son brushing his teeth an hour earlier. In the kitchen, his target and his wife argued. It seemed quite heated, and Blaine could only assume by the way the man kept holding his stomach that the discomfort from the poison had kicked in. It wouldn't be long before Blaine would know whether his plan had worked or if he would have to take further action.

The first slap to the wife's face broke the noise of arguing, but that only lasted a couple of seconds. More furious words followed from her, and then from him. The wife stormed out of the kitchen. The target continued muttering to himself, still holding his stomach. Perhaps, he blamed the meal they'd eaten? The target leant over the sink and dry heaved. Then he turned on the tap and cupped water into his hands and drank from his palm. It didn't seem to help, and the man dashed upstairs and entered the bathroom. He ducked out of Blaine's sight, most probably throwing up in the toilet.

Blaine cursed under his breath, as he'd hoped it wouldn't have to come to this. A few more heaves and the poison in his system would end up useless by the time 10:00 pm came around.

The wife walked into the bathroom, which seemed to annoy the target further. He stood, wiping the spit and sick from his chin with the sleeve of his shirt, and shoved her hard against the wall. Next, he grabbed her hair and, though she slapped him hard, he held tight, forced her head back, and delivered a hard blow to her face with his fist.

Blaine had no time for people like that. He couldn't comprehend how a person could lose control so badly. What must have happened in the man's life to mess him up so badly? During his research, he'd discovered that the man's mother had died when he was young to lung cancer, and that didn't seem to have made a motivating factor in his personality. Some people are just born fucked up. Blaine had grown up with only one parent. His father had died from heart complications at a similar age, and Blaine had joined the Army not soon after. Not that he saw that as a response to his father's death. A military occupation had run in the family for three generations. It was expected of him. Any incidents in his life had never affected the way he lived that much. For as long as he could remember, he had remained calm and collected. Never angry or upset, and equally as level when it came to happiness or excitement. He found joy in a well-executed plan, in watching events unfold as he'd predicted; an effect following cause. Mechanical. Precise. Simple. But any superficial, social happiness had to be faked. Blaine enjoyed fitting in, and over the years, had learned to mimic the people he chatted to, which seemed to relax them. The idea of purposely doing something that you surely knew you would regret later had proven totally alien to him. Until that precise moment.

Blaine should wait until the family fell asleep, fake a robbery, and stab the target when he investigated whatever sounds he could hear. The plan had flaws but held more sense than barging in there right now and taking care of the target in front of his family.

Blaine donned the balaclava and crept toward the house, using the side of the garden so as not to set off the automatic motion-sensor lighting system on the back wall.

Blaine realised why he felt so keen to get it done now. He should have seen it during the weeks he had followed the target. It wasn't one of his work colleagues who had bought the contract on his life, but his wife. Blaine couldn't blame her.

The shouting continued upstairs, and when Blaine took out his lock-picking tools, he heard the sound of the son getting involved and young cries of terror at the abusive man upstairs hurting his mother. Blaine felt unsure if he intended to speed to their rescue or if he simply didn't want to risk the client getting killed before she could pay in full. He put it to the back of his mind and concentrated on the lock.

Blaine considered lock picking, like most of his skills, an art form. He slid the tension rod into place, giving the cylinder of the lock the smallest bit of clockwise stress. Then he pushed the raking tool inside and worked it back and forth while alternating greater and lesser amounts of pressure on the tension rod. With ease, he could feel which tumblers had jammed in place above the cylinder, and with a last push of the lock-picking tool, the tension rod went limp, and the lock turned.

Blaine opened the back door, walked through the utility room, and into the kitchen, where only moments ago, he had seen the couple fighting. A home invasion like this usually made for a big no-no in his line of work. A house clearance meant a big price and numerous kills, but to attempt it solo when anticipating an armed response was considered suicide. Blaine had done his research and, though his target had become angry and violent, he didn't consider him a potential threat. This made part of the reason that Blaine didn't have his gun with him.

The boy upstairs yelled for his mother, and with a slam of a door, he got silenced. Only the muffled screams of a terrified child could be heard while Blaine put his lock-picking tools back in his bag and made sure he had his gloves on tight.

7

FAMILY MATTERS

Silently, Blaine climbed the stairs of his target's house, balling his fists. The target stood on the landing with his wife, who shouted at him for throwing their son into his bedroom. He yelled at her to shut the fuck up, but Blaine knew this would never have the desired effect. She continued berating him, daring him to hit her once more and leave a bruise big enough for the police to see. The sound of a door getting forced open followed, and Blaine reached the top of the stairs and watched the target hold his wife by her throat and shove her into the main bedroom.

The door eased closed behind them. Stealthily, Blaine prowled across the carpeted floor. He passed the son's room and heard him sobbing, trying to catch his breath in between yelps of sorrow.

Blaine burst into the master room and stood in the doorway, looming over the man straddling his wife on the floor at the foot of the bed and holding her face with his hand.

'Who are you?' the target said. 'What the fuck are you

doing in my house?'

Blaine moved forward, causing the target to struggle in haste to his feet. Instinctively, he held out a hand, trying to make Blaine stop.

'Stay back.'

Blaine remained silent. He slapped the target's arm away and blocked a feeble punch with his left arm. Blaine's right fist made contact with the target's nose, breaking it. The man fell to his knees, and Blaine delivered a series of devastating blows to his face until it became swollen and bloody. His body fell to the floor, and Blaine brought out the knife from his jacket pocket. A simple kitchen knife, he had bought it from a department store; half the country had one just like it in their cutlery drawer. Blaine brought it down into the target's chest, under the rib cage and up into his heart. His wife didn't let out even the smallest amount of sound while her husband convulsed in shock and his heart stopped beating.

Blaine turned to face the wife and made sure his voice came out as calm and unthreatening as possible. 'He heard a noise downstairs,' he said. 'He came down and found me. We fought. I chased him up here, where he defended you, and I stabbed him. Call the police.'

Blaine walked over to the bedside table, opened it, and took out a few notes of cash. He made his way back to the stairs. The wife ran to the boy's room, where the crying had stopped. Blaine smashed a vase at the bottom of the stairs and took his black bag off his shoulder. In the living room, he found the Blu-ray player under the TV, disconnected it, and shoved it into his bag. On his way out, he slammed himself against a cabinet, knocking over a few books and breaking the wooden door. Within a couple of minutes of entering the house, Blaine had left and climbed back over the wall.

His blue Vauxhall waited, parked nearby with the false plates he had put on earlier that night. The road got only rare use at this time of night, but Blaine always remained one for caution.

After making his way back into London from Surrey, Blaine pulled up to the garage under the arches in Bow End. He rented it from Tommy and kept any weapons and vehicles he needed there. The electronic doors opened, and Blaine drove the car inside and parked it next to his black Mercedes.

He fired up the small incinerator and stripped off his clothes. Then he put them into the hot metal contraption and got dressed in the dark-grey suit he'd put out before leaving.

Blaine waited until every part of his clothes from that evening had been destroyed and turned off the furnace. All done, he got into his Mercedes and left the garage at just past midnight. As the electronic doors closed behind him, Blaine took out his phone and sent a brief message to Tommy.

Tommy's smartwatch vibrated on his wrist while he sat in his office chair. The message showed a smiley face from Blaine; the code they'd developed to indicate a successful mission. Blaine hated it—thought it too cute—but it amused Tommy knowing that Blaine felt uncomfortable. As long as he had known him, Blaine had been the kind of guy who never cried over spilt milk. Never cursed when angry. Never smiled because he felt happy. Blaine just was. A static event.

And ruthless. It was just like Blaine to discard emotion, dismiss the fallout, and turn an impossible situation into a win, as he had done with the Peterson job. Tommy had a barrier between him and the violence, and staying just that bit removed from the act of killing a man proved enough to settle his conscience.

He covered the watch with his hand, and the face went black. Tommy looked up at Nick, who sat opposite him, where Blaine had only a few hours previously. He looked nervous and kept fidgeting with his hands, grasping the sides of the chair and looking down at the desk. Not finding anything interesting on which to lay his eyes, Nick then glanced back up at Tommy, who still said nothing. Nick awaited a response from the ageing man, reclining in his chair.

'I take it Julie doesn't know you're here?' Tommy said.

'No. She wasn't keen on the idea.'

Nick had just told him that his granddaughter had gotten taken from Julie in broad daylight at gunpoint. Not subtle and not clandestine. Whoever had done it wanted to make a point. Tommy had an excellent idea of who had ordered the snatch.

'How much have they asked for?'

'Five million,' Nick said. 'Five million. God, how the hell do they think we have that?'

'I don't exactly have that just floating around in my bank account.'

'Oh, no ... no, no ... I didn't mean to suggest.' Nick squirmed in his chair, uncomfortable in his skin. 'Julie has a plan ... to borrow the money from work. From her clients' business accounts.'

'She always was a little reckless.'

'She'll go to jail if she goes through with it. I just can't see any other option.'

Tommy stood and walked over to the packed shelves next to the window at the end of his office. The three figures in the photo within the small black picture frame smiled their permanent smiles at him, and he turned back around to face Nick, who looked more desperate than ever. The beads of sweat at his scalp had made their way down to his eyebrows. Tommy worried that Nick was about to lunge forward in an uncontrollable fit of tears, and that he would have to give him a hug.

'You should start thinking about what you can afford to lose,' Tommy said.

'You mean how much money?'

'Sure.'

'Well, we have some money put away but nothing like what they've asked for.'

'If Julie manages to get the cash, I may be able to hire someone to help you out.'

'What kind of someone?'

'A professional someone. After you exchange the money for Jessica, we could have the kidnappers followed and the money retrieved.'

Nick wiped the sweat from his brow, and his eyes widened with hope. Tommy admired the man for coming to him behind Julie's back. For taking initiative. Not too different from his daughter. Maybe that's what she saw in him. Despite the wealth of differences between them, Tommy had an irrevocable link to the problem set before them. His granddaughter had gone missing, and he would get her back, no matter the damage. He would find the people responsible, and they would die.

'How much will it cost?' Nick said.

'Enough to sting.' Tommy turned back to the picture frame and the ten-year-old photo inside. He held it in his hands and looked at the three smiling faces of the soldiers in military fatigues, who had their arms wrapped around each other. Himself, his daughter Julie, and Jason Blaine.

8

CHECKOUT

The new Hunter's chicken meal for two came presented in a silver foil tray and sealed with a plastic lid and promised a nutritious meal free from artificial colours and flavours. Comprised of two chicken breasts, which Blaine could tell weren't large, it also had two slices of streaky bacon and tangy Red Leicester and Cheddar cheese, marinated in the shop's presumptuously titled, satisfyingly smoky sauce.

Blaine picked up the packaged meal, and it felt heavier than he had thought it would. This, among other reasons, led to him placing the meal into his basket. He continued along the aisle, as he would need vegetables to go with it, and settled on croquet potatoes and mashed root vegetables, which he could cook in the microwave.

When Blaine approached the end of the aisle, a craving for a snack hit him, and he considered purchasing chocolate. Every day, he exercised and kept to a strict diet. To have control of his body felt important to him—but so did treats. The odd bit of chocolate encouraged him to work out harder and put in a few extra pull-ups and sit-ups in his training routine.

Blaine's phone rang just as he entered the aisle for cereal. Although the childish, colourful packaging still enticed him, as they did every adult (he assumed), he picked up a cereal that contained dried fruit and put it in his basket. Blaine pulled the phone from his jacket pocket. Tommy came up on the display. He never called. Blaine rarely answered his phone, preferring to text. However, yesterday, he had asked Tommy to gather the millions of pounds that he'd made over the past ten years and that Tommy had invested for him. It could be about the money.

Blaine answered, 'Yeah?'

'Jason.' Tommy sounded more deadpan than usual. 'An opportunity has come up. Something I think you might be interested in.'

'I'm not interested, Tommy. I'm taking a break. I told you that.'

'Client's little girl has been kidnapped. They want five million, but the client can't lose the money they have to pay. I need someone to follow the cash after the exchange and make sure it gets back to the client, who's desperate. A hundred grand.'

'Not interested.'

'Wait ... make it two-fifty. It's a quick job. The exchange is tomorrow night.'

Blaine looked around and made sure that no-one could overhear. 'You're crazy. There's no time for any homework or surveillance. What made you think I'd be interested in this?'

'Jason.' Tommy paused and took a deep breath. Not quite a sigh but enough to make him listen closer. 'It's Julie's kid.'

Blaine stopped at the end of the cereal aisle next to the

pop tarts. 'You saw her?'

'Her husband. She doesn't know he asked for help.'

Blaine said nothing. It had been a long time since he'd seen Julie.

'Look, Jason.' Tommy sounded desperate. 'I'll boost it up to five hundred. That's a half a mil' on top of your invested money, which I will get you—in full—that's about three million in total. If you do this for me. For Julie.'

'I have to go.' Blaine hung up. His attention had diverted from the call to a man in the frozen foods section of the supermarket. Matt Cable stood holding a bag of frozen mince.

Blaine couldn't just stand still, or he would stand out. He walked across the aisle to the edge of the pet food section, where he grabbed a couple of cat treats and placed them in his basket. Wary, he kept an eye on Cable, uncertain whether the man planned to follow him or not. If Cable were, truly, following him, gathering details of his day-to-day activities, it would only mean one thing. Blaine had followed many people over the years, noting down their habits and getting to know their quirks and routines, before developing the best way to kill them.

The supermarket wasn't exactly down the road from Blaine's apartment, but this encounter came far too close for any comfort. Cable put a few more frozen goods in his basket and made his way toward Blaine, who walked down the pet food aisle and made a left at the bottom, reaching for a single pack of AA batteries on a buy-one-get-one-free. He saw a few people in the next aisle and stood next to them, browsing through the soft drinks—blending into his surroundings was a particular skill of Blaine's. A group of people garnered less attention than a single person, alone. That said, if you stood next to a family with a screaming child, you would likely gain a good few pairs of eyes staring at you.

Blaine lost visual on Cable and walked at a slow pace past the fruit-flavoured drinks until he regained his location, walking up the cereal aisle where Blaine had stood talking to Tommy. He could have been right behind him when he answered the phone. Perhaps listening. No. Blaine felt sure that he'd remained alone in that aisle. He wouldn't have taken the call otherwise.

Blaine's basket had grown quite full by the time Cable headed to the checkout counter. Cable walked with some pace, and Blaine watched, a few aisles down from him, as he placed his basket onto the end of the conveyor belt at cashier number four.

Ahead of him stood a middle-aged man, bagging up a packet of bread, tinned food, a few cleaning products, and donuts. As Cable put his shopping on the conveyor belt, Blaine had a decision to make. He should stay behind him and join the queue at cashier number six, but that would mean Cable would definitely leave before him. If Blaine were to exit the shop and not see Cable, he would have to decide whether to risk Cable following him home. Probably, he would have to drive around for a while, maybe stay in a hotel overnight. But, even then, a good tail would wait and stay patient.

Blaine walked into the self-checkout area and placed his basket on the platform. He stood in Cable's direct line of sight, were he to take notice—if he didn't know he was there already—but this way, Blaine had control of the speed of his bagging and could get out of the door before Cable.

Blaine scanned his products, and then realised he didn't have any plastic bags. It had only been a few months since the new law had come in about having to purchase bags from the larger shops for five pence. Blaine still forgot to bring any with him. He had a drawer at home in his kitchen, full of plastic bags, ready to for him to take to the supermarket. None of them had ever left the house. Though the bags cost five pence, at the self-checkout area, you still had to ask a member of staff for them. Blaine looked around and saw the lowly shop assistant helping a short, bald man behind him. The man had placed an item into the bagging area, but it hadn't registered on the checkout screen, and the assistant typed in a long number to cancel the flashing red light above his station.

Blaine continued scanning his items and placing them down where the bag should be, checking over his shoulder to see if he could get the assistant's attention. She still hadn't finished yet. He looked over at Cable, whose cashier had started scanning his items, and he made his way to the bagging area and stood bagging the first couple of items.

Blaine scanned his cat treats, which he didn't need, and then the assistant finished with the man.

'Excuse me, could I get two bags, please?' Blaine remained polite, not wanting to make a scene.

The lady smiled at him and said, 'Would that be the five-pence bags or the eight-pence ones?'

'The five-pence ones are fine.' Blaine went back to scanning. He cursed himself for putting so many items in his basket. The lady came over and handed Blaine two bags, interrupting his relentless scanning by typing in the bag code and adding it to his total.

'Thanks,' Blaine said. He held his Hunter's Chicken to the scanner. An error message popped up, and Blaine looked over at the shop assistant, who had walked away from him to help someone else.

'Hello?' Blaine said. 'This isn't scanning.'

The assistant turned to him with another smile. 'I'll be with you in a moment, dear.'

The red light above Blaine's checkout station flashed red. He looked down at his Hunter's Chicken; the only thing he'd put in his basket on purpose. Then he looked at the screen to see if he could cancel the item and just leave it. The error message flashed at him. He needed a member of staff to continue. Blaine looked over at Cable to see how he progressed. Cable looked right back at him.

Cable's eyes locked onto Blaine's, and within a fraction of a second, the man had doubled his bagging speed.

Blaine walked over to the shop assistant, took her by the arm, and walked her over to his screen. 'I just need this done,' he said.

'I will be with you in a moment, Sir,' she said, blatantly offended by his manhandling of her.

'Now.'

Blaine held her in front of his screen, scared that his tone would have the opposite effect. She seemed sure of herself, and Blaine could tell she was used to being in charge. This self-checkout area remained her patch, and no-one ran it but her. She looked around for help. Then glanced over at the security, who stood chatting by the front doors.

When strong-arming someone, you had to commit to it fully. Any sign of weakness negated any control you may have gained. Blaine had to commit to how he'd proceeded. He squeezed her arm tightly, stared into her eyes, and repeated himself, 'Now.'

The eyes said it all. She scanned her ID card and cancelled the item. Blaine let go of her arm and pressed the button for payment. Cable bagged the last of his items and took out his wallet.

Blaine considered abandoning his shopping and leaving, but that, coupled with what he had done with the assistant, would surely around security's suspicions. The last thing he wanted was them looking at video footage of him and getting the police involved. They could interpret what he had done as assault. He had made a mistake.

Blaine pushed his card into the reader and typed his pin. Cable pushed his card into his reader.

Blaine turned to the assistant as he took hold of his bag. 'I'm so sorry; my wife's in labour, and I'm in such a hurry. Please, forgive my rudeness.'

'Oh ... well ... yes ... there was no need for that, though.'

Briskly, Blaine walked past security. He turned to see Cable grabbing his bags from checkout aisle four and made his way outside the shop. The apology would, hopefully, settle any unease that he'd caused, and now, Blaine's mind focused on dealing with Matt Cable.

Blaine shoved his two full shopping bags into the bin outside and stood in front of the cash dispensers, next to the glass front doors. Cable walked out, and Blaine moved up behind him.

It offered a good location. Lots of people. Very public. Neither of them would do anything here. They were, also— no doubt—on CCTV cameras.

Matt turned around to face Blaine, and they stood looking at each other; sizing one another up. Each prepared for anything. Blaine remained adamant that he not speak first. He would rather respond. Whatever Cable said would give him some clue as to his intentions.

Cable's eyes narrowed. 'Are you ...?'

'Are you?' Blaine said straight back to him. Was he what? Here to kill him? Here to buy chicken?

'Just shopping,' Cable said.

Blaine eased up slightly but only on the outside. He wanted to give the feeling that he felt more relaxed than he did. It also had the effect of making Cable lower his guard. Blaine could see him un-tense his shoulders and lower the shopping bags, still in his hands.

'You live around here?' Blaine said.

'No, you?'

'No.'

Blaine took in a breath of air. Maybe it was just a coincidence.

'So ...' Cable said.

'Yeah.'

Cable sighed, raised his eyebrows, and shrugged. 'You wanna get a beer or something?'

9

A CASE OF THE MONDAYS

Julie grasped the phone with more grip than usual. Not just the fact she'd lied, but also because she felt angry and had to seem calm.

'Yes, she has a high temperature, hot and cold flushes,' Julie said. She listened to the reply on the other end of the line. 'Well, I certainly hope so; Nick's taking the day off to be with her.' Another pause. 'Yes, exactly ... well, we'll see how she's doing tomorrow. Okay. Thank you. Bye now.' Julie hung up and looked over at Nick. He seemed worried to find her so good at lying. Even if just to the school.

'You should eat something,' Nick said.

'I'm not hungry. I don't think I could.'

Nick picked up her work bag and handed it to her. 'You're sure about this?' he said.

'I know what I'm doing.'

'We'll get her back. But you'll be in jail. Me, too, probably. Aiding and abetting.'

'Nick, for God's sake, we'll never see her again. This is the only way.'

'Yeah, I figured you'd say that. You've always had the biggest pair of balls on you.'

Julie let through a painful smile and hugged her husband. She kept it brief. She didn't want to get emotional. She was about to steal five-million pounds.

———

Julie sat at her desk in the open-plan office. A sea of about twenty booths, divider screens separated the space. She had several contracts to type up and even more phone calls to make, but every time she started on some work, she found herself staring at her computer screen not doing anything. When you opened certain account files, it left time stamps, which showed when it got opened and by which computer. She needed a good reason to go snooping around in them, and that meant finishing her work before schedule.

Julie had poured herself a mug of coffee from the kitchen and set it down in front of her computer screen. No time for nerves. She took a sip of the hot, black, sugary liquid and got back to work. She needed this specific contract written up before lunchtime.

'Julie, good weekend?'

Julie looked up. Jasper stood at her booth with a mug of tea in his hand. Her boss always had tea. Tea with two tea bags and two sugars. *Double the pleasure, double the fun*, he would always say when someone asked how he took it.

'Yes, thanks,' Julie said. The interruption made for the last thing she needed right now.

'Get up to much?'

'Just a lazy one, really. Jessica hasn't been well. Think I'm coming down with something too.'

'Well, drink plenty of fluids. That's what they say. How's the Davis contract coming along? Think you'll have it done by the end of the day?'

'Oh, definitely. I'll keep my head down, get it moving.'

'Ooh, that's what she said!' Jasper let out an almighty roar of laughter. The whole office had become used to it. Witty banter and distractingly loud guffaws had become commonplace on a Monday morning and Friday afternoon. Mid-week, Jasper tended to stay in his office, shouting at people on the phone. Julie put it down to the weekly cocaine delivery he would get every Friday. A motorbike messenger would walk through the office to Jasper's room, still wearing his helmet and, five minutes after he had left, Jasper would come out among the ranks, telling jokes and sipping on Vodka, lime, and sodas.

'Well, I'll leave you to it,' he said and walked off to chat to someone else at the far side of the office.

Julie got back to work at double the speed she usually would. It meant that the Davis contract would have mistakes. That didn't matter. She needed it finished. It didn't matter the state it ended up in.

Half an hour before lunch, Julie had finished. A wave of adrenaline hit her when her mind switched from work mode to criminal mode. She had to remain calm. Remain to be seen at ease. Ken dealt with all the larger high-profile accounts but, occasionally, he would ask her to deal with some of the overflow if he got too busy. Julie was about to make Ken's workload impossible.

Julie saved the contract she'd worked on and sent it to the printer. She closed the window and brought up the saved draft for a contract that she'd helped Ken with last week. Investment contracts proved bulky and meticulous, and the slightest concern from a top client meant a lot of work for whoever had charge of that particular account.

Julie dialled the number for the client she'd pulled up on screen and waited. A secretary answered.

'Ah, hello, is Mr Yates available?' He wouldn't be. Any worthwhile assistant would give this set response.

'I'm afraid that he's in a meeting at the moment. Can I take a message?'

'That would be great. It's about the contract dated fourteenth of this month with Cunningham International. If you could just let him know that the corrections are due to be made by the end of today, thanks so much. Bye now.'

Julie put the phone down before the secretary could ask for her name.

The printer lived at the far end of the room, in between the doors to the kitchen and the corridor, which led to the stairs to the first floor. Julie picked up her freshly printed and rushed contract and headed upstairs.

Jasper's office stood at the end of the hall, next to another small kitchen and lounge room. Julie walked past Ken's office and five more doors and knocked on the hard wood surface.

'C'min,' Jasper shouted.

Julie opened the door and poked her head into the office, holding up the bulky contract.

'Wanted to catch you before lunch,' she said. 'Davis contract. Done and dusted.'

'Bloody hell, Jools, did you manage that in half a day?'

'I may have started on it last week a little.'

'Well, great. Leave it with me. Bloody great work. Got enough to be getting on with?'

'A few bits. But if anything needs doing, just let me

know.'

'Will do.'

Julie left the contract on the desk next to the door, littered with other contracts and files that Jasper had to take a look at before hers. She left the office and closed the door behind her.

While walking past Ken's office, she heard one side of a heated conversation.

Julie poured herself another mug of coffee. As she walked back to her booth, her phone rang. She picked up the receiver. 'Julie Jones?'

'Jools, it's Ken. Jasper mentioned your workload is a little thin today. Any chance I could send you a few bits to look over?'

'Yeah, no problem. Anything particular?'

'A couple of drafts need looking over. And I really need the list of last year's investments for each of my accounts put in order. Just the usual.'

'Everything all right? You sound stressed for a Monday.'

'Oh, someone's made some last minute changes to some contract, but Jasper doesn't have a clue about it. Some fuck up their end, probably. Still, muggins here has to go through the entire bloody thing again. Anyway ... I'll email the details now.'

'No problem.'

'Thanks.'

Julie put down the phone and waited for the email. With fifteen minutes to lunch, Julie hoped she'd timed it right. She still needed Jasper in the office for the time being.

As soon as the email came through with details of Ken's accounts and the companies associated with them, she waded through them, searching for the top largest investors. The

Kaizen Group had seven accounts registered with Cunningham Global. Each contained millions of pounds, ready for investment at the whim of the company. £715,000 taken from each account and placed into hers would do it. Julie would get found out within a few days, but all she needed was one. The exchange for Jessica would happen tomorrow evening, and telling Jasper she might be coming down with something would give her the excuse to take the entire day off. The thought of waiting with Nick by the phone for the details of the exchange brought pain. She tried to put it out of her mind. What she had to do now had far more importance than worrying.

Julie opened the office intranet and brought up Ken's accounts, which mirrored those in the email she had. She clicked on the first Kaizen account file, ready to transfer the money. A window flashed up, asking for a password.

It had almost reached lunchtime. The perfect moment to ask Jasper for anything—always so eager to get out of the door. Julie picked up the phone and dialled a three-digit number.

'Hey, Ken, just quickly, do you have the password to the Kaizen accounts?'

'Hmm, I think only Jasper has those. Why do you need them?'

'Thought I'd put together a detailed report of their investments. For the other clients. Pretty decent example of what we can do, considering their returns last year.'

'Yeah, okay. Just keep their name out of the report. Call them an existing client. No names, ya know?'

'Yeah, of course.'

'Okay, I'll call Jasper now.'

'Cool beans. Thanks, Ken.'

She put down the phone, brought up her bank website, and logged into her account. Before long, another email from Ken appeared in her inbox, containing the password to open the Kaizen Group files.

Julie typed in the password, and the intranet screen came to life. The Kaizen accounts listed, complete with separate folders for each investment made on their behalf. Julie clicked on the first folder and looked for the Word document that accompanied each account, which contained the numbers and passwords for money transfers.

She clicked on the document. Another window popped up, informing her that the file had restricted access. No prompt for a password, though. Which meant that only Jasper or Ken's computer could open it.

She had half expected that, however. Julie looked at her watch. 12:59 pm. Jasper would head out for lunch any second now.

Samantha, who worked in the booth next to her, got out of her chair, put on her jacket, and discussed where to have lunch with Paul, opposite.

'Coming to the pub, Julie?' she asked.

'Oh, I may just grab a sandwich. Got a lot on.'

'Ugh, working hard on a Monday? You're a fool to yourself.'

Julie smiled and watched her colleagues walk out. She noted down the password to access the Kaizen files on a post-it note and peeled it off.

When she passed Ken's office on the first floor, she heard him talking to Jasper about the Yates contract. Never before had the hallway seemed so long. Julie couldn't tell if the conversation would go on for a good ten more minutes or if Jasper would storm out at any moment and head back to his office. Or, perhaps, he would just head out to lunch?

Julie strode down the hall to Jasper's office, making sure that the carpeted floor cushioned her footsteps. Jasper's door remained slightly ajar, and that worried her. She entered the office. His jacket still hung in the corner. The computer screen remained on as well. His mobile phone still sat on the table.

Julie made a quick decision and raced behind the desk. She brought up the intranet window and clicked her way into the Kaizen files. The same password prompt popped up, and Julie copied the series of numbers and letters from the post-it note. Frantic, she moved the cursor down to the folder and opened it. The Word document came next. It opened, displaying the account numbers and passwords needed.

Julie's heart beat inside her chest like a pounding bass drum. The voices from Ken's office had disappeared, but she would hear the noise of Ken's office door opening if Jasper were to make his way back.

She took out her phone and brought up the camera app. She held the device close to the screen to capture all the information, but the camera wouldn't focus. Repeatedly, Julie tapped on the screen, but the infuriating phone came up with a message informing her that the camera app had crashed and that it had to turn off. Julie, in a hurry, reopened the camera and held the phone a bit further away from the screen. It focused, and Julie tapped the button to take a picture. Only six more Word files to go.

Fingers trembling, she clicked on the cross at the top left corner of the image on the computer and rushed to bring up the next account folder and the document inside. She took another picture. Jasper's riotous laugh bellowed down the hallway along with the sound of Ken's office door opening.

Hastily, she brought up the next account folder and the password document. Jasper's voice barrelled through the door. 'These bloody corporations; they should just let us get on with the job in hand instead of micromanaging. Anyway … I'm out to lunch. Got it all handled?'

'Leave it with me,' Ken replied.

Julie heard Ken's door close, and then footsteps made their way toward her.

Julie took the third photo. Clicked the cross on the intranet window. All the Kaizen folder windows closed. Julie got up from the desk. Jasper opened his door and walked in.

10

LIQUID LUNCH

Blaine placed the two pints of lager down on the table. The Woodman on Archway Road, a local gastro pub, stood a quick walk away from the supermarket. He had driven past it often but never been inside. Better to have this odd meeting in a place he hadn't frequented. It remained anything but ideal that he stood only a few miles from his luscious church apartment building.

The interior of the pub featured wood panelling with classic paintings hung around. A couple of old blood-red Chesterfield sofas hugged the table in front of the wood burner fireplace, giving the room a cosy but old fashioned atmosphere. Blaine could almost believe this as exactly the way a public house would have looked a hundred years ago if it weren't for the huge sign above the room-dividing arch displaying the words *FREE WI-FI*.

Cable sat facing the main entrance. An ideal position that Blaine had to forfeit in order to buy the first round. Blaine took a seat opposite with his back to the door. He looked over at the fire exit, behind and to the left of Cable.

He also noticed the door to the kitchen at the far end of the bar, which stood to his right. The place seemed busy enough to drown out their conversation and allow them to talk openly. The two bartenders appeared quite occupied, and no-one in the room sat or stood by themselves. You could bet that someone in a crowded room with no-one to talk to would eavesdrop, no matter if they didn't mean to.

As Cable took his pint and sipped from it, Blaine figured that he had surveyed the room already. Blaine did the same with his drink.

They both placed their glasses down on the table and wiped any froth from their lips. Awkward described the situation. Five days ago, this man had come ready to kill him, and now Blaine sat having a beer with him.

'You mostly work in the UK?' Cable said.

Blaine felt unsure how much to reveal. Any conversation would, by definition, aim to learn more about another person. Something to which Blaine had a severe allergy. 'For the past few years or so.'

'I'm mostly in Europe,' Cable said. 'There's work but not exactly prestige stuff.'

'Eastern Europe offered a lot of work around 2007. There and South Africa. Jo'burg was a mess.'

'Heard about that. All sneaky stuff, though, right?'

'Yeah. Sneaky stuff.' Blaine smiled. Cable's accent originated from London—almost East End. Did he put it on to make him seem tougher? Cable stood, perhaps, an inch shorter than Blaine, who reached a modest six foot. Neither of them huge, muscular guys, and Blaine preferred to keep it that way. Big bulging muscles tended to stand out in a crowd, and he preferred to blend in. Cable's laidback attitude jarred with Blaine. He spoke a little louder and reclined back in his chair as though completely relaxed. Sneaky, he was not.

'Yeah, I preferred the work in Europe,' Cable said. 'Easier people to deal with. A lot of work in China, but those guys are a pain. They pay, but fuck me, they want things done a certain way. Precision planning. Down to the last detail. Like they don't fucking understand that things go tits-up sometimes.' He took another sip of beer. 'Came back here six months ago.'

'So, you're—freelance?'

'You think I wanna work for some private security firm? With a pension plan? Ha! I'm not signing my life away. I wanna reap the rewards of my bloody hard work, mate.'

'Agent?'

'Nah. All word of mouth. I have a few contacts; they get me work. Been doing a lot of small stuff. Private security gigs. Ya know? Last Monday was the fist hit I've had in a year.'

'Sorry about that.'

'Yeah, fuck it. It wasn't my gig. I still got paid something. Just no bonus, ya know?'

'Yeah, I know.'

'I swear to God, when I saw you in that supermarket, I thought I was a dead man.'

Blaine let out the slightest of smiles. 'I'm not a huge believer in coincidences, myself.'

'You okay if we talk a little shop?'

Blaine leant back in his chair, matching Cable's relaxed body language. 'Go for it.'

'Do you charge extra for body disposal?'

Blaine smiled again and allowed his middle-class accent to fall into a more casual one.

'Fuck, yes,' Blaine said. 'Ten percent. But I'm rarely asked to do that. Unless it's, specifically, a clean-up job, you shouldn't have to dispose of a body.'

Cable leant forward as if he had something secret to say. A smile lit his face as if he had remembered a hilarious Christmas-cracker joke. He looked giddy.

'My last proper hit was in Budapest. A year ago. Some sleazy porn producer. Owed some money or something. Anyway, I take him down in his apartment—suffocated, right?'

Blaine nodded, intrigued, and leant forward, putting his elbows on the table.

'All immaculate,' Cable said. 'And, as I make my way back to the corridor and head to the lifts, out steps this gorgeous woman. We exchange looks. She's sexy as hell. Had these gravity defying tits that bounced as she walked—and as I step into the lift that she just got out of, and the door starts closing, I see her unlocking the bloody door to this guy's apartment!'

Blaine smiled again. He took a swig of beer and let out a slight chuckle.

'So, I shove my hand in the doors and make my way back to the apartment just as she sees the body on the ground, right? And she lets out the most almighty of screams. Like those bouncing tits of hers were just extensions of her lungs!'

Blaine chuckled again.

'I grab her—get my hand over her mouth, and she's fighting and clawing at me. Now, I don't have a gun. No knife. So, I've got to bloody strangle this bitch right then and there. It takes her five damn minutes to go down. So, I'm panicking, right? I'm thinking surely someone heard that scream. I've got to get rid of these bodies. I hear police sirens. Sounds like one car, out the front. I'm totally fucked. So I drag both bodies to the bedroom. Open the window. And throw them out the back of the building. They land in the alleyway next to my parked car, right? And I'm hoping that the coppers are actually inside the building by now so that they don't hear the bloody splat sound they made. I climb out of the window and make my way down—get the bodies in the boot of the car and drive off.'

Cable paused to take a big swig of beer, but somehow, managed to keep smiling as he did.

'So—as I drive past the front of the building—I only see a bloody ambulance in front of the kebab shop next door. No police. Just some poor fucker who'd eaten a dodgy takeaway!'

'Aw, man that's harsh,' Blaine said, laughing.

'And do you think I was gonna get anything extra for a clean up? Fuck no. But they were in my car now, so I had to go the whole hog. Fuck.'

'Well, that's the job,' Blaine said. 'If you can't improvise, you're fucked.'

———

Jasper walked into his office and headed to his desk. Julie stood behind the door as it swung open, and while Jasper's back faced her, she whipped in front of the doorway. Jasper picked up his phone and saw her standing at the door, sweating.

'Julie?' he said. 'Not out to lunch? What's up? You look terrible.'

'Oh, yeah … just feeling a little run down. And I just threw up in the bathroom.'

'Oh, no. Well, look, if you need to take the rest of the day off.'

'I'll see how I feel after lunch. Thought you'd be out already? Do you need anything?'

'No, no. You look after yourself.'

'I will. Thanks, Jasper.'

Julie left the office and walked back through the hallway. Her heart almost leaping out of her chest.

Back at her desk, she brought up the website for the firm's bank and typed in the account details and passwords that she'd managed to photograph. With the information she had, she could only access three of the Kaizen Group accounts. It meant moving more money from each. About £1,600,000 from each. It would—in all probability—get noticed, but she didn't care. With the press of a button, she had transferred over a million pounds into her current account. Scary how easy it proved. Julie did the same two more times from the other accounts, closed the browser window, and deleted her history. She left the computer in sleep mode and left the building. It would be the last time she would step inside the office.

The tube journey to the station where she had parked her car that morning felt like a dream. Julie had been in life-threatening, stressful situations before when in the Army, but never anything illegal. That remained her father's area of expertise. And, though she loathed stooping to a criminal act, the life of her daughter made it an exception absolutely necessary.

Once in her car, she headed to Brixton in south London. Jasper would have realised by now that she wouldn't come back but, hopefully, the excuse she had given wouldn't have raised any alarms.

Julie parked illegally down an alleyway not far from the bank, just off the high street. A parking ticket wouldn't bother her, but a wheel clamp might give trouble.

This branch, Julie had never been to before, but her local wouldn't have worked. Instead of a few employees behind a booth, her branch had been fitted with an array of automated banking machines. Insufferable computer screens that would, occasionally, not recognise a cheque she would want to pay in. One time, the stupid things forced her to use separate machines to pay in a cheque and then take out cash.

As Julie walked into the building, she noticed every camera in the corners. Every customer. Every employee. Would she have been better dealing with a machine? At least those imposing computer screens wouldn't see the guilt in her eyes. Julie joined the large queue for the cashiers and waited.

'Cashier number four, please,' the pre-recorded voice said.

Julie stepped forward and stood opposite the middle-aged man behind the glass.

'How can I help you today?' he said.

'I'm looking to take out a substantial amount of cash from my account.'

'I see. Do you have your card?'

'Um ... yes.' Julie pulled her purse out of her handbag and took out the bankcard. She slid it into the device in front of her and typed in her pin number. The cashier's eyes widened as he brought up the details of her current account.

'Just how much were you wanting to withdraw today, Mrs Jones?'

She looked back up at him. 'Five million should do it.'

Julie sat alone in the bank manager's office, clutching her handbag. It felt surprisingly cosy, considering she had sat in there for nearly ten minutes. She had no idea what the manager must have thought, but surely, he must have suspected some foul play. Surely they could see that the money had been transferred to her account only a couple of hours ago. However, it *was* in her account and legally hers to withdraw. She felt sure of it. It had to be.

Evan, the manager, walked back into the room, startling Julie, who jumped at the sound. Evan noticed but declined to comment.

'Right,' he said, taking a seat next to Julie. 'As I'm sure you must be aware, it isn't every day that someone walks into our branch and asks to withdraw five-million pounds.'

'I can believe that,' Julie said.

'Yes, well, when this amount of cash gets withdrawn, then usually a security team does it. Not the account holder themselves. May I ask why you wish to withdraw this amount today?'

'Business,' Julie said.

'Well, I'd hope it wouldn't be for pleasure.' Evan expected a laugh, but Julie gave only a smile. His face turned serious. 'A lot of banks have a cap on the amount that they allow a single customer to take out. Now, we don't have that policy but are restricted by the amount we have in the actual building. We're also a little concerned with the fact that only today did that money transfer into your account. I'm sure you're aware that, occasionally, people—when transferring money—will mistype a number and, suddenly, a lot of money gets given to the wrong person. And taking that money is illegal.'

'Yes, I understand,' Julie said. Evan had to fish for any

hint of wrongdoing. Perhaps he even knew it was dodgy as hell, but as far as the law went, Julie felt sure that the money now belonged to her.

A timid knock at the door interrupted, and a female employee opened the door and poked her head into the office.

'Quick word?' she said.

'I'll be right back, Mrs Jones,' Evan said and left Julie alone again.

The door failed to muffle their conversation, and Julie listened intently.

'I've spoken to Cunningham Global,' the employee said. 'They're adamant that they have not purposefully paid that money into her account.'

'Okay, call the police. I'll keep her in there—tell her we're sorting the cash.'

Julie reached into her handbag, grasped hold of her husband's BB gun, and pulled it out.

Evan walked back into the room with a nervous smile on his face. 'Well, we're just going to try and sort the cash now —' His eyes drifted to the handgun in Julie's hand.

She stepped toward him and dug it into his side, not wanting him to get a good look at it but also wanting him to feel its metal composition as opposed to plastic. Wanted him to think that she threatened him with no mere toy.

'Mrs Jones, the police are on their way,' he said. The quiver in his voice let Julie know that she had complete control over him.

'Tell them to bring up all the cash, just as I asked,' Julie said. She moved him out of the office. The other employee in the office opposite held a phone, about to dial.

Julie pushed Evan toward the woman.

'Put it down.' Julie held the gun with two hands, just as taught. Her finger rested on the trigger guard. The gun pointed directly at Evan's chest. Julie kept the gun low enough that he wouldn't see the tell-tale 6mm barrel designed only for small plastic pellets. 'The cash—quickly.'

11

WITHDRAWAL SYPTOMS

Julie held Evan close to her, still jabbing the metal BB gun into his side. They stood in the main part of the bank with the front door locked. Several customers had tried entering the building, but the employees soon waved them away. Three large black bags of cash lay at Julie's feet. Hefty luggage holders with heavy-duty shoulder straps. The cashiers brought up the final one. The man and woman dragged it over to the pile, as sweat dripped from their foreheads. Julie hadn't realised just how weighty five-million pounds would be in cash.

She saw two of the cashiers in the back squabbling; trying to keep their argument to a minimum. Julie pointed the gun at them. 'Hey,' she said. 'What is that?'

The two women froze with fear. The one on the left raised her hand from under the desk.

'The silent alarm,' Evan said. 'Please, don't shoot—they're only doing their job.'

Julie plunged the weapon back into Evan's side. 'How long until the police arrive?'

'Um … should be about two minutes.'

She pushed the gun harder into him.

'At least five minutes!'

Julie looked down at the four heavy bags and wiped the sweat from her brow. A phone rang. The cashiers looked down at the ringing device on their desk.

'Don't answer it,' Julie said.

Evan turned to her. 'What now?' he said. 'You can still just walk out.'

'Now, we take the bags to my car.' She pointed at the cashiers. 'You, take a bag. Take it to the car.'

The middle-aged man, who had sat behind the glass when she'd first walked in, picked up the first bag with a grunt. Julie took her keys out of her handbag and threw them at him. He didn't react quickly enough to catch them, and they hit him straight in the face. Julie felt awful but couldn't show it. She stared at the man until he bent over and retrieved them.

'You lot, too,' she said, looking at the other employees. 'Grab a bag and get it all in the car in the alley.'

'This is crazy, Mrs Jones,' Evan said. 'You can't possibly get away. They know who you are—where you live.'

'I don't care.'

'I can see that.'

Julie walked over to the front door, and Evan unlocked it, letting his employees out with the cash-laden bags.

She watched from the window while the four bags disappeared around the corner. How would they fit in her car? Maybe two in the boot. One on the back seat. Another in the passenger seat. Would the boot even close with two massive bags like that in there?

'What the hell is taking so long?' Julie said.

'My employees are good workers, Mrs Jones. But if they have holiday time to take, they'll always take it. You just let them walk out of a hostage situation.'

Julie pushed Evan to the doorway and walked him out of the building. Several people stared from the other side of the street. They had seen four people carry four large bags out of a bank. Julie couldn't bring herself to look over at them. Instead, she focused on making it to her car.

In the alleyway, her car remained where she had left it. No parking tickets on the windscreen. No wheel clamp. The four large bags of money sat discarded on the ground next to the vehicle with no sign of any of the cashiers. A single police siren echoed in the distance, and Julie dashed over to her car, still holding the gun on Evan. The car was locked.

'The keys,' she said. 'Look for the keys.'

Evan got to his knees and searched around the bags. 'I don't see them.'

The police sirens grew closer. More than one police vehicle headed her way. 'Fuck,' she said. 'Where's your car?'

Evan had parked his car at the back of the bank, against a long wooden fence that backed onto the gardens of the neighbouring houses. Even dragging just one of the bags took them a good thirty seconds. The first bag fit snugly into the boot of the smart Mercedes coupe, but it became obvious that the others would have to go inside the car.

Julie and Evan headed back to the bags just as a police car pulled up. Two officers sat inside, looking at her and talking on their radios.

She pushed Evan toward the second bag, and he picked it up so that it hung from his shoulder. Julie took hold of the third and offered him the strap. Evan grasped it and dragged the bag back to his car. Then she took the final bag and followed him, scraping her bounty along the concrete.

Another police car arrived from the opposite direction. The slam of car doors indicated that the police officers from the first car had exited their vehicle.

Evan pushed one of his bags into the back of the car, as Julie joined him and opened the door to the driver's side. She flung the seat forward and shoved her bag into the back, on top of the other one.

'Get in,' Julie said.

'Please, you have the money. Just go.'

Julie aimed the gun at his head.

Evan pushed the passenger seat back to its normal position and, without questioning her again, climbed into the seat and pulled the huge money bag on top of his lap.

Julie joined him at the wheel and put the gun between her legs.

'The keys,' she said.

'You just push the start button,' Evan said. 'The keys just … have to be in the car … to start it.'

Julie pushed the engine start button, and the vehicle roared to life. She brought the automatic gear lever down to reverse and pulled back in a sharp semi-circle. Back into drive and Julie pushed down on the accelerator and steered down the alleyway, where the two police cars now blocked the exit.

The armed police officers crouched behind the vehicles with their handguns drawn. 'Stop the car, now,' one of them said. 'Right now.'

Julie stamped on the brakes and came to a halt. Close enough to see the policeman's eyes. They stayed steady, confident, and professional. She'd seen plenty of eyes like that in the Army. The eyes of someone who you shouldn't fuck with. Someone in control.

'We should get out,' Evan said.

Julie looked in her rear-view mirror and pushed the gearstick into reverse.

'Get out of the vehicle and get on the ground, now,' the officer said.

Julie slammed her foot onto the accelerator, and the car reversed at great speed toward the wooden fence at the back of the bank and smashed through it, sending splinters and wooden panels flying over the windscreen.

Julie turned the wheel to the right and skidded the car to a halt in the middle of a family garden, destroying a bright-blue slide and setting off the airbags in the front. Quickly, Julie pushed the inflated safety device down and saw that the front of the car pointed at another wooden fence. Another garden. Four houses stood all in a row, directly in front of her, and all with gardens. The main road lay only a swing set, a barbecue, and three tricycles away. Gear shift to drive. Accelerator.

The first fence broke in half but stopped the car as it wedged between the wooden horizontal beams. Reverse. Julie backed up as much as she could. One of the police cars drove toward her. Drive. The wheels spun beneath them, and the car lurched forward and crashed through the remaining beams of wood. The car, in full throttle, exploded through the next fence and decimated a gas-powered barbecue set.

The police vehicle spun into the first garden just as the gas cylinder bumped off the bonnet of the Mercedes with an almighty hiss. It flew into the air, landing in the windscreen of the chasing police car.

Julie smashed through the final two fences and bumped her way over the pavement curb, scraping the front of the car along the street. She held her foot flat on the pedal, and the car bolted down the road.

The remaining police car soon appeared in her rear-view mirror. Its pulsating blue lights and wailing siren felt like a warning that she would never get away.

Julie continued down the busy street as dusk fell. Rush hour, though a painful time for any commuter in London, seemed like a Godsend to her right now. Without anything to lose, Julie drove the Mercedes up onto the pavement, scattering pedestrians onto the busy road. She pulled back onto the street, crossed into the oncoming traffic, and turned into another road. A quick glance in the mirror let Julie see the police car, having to manoeuvre with care across the road. She had bought herself some time, but as soon as a helicopter arrived on scene, the chase would be over. The kidnappers would never get their money. And her daughter would be as good as dead.

The police car had followed her onto the side road and caught up to her quickly. Julie slammed on the brakes sharply, turned into another road on the left, and pulled the handbrake. The car screeched to a halt.

Julie waited.

And waited.

She then put the car into reverse once more and pushed her foot down hard. The car backed up at speed, just as the police car tore around the corner. The Mercedes collided with the pursuit vehicle's front right-hand wheel arch at such force that airbags engulfed the police officers.

Julie turned to Evan, who sat clutching the money bag for dear life as if it made for the only thing cushioning him from all the devastation. 'Get out,' she said.

Evan unclasped his fingers from around the bag and slid out of the car, shaking. Julie shoved the gear back into drive and, with a smoke-heavy wheel spin, untangled the Mercedes from the police car's mangled front end and drove away.

On the main road, Julie lowered her speed and blended in with the other traffic around her, hoping no-one would pay too much attention to the damage at both ends of the vehicle. She pulled her phone from her handbag and double-clicked the home button.

'Call Nick,' Julie said.

'Calling Nick,' her phone replied. After a short ringtone, Nick picked up.

'Julie? How did it go? Are you all right?'

'Nick, shut up and listen. You need to get out of the house, right now. Come meet me at the Travelodge in Balham.'

'In Balham? Why? What's happened?'

'Just do it, Nick. Right now.'

'All right, I'm going now. What the hell happened, Julie?'

'I only robbed a bloody bank, didn't I?'

12

GUNFIGHTS ARE OVERRATED

A third dart hit the treble-twenty of the dartboard. Cable walked up to it and pulled out all three darts. He turned back to Blaine, who readied himself for his turn.

The pub had grown busier as the day went on, and the two of them had decided to relinquish their table and stand. When in a crowded room, Blaine always preferred to stand. The position gave more visibility and less chance of getting overpowered if the situation turned sour. He would have preferred pool to darts. Not that the Woodman had a table. Cause and effect provided his passion. The physics of knocking perfect spheres into one another pleased him greatly. He saw it as a perfect metaphor for the work he did. Life too. All just cause and effect.

'I bet you're a Glock man,' Cable said.

'Until a couple of years ago,' Blaine said. 'I got seduced.' He threw his first dart at the board and hit a treble-twenty.

'Ah, I saw you with a Sig, right?' Cable said.

'P229. Beautiful.' Another dart hit the treble-twenty.

'A little too small for me.'

'Covert is a good thing in our job. I'm not going to carry around a Desert Eagle.'

'How does it compare to the Glock?'

'Well, there's not much in it. The Glock's a bit lighter, maybe. I'll give it that. But what most attracted me to the Sig was the hammer.' Another treble-twenty. Blaine walked up to the board and pulled out his darts. Cable looked mystified.

'Honestly, that little piece of metal can be a real useful tool,' Blaine said.

Matt took his position in front of the dartboard and threw yet another treble-twenty.

'Last year, I waited in someone's house,' Blaine said. 'Mobster type—tough as nails. Middle of the night, he comes in. Goes straight to the fridge. He's browsing the food when I walk up behind him, gun outstretched. I think he took out a bottle of Sunny Delight or something. Just as he's about to take a swig, I cock the gun. He freezes. And I kid you not; he pisses his pants. Stands in a puddle.'

Matt laughed and threw another treble-twenty.

'He knew exactly what was coming,' Blaine said. 'Only, he didn't. It was a warning job. They piss me off. I can't let them see my face.'

Treble-twenty.

'Unfortunately, these days, it's all warnings and small jobs,' Blaine said. 'Babysitting.'

'Yeah, remind me never to hire you as a bodyguard,' Cable said.

His eyes gazed past Blaine and over to some local man in his fifties, who had noticed the amazing score they had both racked up. Blaine saw him too. He stood staring with disbelief.

They both stared right back at the man with dead eyes.

Completely blank looks on their faces. You could tell a lot from a person's eyes. Everyone knew that. Blaine and Cable's eyes said nothing. To look into a blank slate and see complete emptiness in their soul proved highly disturbing. A technique Blaine used as a quick way of letting people know they shouldn't come near him, shouldn't talk to him, and definitely, shouldn't fuck with him.

The man's smile dropped, and he walked away from his small circular table.

'Another game?' Cable said. 'You can go first?'

'Nah.' Blaine picked up his drink from the windowsill next to the dartboard, and the two of them sat at the man's vacated table.

Across the room, a guy leant against a barstool, chatting to three girls. Blaine noticed him touching the middle one on her waist.

Cable took a sip of his beer. 'Ya know, sometimes, after a job—I'll think how easy it was,' he said. 'It's not a challenge.'

The girls in front of the guy asked him questions. Blaine couldn't make out what they said, but it seemed obvious that they all wanted him. The girl he sat touching moved closer while he spoke. He ignored the other two girls.

'You're good at what you do,' Blaine said. 'It's not the job that's easy.'

He watched the guy wrap his legs around the girl and bring her close to him. They kissed. The other girls said something to each other and moved away.

Blaine drank his beer.

Cable finished his drink.

'Have you ever been in a gunfight?' Cable said. 'I mean a proper gunfight. A shootout. Like the movies. Not just involved in a shooting.'

'No. That's how you get noticed. You shouldn't pull a trigger any more than you have to.' Blaine finished his drink. 'I went to considerable lengths to become anonymous.'

'Yeah, but what does that mean?'

'No-one ever knows who I am, and no-one ever will. It's a dangerous game we play.'

Cable made a disgruntled sound as though he thought differently. 'Hm, work is just a job. Life is the game. And such a fun game.' He looked over at the kissing couple leant against the barstool at the other end of the pub. They practically ate each other's faces off. Another man, bigger than the guy, walked up to them, looking furious. He shoved the guy, pointing at him. The girl got between them and tried stopping the man, putting her hands on his chest. Then she kissed his face. The guy put up his hands and backed away, apologising.

'So very true,' Blaine said. 'And, in some ways, more dangerous than the job.'

The guy walked to the exit of the pub and looked back at the girl he'd done so well with, now all over the newcomer. She kissed his face, wrapping her arms around him.

'Therein lies the fun,' Cable said. He held up his empty pint glass. 'Another?'

The streetlights bathed the exterior of the Woodman in sickly yellow light as Cable stumbled out of the pub. Blaine followed, wearing his single-breasted cashmere coat. They walked back up the road toward the supermarket car park.

Cable pulled a pack of cigarettes from his pocket and lit one. He offered the pack to Blaine, who refused. While Cable took a deep breath of smoke into his lungs, he looked out at the incredibly blue night sky. It gave a harsh contrast to the dim yellow around them.

'What's it all about?' Cable said. 'Ya know? Do you think about that stuff? Do you care? Or wonder ... if we're really doomed for who we are?'

'You're not getting religious on me, are you?' Blaine said.

'I don't know. I think about it sometimes.'

'Look—the way I see it ... how you picture the universe is what the universe is for you. What you do, and how you perceive what you're doing, makes the world that you live in. So, you can be as truly evil as you want ... as long as you just don't care.'

Cable nodded along.

'But if you start to wonder what if ... what if what I'm doing is wrong? What if I'm going to hell for who I am? What if I should stop? You're fucked.'

'So, you don't believe in God or any of that?'

'Never met him,' Blaine said. 'Tell you what ... the next person who dies in front of me, I'll ask them what they see as they go.'

'Ha,' Cable said. 'Yeah. Be sure to let me know.'

Blaine saw a few people headed toward them. Blaine grew aware of how drunk he'd become, as the seven hooded guys approached the two of them. He put his mind into mission mode and made a quick assessment of the incoming potential threat. Seven men. Five black. Two white. All wearing hoodies. The two men at the front led the others. With those two put down, the others would be more likely to run. Blaine felt certain that Cable would throw the first punch if it came to it. If that happened, everyone's fists would swing. More bruises to hide. A few probable hospital visits for the hoodies. A lot of attention. Unwanted attention.

The aggressive-looking guys slowed and got right in Blaine's path. 'Just give us your wallets, yeah,' the Hoody said. He pulled a knife from his jacket. A fancy butterfly knife, which concealed the blade within the handle. He didn't seem able to perform the fancy flipping technique that had made them so popular in action movies. Instead, he opened it with two hands and held it forward as if it was a tiny sword.

Blaine could see fifteen ways to disarm and render him unconscious in under five seconds. The guy's accomplices seemed jumpy, looking around, making sure no-one watched.

'Trust me,' Cable said. 'This is something you don't want to do.'

He stared at them with that blank look. To the layman, it would warn them off, but to a group of edgy muggers, it may do the exact opposite. Maybe that's just what Cable wanted. The Hoody didn't take it. He got angry and raised his voice. The knife too.

'No, I fink it's somefin' I do wanna do, actually,' he said. 'Now, give me ya fuckin' wallets before I fuck you up, yeh?'

Two others pulled out knives, and a third had a short, sturdy baton. They all seemed pumped up and full of adrenaline.

'I ain't gonna give you my wallet,' Cable said. 'That's just something you're going to have to deal with. Now, is there anything else I can help you with?'

Blaine looked up at the buildings around them, looking for any CCTV cameras. They remained unobserved. And the yellow glow of the nearest streetlight barely touched them. Even from across the street, no-one would manage to make out any of their faces.

The Hoody took a step closer to Cable and stuck out his chest. 'Listen, bruv, I will beat the shit outta you.'

Blaine could tell this was the line. Cable readied to throw his first punch and, likely, devastate the guy's nose forever. It would mean an ambulance. Hospital. Police. Attention. Unwanted attention.

Blaine stepped between them and turned up the *East End* on his accent dial.

'Listen to me. I've only got a tenner in my wallet and maybe a couple of quid in my pocket. I know, for a fact, that this fucker here spent all his cash in the pub. So, you can mug us for only twelve quid, because we'll cancel any cards in our wallets. We'll also call the police so that they'll be out looking for you, and you'll have to call it a night. All for twelve fucking quid. Split seven ways. Or—you can let us go. We won't call the police. And you can go mug someone else who's far more likely to be carrying more cash on them than us.'

Blaine worried that he had sounded too eloquent. Too precise. He needed them on his side if it were to work. But he also needed them to understand him. Blaine pulled out his wallet and showed them the single ten-pound note inside. 'Because this is all you get if you mug us.'

The Hoody stepped back from Cable and looked at the tenner in Blaine's hand.

'You give me that tenner and your cards, and we'll let you go.'

'Then I'll call the police, and you'll have to go home,' Blaine said. 'Or, you can let me keep this and go and make more money off someone else. And you know there'll be someone else.' Blaine smiled as if he cared.

One of the others grew visibly anxious. He looked over his shoulder. 'Come on, man; it's not werf it,' he said.

'Fuck sake, man,' the Hoody said. 'Come on.'

Blaine put his wallet back in his pocket, as the group of seven hooded men walked past him and Cable.

Cable continued looking at Blaine as if he had just spat in his pint glass. 'What the fuck are you doing?' he said. 'We could've ripped them apart. They think we're some poncy wankers now.'

'Better that way. What if someone got seriously hurt? We wouldn't want any police involvement.'

'Fuck! You didn't want to beat the crap out of them? Tell me you didn't? Come on.'

Blaine shouted back at Cable, losing his temper, 'Yes. I wanted to elbow that prick in the face, take his knife, stick it in his leg, and push him back into his friends. Then I'd grab the others' blades and push them into their stomachs and, maybe, I'd stick one right into their mouth, under the chin. Then, when they're writhing in pain on the ground, I'd stamp on their faces with my boot heel. Over. And. Over.'

'Then, let's do it. We can go and do it. Live a little, man. Can't you feel that?'

Cable stood there, absolutely buzzing. His eyes a frenzy of wild activity, darting around as if his imagination had control over his corneas.

'I rarely feel that,' Cable said. 'And I bet you're the same. That buzz. That adrenaline. That's life. It's emotion. It's—ya know?'

Blaine could feel it too and imagined that he glowed. He closed his eyes and tried to subdue his instincts. 'You want to wander around looking for them?'

Cable didn't answer at first. Didn't even look at where

94

they'd run off to. He looked at Blaine. 'I guess we can always go to plan B,' he said.

'Which is what?'

He leant in close. 'Let's try and kill each other.'

Blaine tried to work out just how serious he was. It became obvious to him, now, that Matthew Cable was an unhinged sociopath. Someone you could never trust. And someone who took a lot of joy in firing bullets into a person.

Cable smiled as if only joking. Blaine gave out a small chuckle to appease him.

'I'm gonna go,' Cable said. 'It's not often I get to talk about this stuff.'

'Yeah, I know what you mean.'

Cable offered his hand. Blaine reached out and shook it, still on guard but fairly certain Cable was just drunk. The smile on his face confused him. He couldn't put it down just to merriment. It seemed to hide something behind it. But then Blaine hid most of his thoughts too. He watched Cable walk back down the road toward the Woodman.

Blaine pulled out his phone and typed a text to Tommy. *Job accepted. Send details.*

13
HEAT

Danny Drake pulled his car over to the curb and turned off his engine. He reached into his pocket and pulled out a small plastic cylinder of cocaine. The lid unscrewed to form a little spoon, which he used to scoop out a mound of the white powder. He brought it to his nose, being sure to breathe out before it got too close. On many an occasion, he had lost a decent bump to a rogue exhale. He shoved the small plastic spoon to his nostril and breathed in deeply.

The effect came almost instantly. Perhaps no more than psychosomatic. Probably, he could snort a line of crushed up Polos and have a similar initial buzz. He scratched his scalp, grazing his fingernails through his short blonde hair. The lethargy left him, and he felt confident to get out and do what needed to be done. The walk to the house would get his adrenaline going.

He placed the coke back in his pocket and opened the door. A beeping sound from the car reminded him that his headlights remained on. He turned them off and got out.

The flashing blue lights from the two marked police cars

lit up the entire street. Monday nights usually made for the slow ones.

Drake walked over to DC Holly Barnes, who stood on the front lawn. Her fitted suit looked smart. A vast contrast to his rumpled grey one. Had she watched him in the car? If so, she made no reference to it.

'Evening, Drake,' she said.

'Holly.'

'You took your time. Miles has been asking for you for the past twenty minutes.'

Holly, in her mid-twenties, had shoulder-length brown hair worn in a professional style. Always on time. Always neat and tidy. Drake felt like she complimented him. Or more that she covered for him?

They walked toward the house. The neighbours twitched their curtains. Eager to get a glimpse of a dead body or a screaming perp in handcuffs.

The house was a mess. A typical family home. Children's toys. Colourful cereal packets. Busy parents with never enough time to keep it straight.

DCI Jack Miles stood in the middle of the open-plan kitchen and living room.

'Drake, how long does it take to answer a simple call?'

'Sorry, Sir, traffic.'

'Yeah, I'm sure.'

'So, we've got a missing family?'

'And missing money,' Miles said. 'Julie Jones transferred five million to her personal account and tried to take the cash out of a bank in Bromley.'

'Five mil? In cash?'

'The bank, obviously, found it suspicious and refused, but it turns out Mrs Jones had a gun on her.'

'She got away with the money?'

'Don't sound so impressed. She threatened the lives of everyone in that bank and caused a lot of property damage.'

'Sounds desperate.'

'I want her found.' Miles walked over to the Constables at the front door. 'I want neighbours spoken to. When did they leave? When were they last seen?'

Drake turned back to Holly as the uniformed officers left the house. 'What about the kid?' he asked.

'Wasn't at school today,' Holly said. 'Julie phoned them, saying she'd taken ill.'

'And then went and robbed a bank with a BB gun,' Drake said.

'BB gun? How'd you know that?'

Drake picked up the cereal packet from the coffee table next to them and held it high. He looked at Holly through the tiny holes in the packaging and shook it. The carton rattled. Drake put his hand up and poured a few bright-yellow plastic balls into his palm.

'I am a detective, Holly.' Drake took another look around the room. The coke pulsed through his blood stream. His mind set on fire. It told him things. A puzzle to be solved. He always loved puzzles. Just a simple matter of putting the pieces together. DCI Miles knew he was good at that. It was why he put up with the attitude.

'She stole five million,' Drake said. 'Why five? You could retire on less than that. And she moved it into her bank account. She knew she'd get sussed.'

'What are you thinking, Drake? You got that look on your face.'

'Remember two months ago? That couple found dead. Six-year-old son missing. Money taken out of their bank.

Borrowed from friends.'

'Yeah, we never found the money.'

'Or the kid. And there was one the month before. A couple had their daughter taken. Asked to pay half a mil.'

'What happened to them?'

'They got us involved, and then no-one turned up at the exchange. We never found the daughter.'

'You think it's the same here?'

'Could be. Although, the five mil seems crazy. Five hundred thousand is, maybe, something a well-off couple could get together over a weekend, but this? It's almost like they never expected them to pay.'

Drake paused in mid-thought. 'Fuck,' he said. He ran past Holly and over to Miles, who stood by the front door. 'Sir, we have to get these units out of here. And we can't question the neighbours.'

'What're you talking about?' Miles said.

'Sir, I think this is a kidnapping. And if that's the case, we can't let the kidnappers know that we're involved. All this attention is only—'

'Drake, there is no evidence that this is a kidnapping. The more information we have, the easier it'll be to locate them.'

'With respect, Sir, you haven't got a fucking clue what you're doing and may well be putting their little girl in danger.'

He realised that he had said the wrong thing almost immediately. Miles, a hard case, hated getting told what to do. Much like himself. Drake had to appease him. Put the idea in his head.

'Drake, I'm in charge here.'

Drake lowered his voice. 'Then, take charge, Sir. I'm

telling you; I think their girl has been taken and they were forced to get that money. Now, every second we're here, flashing our lights and talking to neighbours, the more likely the kidnappers are to know that. We need to do this covertly, Sir. I'm just telling you my thoughts. You make the decision.'

Miles stood there, mulling it over. It would be painful for him to do what he'd suggested, but it remained the right decision. Surely, he could see that.

'Sorry,' he said. 'We're doing this my way.'

Drake walked out of the house, annoyed at his boss's stupidity.

Holly ran after him.

'Drake? You really think that girl's been taken?'

'Yeah. I do. It's the only thing that makes sense.'

'I've got an idea. But it's a bit fucked up.'

'Now, you're talking my language.'

She pulled out her phone and dialled. Then pressed it to her ear and waited. 'Oh, hi, is that the station? Yes, look, it's Deborah Miles here, I've been trying to get through to Jack, but his phone seems to be off. I've been in a minor car accident and am in the Royal London Hospital in A and E. Is there any chance you could let my husband know?'

She looked over at Drake, who smiled back. He couldn't believe the balls on this girl and liked her attitude. She'd always done what she thought right. Not what people told her to. This made him happy to have gotten partnered with her for the past few years.

'That's great, thank you so much.' Holly ended the call and raised an eyebrow.

'You know, you sounded nothing like her, right?' Drake said.

'Didn't seem like it mattered.'

They looked over at Miles in the doorway of the house, who responded to a call on his radio. He nodded and looked around. 'Drake,' he said, walking over to his car. 'I have to go. Keep uniform asking questions and see about tracking their mobiles and their cars, okay.'

'Will do, Sir,' Drake said.

Miles got in his car and pulled away at speed.

'Looks like you're in charge, Sir,' Holly said.

Drake smiled and looked over at the uniformed officers going door-to-door. 'Holly, get them away from the neighbours. And out of sight. I want the cars away from the front of the house. And no uniforms or lights anywhere near this place.'

'You got it.' Holly walked off to round up the officers. Miles had it right about one thing. If they had a smartphone, they might be able to track it.

14

A ROOM WITH A VIEW

Julie pulled up to the Balham Travelodge car park in the stolen dented Mercedes. Glad it had grown dark already. Paranoid about getting looks from vehicles passing her on the motorway, she had kept her speed at seventy. Not that anyone else did. If anything, it brought more attention than the messed up bumper and bonnet.

The car park stood quiet and, from the outside, the hotel seemed the same. Julie took out her phone and called Nick, who answered quickly.

'Julie? Are you all right? Where are you?' he said.

'I'm in the car park. I'm fine.'

'Jesus, so you got the money?'

'Yeah, it's in this car in four huge bags.'

'Okay, I'm coming out.'

Nick hung up, and Julie waited, looking at her phone. Her phone. The kidnappers had told Nick that they would call again tomorrow. But they'd called on the house phone. Not either of their mobiles. A wave of panic cascaded through her body while she imagined all the police, searching her house. Searching for her.

Nick knocked on the window and gave Julie a fright. 'Who's car is this?'

She opened the door in a panic. 'They have no way of calling us,' she said.

'What?'

'They fucking called on the house phone, Nick. It's not like we can just creep back home and hope nobody's watching.'

'Okay, let's get inside first,' Nick said.

'I've got four bags.'

'Okay.'

Julie opened the back door and revealed the first two bags. She tried pulling one of them off the chair but struggled.

'Here, let me do it,' Nick said.

'I can manage.' Julie pulled the strap over her head and used her body to lift the heavy bag. Nick took hold of the other one, and Julie took satisfaction in watching him struggle just as much as she had.

The first-floor hotel room looked small. With the four bags of cash on the bed, it looked even smaller.

'I didn't think five million would be so heavy,' Nick said.

'They only had a limited number of fifties and twenties in the bank and put tens and fives in there too.'

Julie shook her head, trying to rid herself of the inane conversation they were having and get back on track. 'Nick, we need to get back to the house.'

'You're crazy. You just said we can't go back. You told me you used my silly gun to rob a bank, and I'm pretty sure the house is swarming with police by now.'

'They're gonna call tomorrow. They're gonna call, and we won't be there. The police will answer, Nick. And then Jessica is gone. Forever. So, we're gonna figure this out.'

'Okay, I'll think of something.'

'And the car,' Julie said.

'The stolen car?'

'I should take it somewhere else. Where no-one can see.'

'I'm sure it's fine parked here. It's bloody Balham Travelodge. After tomorrow, nothing matters, right? Shouldn't we do something about our phones?'

'How do you mean?'

'Well, can't the police track them? You see it in movies all the time, but can they do that for real?'

'I don't know. Get rid of it anyway. Take out the battery.'

'It doesn't come out.'

'Then, smash it.'

'Okay. Let me just copy down some numbers.'

Julie took out her phone and pulled the battery off the back. Nick wrote down a number on a small pad of paper provided by the hotel.

Julie walked over and looked at the phone screen in his hand.

'What are you doing?'

Nick turned. He looked guilty and tried to hide his phone. 'What do you mean?'

'Why are you writing down my dad's number?'

'Look, I know you're going to be mad.'

'What have you done, Nick?'

He didn't have to talk. Even as he stuttered his way though his explanation, Julie guessed that he'd spoken to her father already. Nick laid out the plan suggested to him. Hire someone to follow the money. Get it back. Julie had no doubts at all as to who Tommy would hire, and it meant that this whole affair could end badly for her and Nick.

'Fine,' Julie said. 'Call him.'

'I think this guy he knows can help.'

Julie closed her eyes. 'Yeah ... yeah, I'm sure.'

———

Blaine pulled his car over to the side of the road a hundred meters from his destination. The sun remained low in the sky and shone through his rear window. He reached up and adjusted the mirror until the glare of light reflected away from his face.

The car across the road from Julie's house was supposed to fit in. Just another BMW belonging to a neighbour. However, the two people seated inside gave it away. The police watched her house. Probably procedure. He doubted anyone actually expected anyone to turn up there.

It had surprised Blaine to get the call from Tommy a couple of hours ago. The slight hangover he'd woken with hadn't helped his concentration when listening to the problem. Tommy thought they could plug some kind of call-forwarding device into the phone socket. It didn't need to be that complicated. The landline company offered a call-forwarding service, but it still required activating from the home phone.

He doubted the two officers in the car would be the only ones on scene. Others could lie in wait in the house. No way to know for sure. Best to create a significant diversion. Get people on the streets. A bit of panic. Any police officers inside would have to come out. And Blaine would be at the back door ready to head inside.

The bright sunlight bursting through the sky to his rear masked his exit from the car. He doubted the police in the vehicle he had spotted had even noticed him pull over. In five minutes, however, all their attention would turn this way.

Blaine took out the timed IED from his boot. Over the last ten years in this industry, he had made hundreds of explosive devices. Some designed to kill. Some to open doors. And others, like the one he had in his hands, designed for spectacle. The detonator would create a simple spark, which would ignite a small pouch of black powder. That, by itself, would create a tiny explosion. Blaine had placed the detonator into a sealed plastic bag, filled with crushed mothballs and black powder. The naphthalene in the mothballs would create a large flame and a lot of smoke.

Blaine set the detonator for five minutes. He took out one of the new pay-as-you-go phones that he'd picked up en-route and activated the stopwatch app. He closed the boot, walked to the car parked in front of his, and placed the device underneath. With one fluid movement, he straightened himself and continued walking to the post box ahead of the car and pretended to mail something. Then he walked back to his car, got into the driver's seat, and drove away. He took the next left and headed around to the back of Julie's house.

Blaine pulled over once more. A neighbour's garden lay between him and the back door. Two fences he would have to climb over. All at 10:34 am on a Tuesday. Most people should be at work. But a good few people would still be around. Though not a busy street, he had noticed several dog walkers when he pulled over. Just a matter of waiting. He looked at his phone. Only a minute more.

He gripped the steering wheel with his black leather

gloves and looked over at Julie's house. Or was it her husband's? Did they co-own it? More than likely. They hadn't spoken in a long time. Tommy mentioned that Julie herself had called last night. Looked like hubby let the cat out of the bag. Blaine wondered if he would find an excuse to see her. Talk to her. Had she changed? Did he still have any effect on her at all? Or had she become just an average wife, in an average house with an average family? An image stuck in his mind of Julie holding up the bank. It had been all over the radio on his way there. Not so average.

The explosion sounded just loud enough to grab attention. But what would get them out of their houses, or at least peering through the windows, was the smoke. It plumed up into the sky above the rooftops. The two officers sitting in that car would have jumped out by now, running over to see what had happened.

Blaine got out of his car, checked his gun held secure in his hip holster, and walked to the first fence. He vaulted over the top and walked calmly across the grass to the opposing fence. Another quick vault and he stood in Julie's garden. The back door stood ahead of him. When he reached the door handle, he studied the lock. An old-fashioned five-lever mortice deadlock. Pickable if he had half an hour on hand, and the right tools, but Blaine guessed he had maybe two minutes to get inside, activate the call forwarding, and get out without alerting anyone to his presence.

He looked around at the back of the house. Blaine didn't fancy climbing to the first floor and considered simply smashing the window and turning the key from the inside. It would tell the police that someone had broken in, though. And he needed to leave no trace.

The thought hit him hard in the back of the head and

travelled quickly to the front. Julie's husband had probably left the house in haste. And, likely, the police had traipsed in and out of the place for a while yesterday. Blaine reached for the handle and turned it. The door opened without a sound, and Blaine rolled his eyes as he entered the house.

He walked through the kitchen and looked around for the phone. Nothing on the walls. Nothing on the counter. The living room looked a mess. He assumed the police had searched through everything. Next to the TV stood a docking station for the phone. The phone, however, he could see nowhere. A quick search of the living room turned up a few kid's toys under a chair and the TV remote down the back of the sofa. Blaine wandered through into the hall and upstairs.

The kid's room lay on his right. He stopped outside and peered in. Toys. Clothes. Statues of ballerinas. She had been spoiled.

The main bedroom loomed up ahead. The door hung open. It appeared lived in. On the floor lay piles of clothes, waiting to get put away. And on the dressing table stood framed pictures of Julie, her husband, and the seven-year-old Jessica. The phone sat on the bed.

Blaine picked it up and dialled the star key, followed by two and one and the star key again. He pulled out a piece of paper from his pocket and typed in the number written there. When he'd done, he pressed the hash key. Now, all calls would divert to the other phone that he'd brought. All he had to do was get it to the Joneses.

'Put down the phone and put your hands on your head, right now.'

Blaine dropped the house phone on the bed, raised his hands to his head, and turned to see a police officer in a crumpled grey suit, holding a Glock 26 on him.

15

PREPARATIONS

Blaine looked the officer dead in the eye. He appeared nervous. Hadn't expected to find some guy in the house. He seemed tired too. Had sat outside in that car all night, waiting for someone to show. Doubtful that he'd slept at all. Blaine could disarm him in half a second with ease. Knock him out in another half. But the cop had seen his face. Blaine didn't want to kill him. One manhunt for Julie was enough heat. The main objective was getting Jessica home safely. And getting paid for it.

The officer's radio crackled to life on his belt. 'Drake, you there? Everything okay?' He grasped it with his left hand, maintaining eye contact with Blaine. His trigger finger moved from the trigger guard to the trigger. This was the moment. A slight distraction meant Blaine could slap the gun out of his hand and deliver a devastating blow to his head. But he didn't.

'Don't answer that,' Blaine said. He felt tempted to draw his gun. Show this Mr Drake just how fast he was. But risking a gun fight would be madness. 'You have to let me go.'

Drake hesitated with his radio. His left hand still grasped it, but he didn't lift it from his belt.

'And I'm sure you have a good reason why I should do that,' Drake said.

'The little girl got taken.'

'Yeah, I figured.'

'If the police get involved, she dies. It's my job to make sure that doesn't happen.'

'What were you doing with the phone?' Drake pulled his hand away from the radio and clasped it around his right, which still held the gun trained on Blaine.

Unsure how much to tell him, Blaine gave it some thought. If the police checked with the phone company, they could find out to which number the calls would forward. Maybe it would be best to level with him.

'Call forwarding,' Blaine said. 'The kidnappers plan to call with a time and place for the exchange. You have to let me go.'

'I can't do that. Let us help. We can do this together.'

The officer's radio crackled to life once more. 'Drake, nobody saw anything down here. Anything at the house?'

Drake reached down and lifted the radio. He raised it to his mouth slowly and pressed the talk button. 'Holly, it's Drake,' he said.

Blaine lashed out and grabbed the barrel of the cop's gun. Then he pushed it upward and out of his palm. His finger got trapped in the trigger guard, and Blaine put pressure on the weapon, forcing Drake to his knees. The officer dropped the radio and held the gun with both hands. Blaine couldn't risk a shot going off and managed to press the magazine eject button. It slid out of the bottom of the gun and hit the ground. Drake let out a muffled grunt of pain, and Blaine managed to wrench the weapon from his grip.

'Listen to me,' Blaine said. 'The only way the daughter gets back safely is if I'm there to help. So, you're going to let me go. Julie Jones will give herself up as soon as the exchange is done.'

Drake looked up at Blaine and held his right hand as though it throbbed in pain. 'You don't get it,' he said. 'This isn't the first time they've done this. Nearly once a month now. They ask for £500,000 then kill the parents at the exchange. They keep the money. And the kids.'

Blaine took this in and ejected the chambered round in the Glock. It fell to the carpeted floor, and Blaine handed Drake back his gun.

'Drake?' Holly said over the radio. 'I'm headed to the house.'

Drake reached over to it, picked it up and raised it to his mouth. He glanced up at Blaine and pushed the talk button. 'Don't bother. All clear here. I'll meet you out front.'

He got to his feet while Blaine walked away, headed downstairs. 'You should let me know where the meet is,' Drake said. Blaine continued walking. 'Someone's gonna end up dead.'

'Someone always does,' Blaine said. He exited the house via the back door and hopped back over the two fences to his car.

As Blaine drove his way to Brixton to meet Nick and Julie at the Travelodge, he thought about his plan for that evening. He would have to wait to know where the exchange would happen. No preparation time to stake-out the location. Ideally, he wanted to watch the whole thing from his car. His priorities were following the kidnappers and returning the money. But that may change, now. If they killed whoever went to the exchange, should he let it happen? Still follow the money? Should he tell Nick and Julie? What a clusterfuck. He had to get it straight in his head. Foresee all possibilities. He could bring a sniper rifle along with him. Protect Nick and Julie, but then his position would get compromised. Impossible to follow the kidnappers back to where they had Jessica. Could he let them shoot Julie and Nick? Would Tommy still pay him? Too many questions. A clusterfuck. If Blaine wanted any chance of success, he needed answers.

The Travelodge looked quiet when Blaine drove past it and pulled into the petrol station a hundred meters further along. He parked and walked back to the hotel, taking in all escape routes, CCTV cameras, and how many cars in the car park. He had stayed cautious enough to make sure that Drake hadn't followed him. It meant taking his time driving to Brixton, but he figured it worth it.

Blaine walked past reception with his head hung low and pressed the call button for the lift.

He arrived on the first floor and took the corridor along to the last room on the left, passing several other rooms and a couple of fire alarms. He knocked on the door. Nick greeted him and held open the door, but only a tiny amount.

'Hi, you must be Tommy's guy, yeah?' he said. 'Please, come in.'

Blaine stepped inside. The four bags of cash sat by the window. Next to them stood Julie. Had she told Nick about their history? Unsure, he made the decision to treat it as though she hadn't and just go along with however she played it.

'Did you manage to get the phones to forward to a

mobile?' Nick said.

Blaine pulled out the cheap phone and handed it to him. 'No problem.' Julie still hadn't said anything. He glanced at her. She stood staring at him, but Nick hadn't noticed yet.

'Thank God,' he said. 'We do appreciate this. Look, I have your number, and I'll let you know the address of the exchange as soon as they call.'

'They'll likely do it last minute,' Blaine said. 'Which isn't a good thing for me. They'll have people there already, and I won't be able to stake it out.'

'You can still help us, though, right?'

'I just want you to know the risks. I'll be there. I'll watch it all go down. As soon as you have your daughter, and the kidnappers drive away with the cash, I'll follow them and attempt to retrieve it. But nothing's a hundred percent.'

Julie let out a breath of air with a smirk. 'And how do we know you won't just keep the money?'

'If you don't want my help, I can just go.'

'No, no,' Nick said. 'Sorry, we do want your help. My wife is still a little shaken by yesterday's events.'

Julie walked toward Blaine. 'Jason, I don't care about anything except getting my daughter back. So that's what you're going to make sure happens.'

Nick turned to Julie with a confused look on his face. 'You know him?'

'You asked my dad for help,' Julie said. 'Yes, I know him.' She stepped closer to Blaine. 'You think this will work?'

'Too many variables to be sure.' Blaine took out the second cheap phone and handed it to Julie. 'Figured you may need an extra one.'

She took it from him with a worried frown. He could see her

frustration. Her anger. She'd been willing to rob a bank to get Jessica back and wouldn't like what he was about to tell her. 'Only one of you should go and meet them.'

'No way,' Julie said. 'You are not going to tell me to stay here. I won't do that.'

'Isn't one of us going more dangerous than the two of us together?' Nick said.

'The risk levels increase if Julie goes,' Blaine said. 'She's wanted by the police, and if she's recognised or stopped on the way, you risk Jessica's life.' He focused his gaze on Julie. 'You said you wanted me to make sure your daughter gets back safe. I'm telling you how to make it happen.'

'We should listen to him,' Nick said.

'You don't know him. He kills people for money. He doesn't care.'

'But what he's saying makes sense.'

Blaine left the room, satisfied he had persuaded Julie to stay behind. His next concern was the location of the meet. He drove back to London and his apartment.

Drake had mentioned other kidnappings, once a month, which left the parents dead and the children missing. News pages online gave him more information about the locations at which these other parents had been killed. Last month, a couple were found in Cobham Wood; their son remained missing. The month before, a single mother got shot in a small car park on the outskirts of Nottingham; her daughter missing. The month before that, a couple shot to death in a park in Exeter; their son never found. The more he looked, the more cases he discovered. All within the last year and, in every case, the children never got recovered. The meet locations all happened outside. None of them had CCTV cameras anywhere nearby, and all occurred within a twenty-mile radius of the family's home address.

He brought up a website that would place a highlighted radius around a designated point on a map and typed in Julie's home address in Hertford. The kidnappers would look for an open area, out of the way of the public. They wouldn't choose an area on the inside of the M25, so that narrowed his search by fifty percent. Welwyn Garden City had plenty of suitable places, as had all the surrounding areas. Blaine would put money on them choosing somewhere near there. Quiet and out of the way with plenty of access to main roads. It would make following them difficult. On the small back roads, it would be rare to see another car late at night.

After having a quick bite to eat, Blaine drove to his lock-up and set about deciding what weapons and gear to take with him.

He opened the locked walk-in safe inside the lock-up and stepped in. Then he pulled down two P229s and a couple of suppressors. Next, he took six magazines from a drawer and placed them next to the guns. He looked at the sniper rifle on the rack above him. Originally an M14, he'd customised it to include a folding stock and removable barrel, allowing him to transport it covertly. Blaine took it down and placed it next to the two semi-automatics. Best to be prepared. The scope on top of the rifle, he had used his entire career. Fifteen times magnification and a night-vision option too. Guns had come and gone, but that scope felt like a part of him. He knew it inside and out, and it had never let him down. With every new rifle he had gained, he had meticulously made sure both scope and rifle worked in perfect synchronisation.

The middle drawer at his knees housed a couple of flack jackets and body armour. While he pulled out the armour and laid it on the table along with the rest of his equipment, he ran through in his head what he anticipated happening that night. Perhaps Drake had it wrong. Maybe this *was* just a simple kidnapping. In all the other cases, the kidnappers had asked for an exact five hundred thousand from each family. To ask for five million now felt off. Hopefully, he would watch Jessica step out of a vehicle and run toward Nick. With any luck, the kidnappers would drive off, not knowing that he trailed them. If all went well, it would prove simple to retrieve the money without putting himself in too much danger. He hoped. But, nine times out of ten, a plan was just a list of things that didn't happen.

16

THE EXCHANGE

Blaine received a phone call from Nick at 1:15 am, explaining that the abductors had given them a set of co-ordinates to get to in one hour. He got stressy, saying that he couldn't get to the place in time. Blaine sat in his car on the side of a road near Welwyn Garden City and wrote down the numbers that Nick dictated; 51.934689, -0.295983. When placed into his sat-nav, they came up as a spot on Temple Close near Hitchin. A nineteen-minute drive from where he had placed himself. His only words of advice to Nick were, *drive fast and don't get pulled over.*

Quickly, Blaine moved onto the A1 and drove up past Stevenage. He turned off at the next roundabout and drove closer to the location. Before reaching Temple Close, he pulled off onto Windmill Lane; a public footpath, which ran parallel to it, and drove along a few hundred meters.

Blaine got out of his car and closed his door silently. He glanced at his watch. It showed 1:31 am. He had made good time. Still quiet, he opened the boot of the car and took out the sniper rifle. Blaine walked from the footpath and into the field next to it. He could see a small telecom station about 400 meters away. Elevated by a good fifteen degrees, Blaine sat himself on the ground and lifted the rifle to his shoulder. He activated the night vision on the scope, and the entire area burst to life in different shades of grey.

The gate to the area stood open, and a black van had parked next to a large brick hut and opposite a small metal telecom box. Outside the van stood a man in glasses, smoking a cigarette. The van parked at such an angle that he couldn't see if anyone sat in the passenger seat. And he had no way of knowing how many people might wait in the back, or if Jessica had come with them. The night seemed pleasant and not too cold. Blaine would now have to wait a good three-quarters of an hour for Nick to arrive. He got himself settled and waited.

———

Nick wiped the sweat from his brow and took the phone from his pocket to glance at the time. He had lugged three of the bags of money into the car and come back to the hotel room for the last one. He picked it up. Each one felt heavier than the last. Julie touched his arm.

'Nick,' she said.

He put down the bag. 'I need to get going. I've already spent ten minutes dragging these things around.'

'I know. I just wanted to say I'm sorry.'

Nick shook his head as if to tell her it wasn't necessary. 'We'll deal with everything as it comes. The money. The bank. All of it.'

'Just bring my little girl back first.' She kissed him on the lips. 'You have been amazing. I love you.'

'I love you too.' He smiled and held it for a while, letting her know that everything would turn out okay, and lifted the heavy bag with ease.

Nick drove his way through West London and past the M25, finally getting onto the A1. He had his foot to the floor whenever he could but made sure to keep to the speed limit in the city. On the motorway, he pushed his foot down hard and raced along the fast lane toward Hertford.

His satnav continued to call out instructions as Nick pulled off the A1 and headed at speed toward the little flag that marked his destination on the small screen. After a couple of minutes, he pulled off onto Temple Close and drove along a dark, narrow road. His headlights on full, he approached the telecom station. A black van sat parked inside the gated area with two large men in black jackets standing next to it. He pulled in and parked opposite. Then he looked in his wing mirror. Another man, this one in glasses, stepped out of the front. Nick took a deep breath and opened his door.

He walked to the back of his car and stopped while the man in the glasses approached him with a smile.

'Mr Jones?' he said with an American accent. 'My name is Richard. Over here, please. My associate will take a look at the money.'

Nick stayed rooted to the spot. 'Where's Jessica?'

'In the van.'

'Let me see her.'

'You're in no position to be making demands, Mr Jones. Let my associate see the money, and we will show you your daughter.'

Nick turned to the car and opened up the boot. The associate that Richard had mentioned walked over, opened the bag in the boot, and rifled through the contents. Casually, Richard walked over to Nick and smiled once more.

'Do you know how long it would take to count five-million pounds properly?' he said. 'I have no idea, but it would take quite some time. A long, long time. So, there's no real way we could possibly know just how much you actually have right here and now. You could, very easily, be light a hundred grand, and it would be impossible to tell. I know I've never seen five million in cash before.' He let out a small laugh and placed his hand on Nick's shoulder. 'A bit of trivia for you—you know—in case you find yourself in this situation again. God, could you imagine? But, then, I'm sure you would never risk your daughter's life, would you?' He glanced over at the man looking through each of the bags in the car. 'How's it going?'

He settled his gaze on Richard and nodded.

'It seems we're all good, Mr Jones,' Richard said. He smiled once more, turned back to the van, and walked up to the back door.

———

Blaine held the scope to his eye and watched while Nick arrived in his car and pulled up opposite the black van. He reached into his pocket and placed the Bluetooth speaker in his ear. Then he looked down at his phone and dialled the most recent number he had added in his contacts list.

Julie answered with a nervous, 'Hello?'

'It's Jason.'

'What's happened? Is Jessica okay?'

'I don't think Jessica will be here.'

'What do you mean?'

'I had some intel come to me. These guys have been taking kids all year, from all over the country. And then killing the parents when they turn up with the cash. The children are never found.'

'Why the fuck didn't you tell us this? Don't let Nick go. Shit ... what's the number of his phone?'

'Listen to me, Julie. Listen carefully. Nick is with them now. They're counting the money. They *will* kill him. I can stop them. But if I do, there's no way they'll lead me back to where they're holding Jessica.'

'What the fuck are you telling me?'

'I need you to choose. Right now.' Blaine watched the man in glasses walk back to the van. 'I can't save them both, Julie. If I let them do this, I can follow them and get her back. But if I shoot, they'll know I'm here. Julie? I need an answer, now.' Blaine listened to the painful silence on the other end of the line. He watched through the scope as the man in glasses opened up the back of the van. Out stepped another couple of guys in black. One held a suppressed handgun.

Blaine trained the crosshairs of his scope on the man's chest and rested his finger on the trigger. 'Julie?'

'Let them do it,' Julie said.

Blaine watched the man raise his gun and shoot Nick in the chest three times. His body convulsed with the shock of the impact and fell to the ground in a heap. Blaine felt a sensation in his shoulder as though someone had punched him hard. It took him a brief moment to realise he had also gotten hit. He reacted at speed and dove to the ground, but another shot whipped into his chest before he hit the deck, quickly followed by the crack of a suppressed rifle. Winded and in pain, Blaine scrambled across the field. He pulled his way through the fence and onto the footpath where his car waited. Another bullet impact slapped across his leg and hit Blaine's rifle. Blaine dashed behind his vehicle, still clutching his damaged weapon. He looked back at the black van across the field. Near it, the men shouted at each other. Guys hauled the large bags of cash into the van while others brought out automatic weapons and aimed into the field.

Blaine had assumed the sniper must have come with the kidnappers, but they seemed as blatantly surprised as he was. Another suppressed shot rang out and hit one of the men in the chest. Blaine brought up his rifle and leant out from the side of his car. He looked to his right, across the field. Searching for movement. Tense, he waited for another shot, knowing that the sniper now aimed toward the kidnappers. About a hundred meters away from Blaine, a figure crouched in the dirt. A rifle in his hands. Another shot. Sounded like it hit the side of the van. A series of automatic weapons fire caused mini fountains of dirt to erupt in front of the figure. They had spotted him. He stood and returned fire, but the men had placed the bags of cash into the van already, and now drove away. More shots from the sniper, presumably aiming for the tyres. The van drove out of the telecom station at speed. The sniper cursed, loudly. Then turned his attention back to Blaine. Through the night-vision scope, Blaine could see his face plainly. Matt Cable.

17
EXIT WOUNDS

Blaine ducked down behind his car. Another couple of shots rang out, hitting the front bumper. In pain and bleeding, Blaine managed to get to the back of the vehicle as Matt Cable ducked through the fence and stepped onto the footpath. Blaine reached up and opened the boot. He could hear Cable running while he rushed to find the bag inside, which contained his P229s. With a thump, Cable jumped onto the front of his car and stepped onto the roof. Blaine leapt out of the way when Cable fired three semi-automatic shots through the boot door and jumped to the ground. Blaine put all his weight on his good leg and launched himself into Cable, who managed to get off another shot, which hit the ground next to them. Blaine punched Cable in the face as hard as he could, which loosened his grip on the gun. Blaine grabbed it and pushed it back so that the barrel pressed against Cable's chest. Blaine took a swift fist to the face but stayed his ground. He pushed Cable back against the car. His concern stayed on not letting the van get too far away, although they would expect someone following them because of the sniper shots. They would do everything they could not to lead anyone back to where they kept Jessica. He had to deal with Cable fast. Blaine head-butted him in the nose, and a warm spray of blood hit his face. The force pushed Cable away from Blaine, and he gained back control of the gun. Cable fired three shots into Blaine's chest.

Blaine dropped to his knees, gasping for air. Cable stepped closer for the kill-shot to his head. Blaine sprung his left arm upward, grabbed the gun, and pulled Cable down. Then he delivered a powerful blow to his face, and Cable dropped the gun and staggered backward. He fell hard to the ground beside the car.

Blaine crawled to the front door and opened it. In pain, he got into the driver's seat and closed the door. Then he started the engine, put the gear into reverse, and pushed the accelerator. Cable got up as he backed his way out of the footpath and back onto the road. More gunshots rang out but failed to hit anything solid. Blaine put the car into drive and sped toward Hitchin, searching for the van. It would be long gone by now, though. Both the cash and Jessica had gone. He slammed his hand down on the steering wheel, cursing Cable. Blaine had no clue how he could have been there if not with the kidnappers. No way could he have known the co-ordinates before Nick. He could have come with the kidnappers; hired to look out for people like Blaine. And he could have turned on them for the cash. There would be better ways to do it. Cable didn't seem like the kind of person to make decent plans, though. Blaine's head hurt, and he could feel himself losing consciousness. And thinking about Cable only made things worse. Blaine leaked blood, and Cable would, likely, keep looking for him. He had to pull over and get his wounds sorted, or he would die.

A small town lay up ahead, and Blaine drove past a local pharmacy. He turned at the next left and pulled over to the side of the road. Then he pulled open his black shirt, revealing the body armour underneath. What a mess. Blaine unclipped it at the sides and stepped out of the car. Then he took off his jacket, then his shirt, and finally, the armour. He threw them in his car and put on his black coat. In pain, he walked to the back of the car and opened the boot. After pushing aside the emergency petrol canister, he pulled out the black duffel bag, which contained his P229s and shoulder holster. Done, he lowered the boot and staggered toward the pharmacy. In this residential area, people would awaken at his next actions, but he didn't have much choice.

Blaine stepped in front of the glass window at the front of the pharmacy and pulled out his suppressed gun. He fired a shot at the corner, and the entire pane smashed to pieces. For sure, he had no time to pick the back door and felt unsure he would have been able to make it over the back wall to get to it. He had to be quick. In and out before any police arrived.

As the alarm rang out with a piercing sound, he stepped in, grabbed some powerful pain killers from the shelves at the back, some gauze, bandages, and tape, and placed them in his bag. His shoulder hurt badly, but the wound on his thigh worried him most. He dripped blood at an alarming rate and needed to stop the flow. With his bag now full of everything he needed, Blaine walked around the counter and toward the smashed window, only to see Cable screech to a halt on the street outside. He got out, holding his handgun, and ran toward the shop. Blaine limped behind the counter and through the back door, into a corridor, which led to a small bathroom, a kitchen, and a flight of stairs. In the dark, he stepped through into the kitchen and found a locked door, which led outside. The key sat in the lock. He turned it and pushed open the door, nearly collapsing onto the ground. Behind, Cable crunched his way through the broken glass on the shop floor.

Blaine fell onto the wall at the back of the shop and used all his remaining strength to launch himself up on top of it, where he fell over the other side and into a small car park at the back. He limped toward his car. Another vehicle pulled up to the front of the shop, and the door opened. Then came voices.

'Hold it right there. Don't move.'

Blaine walked past his car. Police lights flashed at the front. Cable walked out of the smashed window toward the two unarmed police officers. Another police vehicle pulled up with its siren wailing and blue neons flashing.

'Get down on the ground, right now,' the officer said. Casually, Cable pulled his gun from a holster on his belt at his lower back, fired into the officer's chest, and then at his partner. Blaine hurried back to his car while more shots rang out. The tinkling of smashing windscreen glass reached him. Voices screamed orders into radios, and the police car backed up as more shots rang out.

Blaine got into his car and drove off in the other direction, leaving Cable and what he assumed were four dead police officers behind.

Blaine stuck to the speed limit and munched away on several pain killers. He had to pull over soon. His leg had grown numb, and his control of the car became questionable. Cable had followed him. It offered the only explanation that made sense. A reason lay behind how he'd found him at the pharmacy. It was how he'd known about the exchange location. Blaine's car must have gotten tracked. Somewhere underneath his car, a small GPS device had given Cable the destination. Blaine pulled over one last time on a quiet, solitary road outside Stevenage. Only fields surrounded him. No onlookers. No houses. No witnesses. Blaine took the petrol can from his boot and used it to cover the vehicle in flammable liquid.

He patched up his leg as best he could—enough to stop the bleeding—and applied gauze to his shoulder, sticking it in place with tape. With a toss of a lighter, the car went up in flames, and Blaine limped his way toward town, staying out of sight of the roads. If he had it right about the tracking device, Cable would drive by soon.

Blaine took out his phone, scrolled through his contacts to the name *Repairs,* and pressed the dial button. Several rings sounded. Blaine pulled the phone away from his ear when someone answered.

'Yeah?'

'I need a repair job.'

'Body or tech?'

'Body.'

'Location?'

'Stevenage.'

'Heat?'

'Probably. I need a pick up too.'

'Can't do it. Wrong side of London. If you can get here, fair enough.'

'Understood.' Blaine hung up and looked behind him to see another vehicle approaching. He laid in the field by the side of the road and watched as Matt Cable's car drove by slowly, obviously looking around for Blaine. When it reached the distance, Blaine picked himself up and walked further into the field, clutching his duffel bag, which contained everything he needed. He limped toward the edge of a large back garden and saw a shed. Shelter. He remained dangerously close to the burning car, which would attract attention soon enough, but he needed rest. His body ached to stop and collapse, but he wouldn't allow it. Not until he got out of harm's way. Blaine crept into the back garden and entered the unlocked shed.

It contained a sit-on lawnmower, a metal desk with a few tools and woodwork equipment on it, and a lot of junk. Blaine laid on the ground underneath the metal desk. If the police helicopters used thermal imaging cameras, it would shield his body heat. Enough to relax, anyway. Blaine closed his eyes and breathed deeply. Someone had tampered with his car. Someone got to it. Someone knew more than they should about him. Blaine came to the only logical conclusion. The best answer that fit all the facts. Cable wanted to kill him. He had said so when they'd met. Only now, Blaine knew he was getting paid to do it.

18

MOURNING

Detective Sergeant Danny Drake got out of his car and walked up to the crime scene. He and Holly had just come from the high street in Hitchin where four police officers had been gunned down. The street lay awash with blood and a pharmacy broken into. No CCTV footage at the location. Local officers canvassed the area, talking to residents. Two bodies had been reported found nearby, and one matched the description of Nick Jones.

Several Constables worked on site along with some plain clothes detectives. They informed Drake that they hadn't touched the bodies but had commenced a search of the area. Drake looked down at the body of Nick Jones. The early morning sunshine hit his eyes when he looked up at the other body laying not too far away. He raised a hand to shade his vision and glanced over at Holly.

'What do you think?' Holly said.

'Looks like he tried to pay the kidnappers but, just like the others, he's double-crossed and killed.'

'Looks like it.'

Drake pointed at the vehicle near the body. 'Nick Jones' car?'

'Yep. So, did they take Julie too?'

'I don't think they both came. I'm willing to bet she's still alive and still wherever they were hiding out. Now without a usable car ... or a husband.'

Drake pulled on a pair of white evidence gloves and crouched down. He opened Nick's jacket and searched his pockets. Then he pulled out a cheap mobile phone and handed it to Holly. 'See if it has any numbers saved on it. Last ones called, you know?'

Holly took the phone, slid it into an evidence bag, and proceeded to turn it on and tap away at the screen from outside the plastic.

Drake found some loose coins, car keys, and a folded piece of paper from Nick's trouser pockets. He unfolded it and revealed two phone numbers. One labelled Tommy, and the other, Tommy's guy.

One of the detectives walked over with haste and informed them that they had found a sniper rifle up on the footpath across the field.

'The kidnappers had someone watching over them?' Drake said.

'It has a bullet in the middle of it,' the detective said. 'The entire area up there is covered in blood and tyre tracks.'

'Thanks, we'll take a look,' Drake said. He stood up and looked over to Holly, who still looked at the phone. Drake searched his suit jacket for his sunglasses, failed to find them, and brushed his fingers against the small, now empty bottle of cocaine he still had in his pocket. 'That damn sun,' he said and manoeuvred himself around Holly so that the sun shone from behind him, and he cast a shadow over her.

'No numbers saved in the contacts list,' Holly said. 'Looks new. The last number to call it is private. It has a last number dialled, though.'

Drake handed her the piece of paper. 'One of these?'

Holly looked at the numbers and nodded. 'Yep, Tommy's guy.'

'Well, all right,' Drake said. 'Let's find out who Tommy is.'

<hr />

Blaine stood in front of Tommy's office in Charlotte Street in London. He wore jeans, a grey T-shirt, and the black jacket from the night before. The small bullet hole in the shoulder didn't look too obvious, and any blood stains proved dark enough not to draw notice. He had slept for four hours in the shed in Hitchin. When he'd awoken, he had replaced his bandages on his leg and shoulder and changed into the spare clothes from his duffel bag. Without much trouble, he had managed to walk into Stevenage and call for a taxi. The sunglasses and ruffled, messy hair covered his bruises, and he didn't get any funny looks from anyone at the tube station. At past 9:00 am, Blaine took one last drag from the cigarette and threw the stub onto the ground. He reached into the duffel bag around his shoulder and grasped hold of the P229.

Blaine walked across the concrete to the front door of Tommy's office. He pushed the buzzer.

'Yes?' a voice said.

'It's Blaine. I want to see Tommy.'

'He's not here.'

'I'll come in and wait.'

A moment of silence. Blaine gripped the gun in his hand tighter.

'He's not in at all today.'

Blaine shoved the end of the bag against the lock and pulled the trigger. A loud crack sounded, and the door lock blasted apart. Blaine barged into the door and forced it open.

Smoke and debris from the door covered the hallway. Blaine rushed up the stairs, pulling out the P229, complete with the large suppressor on the end. At the top, Blaine kicked open the door to Tommy's office and came face-to-face with the pair of guards he'd encountered two days ago. He aimed his gun at them, and they backed off.

'Where is he?' he said.

Neither of them said a word. They simply glanced at each other, not sure what to do. Blaine put a bullet in the one on the right's leg. He screamed with pain and fell to the ground. Blaine aimed his gun at the other guard's legs. Quickly, he waved his arms, begging Blaine to stop.

'He went to a safe house,' he said. 'A caravan out of town.'

'Where?'

'I don't know.'

Blaine fired a shot into the first guard's right leg, and tears welled up in his eyes as another cry of pain left his body.

'Fuck, just stop,' the first guard said. 'He'll have looked up the postcode on his computer. He always does.'

'Get the postcode,' Blaine said.

The guard with usable legs walked into Tommy's personal office and woke up his computer. Blaine pulled the other gun from his bag and trained each one on a guard.

'Here it is,' the guard searching the computer said. He grabbed a pen and wrote down the address. 'Here.' Pale-faced, he handed Blaine the post-it note. Blaine put away the gun that he had pointed at the bleeding guard and took the small yellow piece of paper.

A bullet whizzed past his cheek and into the wall behind him. Blaine spun to see that the guard on the ground now lay armed and attempting to aim at him. Blaine darted over the desk and across the room, and more bullets came flying.

The guard on his feet opened a drawer in the desk and pulled out a black Colt 1911. Blaine collided with the shelves at the end of the office, knocking a picture frame onto the floor. He turned when shots got fired at him. A mess of wood and plaster exploded around his head. Blaine lifted his gun and fired twice, stepping back onto the picture frame with a crunch of glass. His bullets ripped through the rear of the computer screen and into the guard's chest. He flew back against the wall, and the computer screen burst with flickering light. Blaine kept his gun aimed at the doorway. He could hear the wheezing sound of the bleeding guard trying to breath properly and to keep that heavy gun he had up in the air.

Blaine stepped off the picture frame and walked with caution to the door. He waited and listened to the guard on the other side.

'Son of a ... I'll ... fucking ... kill you ...' the guard said.

Blaine waited until he heard the clunk of gun metal against carpet and strolled out of the office. Without bothering to lift his arm, he put one final bullet in the man's head when he walked past.

Blaine didn't fancy heading back to his apartment. Or to the lock-up. He needed a warm shower and decent clothes, but going anywhere that Tommy knew of was out of the question.

Blaine exited the offices and walked with haste to the nearest underground station. He looked up at the street corners. Cameras watched the populace. The trains had them too. So did all the taxis. If his phone had any charge left, he would have called for an Uber.

He looked down at the piece of paper that the guard had given him. He recognised the postcode as Surrey. Blaine needed a car, and that meant going to his failsafe garage, which Tommy remained unaware of. It contained a cheap, unassuming silver Ford Focus, five-thousand pounds in cash, a few weapons, and a passport in a different name. Blaine always liked to be prepared, and when Tommy had suggested the lock-up all those years ago, Blaine took it upon himself to create his own miniature version. A failsafe. A place he could go to if shit hit the fan. And the fan had well and truly been shat on.

19

MOVING ON

The garage, a small, unassuming affair, stood in Stratford, East London. It looked the same as the four others next to it. White metal up-and-over door. Brick construction. However, the lock on Blaine's probably cost ten times as much as any other. With the padlock unfastened, Blaine pressed a button on his key ring. A deep click came from the inside, and Blaine pulled up the garage door, revealing a metal shutter with a number lock. Blaine dialled in the number he had memorised years earlier and slid open the metal shutter.

Once inside, he slid it back down and flicked on the light switch. The car took up most of the space but, at the back, there remained enough room for a large storage chest. Blaine took out a USB phone charger cable and a thousand pounds in cash. He stripped out of his clothes and changed into fresh underwear and clean attire; casual trousers and black shoes with a dark shirt. Then he took out a black, knee-length single-breasted cashmere coat from the chest and placed it on the passenger seat of the car.

Seated in the vehicle, he turned on the engine and made

sure the car ran okay. He only checked it once a year, and the last time occurred seven months ago. When ready, Blaine pulled the car out of the garage, locked everything up again, and activated the car's satnav.

It took an hour to get out of London in the busy mid-week traffic, which gave him time to charge his phone. He considered calling Julie. She must be going crazy by now, and would hate him for what he had made her do, but he had to put that out of his mind. It was over now. No way to save Jessica. No way to get the money back. The only thing left was to force Tommy to pay him what he owed and put a bullet in his head.

Tommy's caravan wasn't quite what the two guards at the office had made it out as. A large recreational vehicle, it certainly came with every luxury imaginable. Tommy had mentioned it a few times during the sparse conversations they'd had over the years. Blaine recognised it immediately. It didn't sit in a caravan park or random field. Tommy, evidently, owned the elegant forest clearing in which it sat parked. Had the bastard used Blaine's money to pay for it? Business mustn't be that bad for him.

The huge blue-and-silver motorhome dwarfed Blaine's car when he pulled up next to it. With speed, he got out, holding his gun in his hand. He knocked hard on the motorhome door. 'Tommy?'

Tommy opened the door and looked surprised to see him. 'Jason? What's going on? What the hell are you doing here?'

Blaine stepped inside and pushed Tommy backward and into the driver's seat. He aimed the gun at his chest. 'You set me up.'

'What are you talking about?'

'There was a sniper at the exchange. Matthew Cable. He put three bullets in my chest.'

'You think I sent him? Why would I risk my granddaughter like that? Where is she? What happened?'

Though real concern creased his face, Blaine knew Tommy well. Always hiding something. 'Does he get work through you?'

'Everyone gets some work through me. But if he was there, it wasn't because of me. Jason, what happened?'

Blaine took a step closer, moving the barrel of the suppressor inches away from Tommy's chest. 'He tracked my car. And there's only one way he could have got to it. Through you.'

'Christ, Jason, if he turned up at the location then he was obviously with the kidnappers.'

'He shot at them.'

Tommy breathed deeply. 'The money.'

'What about the money?'

'Julie worked for a specialist investment company. They'd take huge amounts of cash from not so strictly legal companies and invest it for them. That's where she got the money from. Someone's missing five million ... the kind of people who know how to get it back.'

'Julie would never work for a place that had anything to do with things like that.'

'She doesn't know. I arranged the job for her.' Tommy sat up straighter, looking a little more at ease. 'She doesn't want me in her life. But that doesn't mean that I can't still help her out. Even if she doesn't know about it. I'll make a few calls, see what I can find out. Is Jessica okay?'

'They never brought her.'

'Nick?'

'They shot him.'

'Jesus.' Tommy glanced upward. He kept something from him. Blaine could see him in deep reverie, thinking something through. 'How do we find Jessica now?'

'She's gone.' Blaine waited a moment and stared at Tommy's face, looking for any suspicious micro expressions. Anger and frustration met him. 'Their van got pelted with bullets. Windows smashed. And one of them is dead. The police are probably all over the scene now.'

'I'll see what I can dig up. A van with bullet holes tends to stick out. This isn't over yet.'

'It is for me. Forget the extra money. I just want what you owe me.' Blaine lowered the gun and stepped back out of the vehicle.

'Where are you going?' Tommy said.

'If it *was* the money, Cable will go after Julie.'

'You should stay away from her, Jason.'

'I'll bring her to you. Then you get me my money. Then I'm gone.'

Blaine got back in his car and typed in the address of the Travelodge in Brixton. Tommy was an accomplished liar, but Blaine could see he was visibly upset. He grabbed his phone and dialled Julie. He was twenty minutes away, but if Cable had followed his movements for the last couple of days, he would have seen that Blaine had parked near the hotel for a few minutes. No answer. Cable could have gotten to her any time since last night. He cursed himself for jumping to conclusions. By going after Tommy, he had left Julie in danger. He remembered why he hadn't had any contact with her for the past several years. Caring was too hard. A liability. His decision to leave was the right one. He just needed his money safely in his bank account and could just leave everything else behind.

———

Drake drove through the busy North London streets. He yawned and turned away from Holly, who sat beside him in the passenger seat, using the phone. The late nights had caught up with him. He had made the wrong decision in letting the guy in the Jones' house go. If he would have just taken him in as per protocol, then maybe, they could have helped properly.

Holly put down the phone and turned to Drake. 'Tommy is Thomas Carmine, Julie's dad.'

'What does he do?'

'Owns a private security firm. Deals with military personnel.'

'Exactly the kind of person you could go to for help with a kidnapping.'

'You think he tried to help? Botched it?'

'Back at Julie's house, yesterday ... I found a guy in there, redirecting incoming calls to a mobile.'

'What? Why didn't you say?'

'I let him go. Thought he could help. Guy seemed to know what he was doing.'

'And now we have two dead bodies and a missing girl. For fuck's sake, Drake.'

'Where do we find Tommy?'

'He has an office in central. Charlotte Street.' Holly's phone rang, and she answered. The call lasted maybe seven seconds before she said 'thank you' and hung up. 'They've found the bank manager's car at a Travelodge in Brixton. Could be, Julie's still there.'

'Okay, let's get uniforms over to Tommy's place. We'll go get Julie. No-one else approaches her.'

Holly dialled a number and relayed his instructions. Drake gripped the steering wheel and sounded the siren. The cars in front of him parted, and they accelerated through the sea of vehicles.

———

Blaine pulled up to the Travelodge and exited the car quickly. He had tried Julie's phone a few times but either the battery had died or she'd cancelled his calls. Either were likely. He took his duffel bag with him and made his way through reception and into the upstairs corridor. Julie answered the door before Blaine even finished knocking. The slap hit him square in the cheek and took him by surprise. He could see the second coming and could avoid or stop it but, under the circumstances, he figured it best to take it. Julie clocked him in the exact same part of his face, and his left cheek tingled.

'What happened? Is he dead? Where's Jessica?'

Blaine lowered his head.

'Nick's dead. Someone else was there. He shot at the kidnappers. And me. They drove away with the cash, and I only just managed to escape.' Blaine pushed his way into the room. He didn't like talking about this stuff in the hallway. The door closed behind him, and Julie stood in front of it. Her eyes welled with tears.

'You said you'd get her back. You made me choose between them, you son of a bitch. Holy fuck, you ... you made me let Nick die.'

'Julie, this other guy, Matt Cable—Tommy think's he

142

works for the guys you stole the money from.'

'What?' Julie frowned. She looked offended at the proposal. 'What does he know?'

'He said he pulled some strings and got you the job. That the people who invested were dodgy companies.'

'That's utter bullshit. Kaizen, the company I took money from, deals in tech. It's all insured, regardless.'

Adrenaline pumped through Blaine's body. He walked to the window and ran it all through his head. Tommy had reeled off a load of utter crap to him, and he had bought it. 'We need to get out of here, now,' Blaine said.

'I'm not going anywhere with you.'

'If that company didn't hire Cable to get the money back, it means Tommy hired him to kill me, and he likely knows about this place.'

'Why would he want you dead?'

'I told him I wanted to leave. That I wanted all the money he owed me. No wonder he offered me half a mil for this job; he knew I'd never get it.'

Blaine looked out of the window at the car park below. A car pulled up to the reception doors. A man and woman got out and hurried into the building. Blaine recognised the guy as Drake, the police officer he had met at Julie's place yesterday. 'Police are here,' he said. 'Come on; we can take the stairs.'

'No, I'm not going anywhere; this has all gone too far.'

'Tommy said he would make some calls about the kidnappers. I think he knows more than he's letting on. There's still a chance we can find Jessica. But we need to go. Now.'

'Why do you care?' Her face looked tense. The lines on her forehead painfully present. 'Right ... the five million.

Well, when you find your money, would you be so kind as to return my fucking daughter.'

Blaine opened the door and stepped out into the corridor. He smashed the fire alarm, which wailed, and pushed open the fire exit at the end of the corridor. He glanced back at Julie, who seemed torn. He could tell she wanted to go to the police; anything would look better than coming with him. But Julie always saw things through to the end. Like him, she would always calculate the best possible strategy. Blaine held the fire door open for her, and she hurried through and onto the fire escape outside. The two officers ran through the door at the end of the corridor, and people stepped out of their rooms to see what all the running and door banging was about. The officers made their way to Blaine, following him to the emergency stairs. Then they pushed their way through the small crowd of people, and Blaine followed Julie outside and ran down the grated metal stairs.

Blaine looked back up to see the two officers run out onto the steps, pushing their way through a couple of guests.

'Armed police, don't move,' Drake said, brandishing his gun.

Blaine urged Julie on, and they ran around the building to the car park at the front. 'I don't want them to see my car,' Blaine said. He pulled her toward the fence beside the car park and hopped over. 'We have to lose them.'

Two marked police vehicles pulled into the car park just as Julie swung her legs over the fence. Two officers got out and ran toward them, joining Drake in pursuit.

Blaine and Julie raced down the path, headed for the train tracks of Balham Station. 'We have to double back,' Blaine said. 'Through here, onto the tracks.' Julie thought him crazy, but before she could protest, he waded through the hedgerow and pulled himself up and over the metal railings. Quickly, Julie did the same. They dashed over the train tracks. Their pursuers ran past the other side of the hedges. As Blaine and Julie reached the end of the hedgerow, they came parallel to the Travelodge car park, but the railway line ran over a bridge, and they now stood a good twenty-four feet from the ground with an incoming train heading straight for them.

20
BANDAGES

The train heading toward them on the tracks spurred them on. Blaine helped Julie back over the railings. As the train rushed past them, Blaine leapt over too, and they hung from the top of the metal structure. Julie climbed down the side of the bridge, gripping the iron bars on the side. Blaine followed her, and when they reached a good twelve feet from the ground, Julie let go and landed, rolling with her movement. Blaine dropped and did the same, and the wound on his thigh split open again. He held his leg, putting pressure on the wound, and limped back into the car park.

Two police officers had stayed out in front of the hotel. They talked on their radios. It wouldn't take long until Drake made his way back. 'Stay here,' Blaine said.

Julie turned her face to the bridge and tried to stay out of sight. 'They'll see you.'

'They won't.' Blaine pulled the P229 from his bag and hid it under his armpit so that the barrel of the suppressor pushed against the back of his coat. He stood with his back to the hotel and glanced over his shoulder, adjusting the angle of the gun. Then he pulled the trigger. A pop echoed around the car park, but due to the size of the buildings, no-one could feel certain of where the sound had originated. A window on the third floor smashed open and showered glass down onto the concrete below. The police officers looked up at the window, and then ran inside the building.

Blaine, calmly and slowly, ambled toward his car, trying his hardest not to limp. He took out his key, unlocked the door, and climbed inside. Then he started the engine and backed out of the space. Slowly, he drove to the car park exit where Julie waited for him. She jumped inside, and they drove away, leaving the police behind.

Blaine took out his phone and dialled Tommy's number. Tommy answered after the first ring, and Blaine could hear the hum of a vehicle as though he was in a car. 'It's Blaine. I've got Julie. I'm bringing her to you.'

'Good,' Tommy said. 'I'll text you the address of an apartment. Meet me there.'

'Okay, make sure you have a laptop with you. Whatever happens, you're transferring my money today.' Blaine hung up before Tommy could reply.

'You said someone was after you,' Julie said.

'Yeah. Cable will probably be waiting for me.' Blaine held his leg. Blood trickled down his thigh and onto the seat.

'We should stop somewhere and look at that,' Julie said.

'I'm fine.'

'You're not fine. You've been shot. You need medical attention.'

Blaine's phone vibrated, and he looked at the message from Tommy. An address in Hackney. 'We'll pull over when we get further away.'

Tommy pulled into a car park in Hackney and turned off his engine. He dialled a number on his phone and held it to his ear.

Matt Cable answered with a 'Yeah?'

'Where the hell have you been? I've been trying to call you for hours. What the fuck happened?'

'He wore a vest. The fucker's got nine lives.'

'You shot at the kidnappers too? I didn't order that. You may have just earned my granddaughter a death sentence.'

'She wasn't there. I figured I could take the money back there and then. Didn't work out as planned, but listen, I recognised one of the men. Richard Harrington.'

'Harrington?'

'You know him?'

'I do.'

'Did some work with him a while back. Classy motherfucker. American but polite.'

'Any idea where he might be?'

'Hell, yes. But if you want me to drop in on him, you're fucking dreaming. This guy runs a tight crew of professional mercs. I'd need time to get a team together. What do you want to do about the Blaine situation?'

'How fast can you get to Hackney?'

Blaine pulled into the car park of a coffee shop next to a petrol station and manoeuvred into the first available space.

Julie rummaged through her jacket and pulled out a

wallet. 'You think they'll have first-aid kits in there?'

'I'll go,' Blaine said. 'Your face is all over the news. Besides, using your debit card is a big no-no.'

'You can hardly walk, and blood is dripping from your arse.'

Blaine handed her some cash from his duffel bag, and she opened her door. 'Thank you,' he said.

'Don't fucking thank me. I'm not doing this to be nice. If I could leave you bleeding, I would, but I have a feeling I'll need you.' Julie slammed the door closed.

Blaine watched her walk over to the petrol station. He glanced down at his leg. It looked a mess. His trousers had soaked up a lot of the blood and had turned a dark crimson. He checked the shoulder wound. His taped up bandage had started to peel at the edges. He felt like he was being held together. Blaine didn't like to have to rely on someone else. The fact that he had to rely on Julie, of all people, made him uneasy. To go from being so close to someone to making them hate you was a new sensation for him. He tried to put it out of his mind.

Julie walked back to the car with her head held low and sunglasses on her face.

She got back into the passenger side and placed the first-aid kit on her lap. Then she pulled out bandages and gauze and looked over at Blaine. 'Trousers down.'

'Right here?' Blaine undid his belt and worked his trousers down his thighs, exposing the hastily tied bandage around his leg.

'Jesus, did you do that one?'

'I was in a hurry and semi-conscious at the time.'

Julie took the small pair of scissors from the kit and cut off the stained bandages. Underneath was a large open wound where the bullet had shot across him.

'You got lucky,' Julie said. 'A centimetre deeper and the blood loss could have killed you in minutes.'

'It didn't feel lucky.'

Julie opened a small packet containing alcohol wipes and cleaned the area.

Blaine winced.

'It hurts?'

'It stings.'

'Good.'

Blaine looked at her. Still beautiful. Older and wiser. A few more lines around her eyes. But her face had always shown natural beauty.

'I'm sorry,' Blaine said.

She didn't look up at him. 'No. You don't get to say that. There's a reason I wanted to get as far away from you and my dad as possible. And I was right. The instant I have something to do with you, my entire life gets completely fucked up.' She brought out the tape and set about patching up Blaine's leg. 'They didn't have needle and thread, so this will have to do.'

'It'll be fine.'

'I doubt it.' Julie took the fresh bandages and tied them tight around Blaine's leg. She pushed the rest of the first-aid kit into the foot well and let out a frustrated sigh. 'I know it wasn't your fault. I know you were trying to help. Please, Jason, just tell me that you'll get her back.'

Blaine pulled up his trousers and buckled his belt. He didn't want to lie. They had a slim chance of finding Jessica. He hoped that Julie's dad might have a few more answers for him and couldn't believe Tommy had put his granddaughter in danger the way he had. Not if he didn't know something.

Blaine got himself comfy in the seat and started the engine. 'I'll do everything I can to get her back. We should ask Tommy some questions. Are you ready?'

'Ready.'

———

Matt Cable attached the sturdy stock to his rifle, rested the butt on the floor of the apartment, and screwed the large suppressor onto the barrel. Out of the window ahead of him, he could see the large building opposite. The window hung open as far as it would go, and he had a direct line of sight into the room in which Tommy paced around. His phone vibrated. Tommy calling him. He answered. 'Yeah?'

'They've just arrived outside. I take it I don't need to stress the fact that if my daughter is in any way harmed, you won't get paid?'

'Yeah, yeah. I *have* done this before.'

'Does he have your number?'

'Yeah, why?'

'Turn off your phone. If Blaine suspects something, I don't want him talking to you. He can talk his way out of anything.'

'Fine.'

Tommy hung up, and Matt turned off his phone and threw it onto the hotel-room desk. He had piled the cushions from the sofa on top of the bed so that he could aim out of the window by laying down on top of them. Ready, he climbed up and lay on his front, resting the barrel of the rifle over a pillow. He looked through the scope and trained his crosshairs on the window to the far left of the room. Tommy walked from the large desk, and then passed the first window, disappeared behind the wall, and emerged in the second window in the middle of the room where Matt had a perfect view of the door. Tommy grabbed the handle and opened it. Blaine stepped inside, directly in the middle of Matt's crosshairs.

21

CROSSHAIRS

Blaine stepped closer to Tommy and watched as he looked at Julie next to him.

Tommy walked in front of Blaine and extended his hand to Julie.

'So good to see you.'

'No, Dad, you don't get to say that. You don't get my husband killed and then expect me to run into your arms.'

Tommy glanced over at Blaine as though looking for backup. He wouldn't get any. From the start, Blaine had thought this whole plan rushed.

The frown lines on Julie's forehead came back. 'Now, will one of you tell me how we're going to get Jessica back.'

'Yes, right.' Tommy walked from the door and toward his desk at the other end of the room.

Blaine gripped his duffel bag tightly and stayed close to him so that they walked almost side-by-side. He stopped as soon as he passed the window and stayed in place beside the wall.

Tommy carried on to the desk and tapped a button on

his laptop. 'Jason, come look at what I found.'

Blaine didn't move. 'What?'

'I spoke to a few colleagues and contacts about the man that got killed. I've managed to get a few locations his known associates used. Come and see.' He looked up at Blaine, who simply stared right back at him.

Julie crossed to the desk. Blaine put out his hand and grabbed her arm, stopping her next to him.

'Let's get the money out of the way first,' Blaine said.

Julie took hold of his hand and wrenched it away from her. 'You can sort out your money later.'

Blaine allowed Julie to take his hand off her arm and looked dead into Tommy's eyes. 'Let's just get it done.'

'Fine.' Tommy sat at the desk and moved his finger across the track-pad. He typed in a web address and seemed to be logging into a bank account. 'It'll take a few minutes. I need to take money from different accounts.'

Blaine took out his phone and opened the messaging app. He typed out the bank account number that he'd prepared to receive his funds and sent it to Tommy. 'I've texted you the bank account details. It's funny, a few days ago, you said it would take a few weeks.'

'It will take weeks to get the invested money out. Money is complicated. You never quite understood that. You were lucky to have me look after it.' Tommy moved his finger around the track-pad and clicked a few times, using his other hand.

Blaine opened his contacts menu and found the number for Matt Cable. He touched the call button and rested the phone against his ear.

'I'm getting you as much as I possibly can, Jason. But you can forget the money for last night.' He entered a figure into the laptop, stood, and turned the computer around so that the screen faced Blaine. 'Is this enough for now?'

The screen stood too far away for Blaine to see. He didn't move closer. Matt Cable's phone went straight to a generic voice mail. Blaine put away his phone and took his gun from his bag. The P229 felt light in his hand, even though it had the extra weight of the suppressor on the end. Adrenaline rushed through his body. Cable would lie in wait somewhere close. Across the street with that high-powered rifle of his, most likely. He had spotted the handy, tall hotel next to the building when they arrived. And seeing the layout and the two tall windows in the room gave his theory weight. Tommy trying, constantly, to get him to move out from the safety of the wall had cemented it for him.

Julie looked at Blaine's gun. 'What are you doing?' She moved toward Tommy.

'Julie, get away from the window,' Blaine said. 'Stay against the wall.'

'What is this?' Tommy glanced to his right and out of the window. When his eyes came back toward Blaine, they looked full of anticipation.

Blaine smiled the slightest of smiles, which quickly turned to a frown. 'Finish the transfer.'

'You gonna kill me?'

'You're the one with a sniper across the street just waiting for me to step in front of that window.'

Julie looked over to Tommy and stayed by Blaine's side. 'Is it true? Did you send someone else to the exchange?'

Tommy hesitated. He looked back at Julie and couldn't quite seem to find the words.

'Tell me, Dad.'

'Our world is vastly different, Julie,' Tommy said. 'Every

life has a price. I run a business where I have to assign a value to life and death. Jason came to me wanting to take a huge chunk of investment money. He wanted to quit and go retire somewhere; raise a family. Right, Jason? At first, I thought Harrington had got to you. Managed to poach you away from me.'

'Who's Harrington?' Blaine said.

'Yeah, I figured,' Tommy said. 'I thought you were making it all up so that you could tear down everything we'd built and go work for him, but you really did want to retire, didn't you?'

'Harrington,' Blaine said again.

'I'd never heard of him until a few months back. American. Deals with a lot of military related projects, apparently. He tried to buy me out. I told him I wasn't for sale. But he had no interest in me, just my contacts. Wanted my clients. I told him no. He seemed a little used to getting his own way. And soon, threats came. Then he started surveillance on me and everyone around me. He took jobs from underneath me. Sabotaged others, like that simple protection gig a few days ago. For months, he's tried to break me down. My client list is small, but in Europe, it's incredibly valuable. Then you say you want out. What else am I to think?'

'Did he have something to do with Jessica?' Julie stood akimbo.

'I suspected. It wasn't until Cable said he recognised one of the kidnappers at the exchange as Richard Harrington that I was sure.'

'So, they want your contacts? We can use them to get her back?' Julie said.

'They haven't contacted me,' Tommy said. 'I think

Harrington just wanted to piss me off.'

Blaine lowered his gun a little. 'According to the police, he's taken children every month or so for the past year.'

'I don't know anything about that,' Tommy said. 'I just know the five million he has now probably means this is all over.'

'It's far from fucking over,' Julie said. 'He spoke to you, right? You must know where he is.'

'I never met him in person, and I haven't managed to dig up anything on this company of his. Cable, however, says he's worked with him. Knows where he might be.' Tommy allowed his face to soften while he looked at Julie. 'We have a chance.' He looked at Blaine, pleased that he had taken control of the situation. 'Put the gun down. You kill me, you don't get your money.'

Blaine increased his grip on the gun and raised it once more. 'Finish the transfer and tell Cable to stand down.'

'I will. I'll call him just as soon as you slide the gun over.'

Blaine stared at Tommy. What to do? He knew the outcome. Had known it before he'd stepped into the building. Tommy looked as though he believed that Blaine believed him. 'Something tells me you're paying Cable after the job gets done.'

Tommy's eyes widened, and the hairs on his bare arms raised.

Julie's breathing increased, and she touched Blaine's arm. 'Jason. Don't. Please.'

Blaine continued staring into Tommy's eyes. He had manipulated him his whole adult life. Chose to have him killed instead of paying what he owed. To him, it made a logical business decision. A chess move. Blaine had grown tired of his games. 'Dead men don't pay.' Blaine brought his left hand up to cup his right and aimed the gun at Tommy's middle. He fired two bullets into Tommy's chest. Blood splattered the wall behind him, and the two bullets impacted the plaster. Tommy slumped on his chair, and Blaine put one more into the centre of his forehead, which exited the rear of his skull with a collection of bone fragments and chunks of red flesh.

Julie's screams of anger and hurt slid over Blaine. She berated him. Punched him. Shoved him. He put it to the back of his mind. First, he had to deal with any imminent hail of bullets from across the street. Blaine took a deep breath, stepped out from behind the wall, and stood in front of the window. He stared out, trying to pinpoint the exact room in which Cable waited.

Blaine placed his gun back in the bag and took out his phone. He shook it in full view of the window, as though he were some scantily clad girl on a late-night TV channel. Then he placed it on the desk and looked at Tommy's laptop. He had a measly £75,000 ready to transfer. Blaine clicked on the enter button while Julie tried to get herself together. A new smaller window opened, asking for a password. Blaine typed in Julie's name. Incorrect. He typed it again and added her date of birth. The entire webpage shut down. Julie grabbed his arm.

'You absolute fucker.' She swung her fist at his face.

Blaine caught it in the palm of his hand. 'Listen to me,' he said. 'It was the only way. Tommy didn't know a thing about Harrington. Cable does. If he shot me, and Tommy paid him, he'd be gone. And there'd be no-one to find Jessica.'

'And what the fuck make's you think this Cable will help

us now?'

Blaine's phone rang.

22

COFFEE

Blaine stared at Cable from across the booth of the coffee shop. His duffel bag sat close to him. He had told Julie to wait in the car. With her temper, he didn't feel it in anyone's best interests for her to meet the man who'd ruined her daughter's rescue plans. Julie, however, had felt differently. She sat next to Blaine, also looking at Cable, who smiled back at her.

'Yeah, that kind of money has quite a bit of pull,' Cable said. 'Five million? Shit, anyone would have done the same thing.'

'You may have killed my daughter,' Julie said.

'Look, you said you had a proposition, but if you're here just to tell me off, I'm fucking leaving.' Cable moved across the bench.

'You can still get the money,' Blaine said.

Cable stopped and sat back down.

'There's still five-million pounds out there, and it still be yours.'

'If I help you find the girl?'

'Exactly. Tommy said you knew this Harrington guy?'

'Yeah. The American. Richard Harrington. Recognised him straight away. Wears glasses. Hair slicked back. We did a job together in London about a year and a half ago. Some kind of gang war was raging, and we got hired as enforcers. One night, we got forced to hide out at one of Harrington's pal's flats. They seemed pretty chummy. Like they properly knew each other. Like more than just business acquaintances. Don't remember his name, though.'

'Do you remember where?'

'Yeah.' Cable smiled once more, as the waitress brought the coffee.

Blaine thanked her, and she smiled and left. 'Would you mind telling us?'

'Sure, so you're free to kill me?'

'I doubt getting to Harrington will be easy. I'll need you. You said you wanted a gun fight.'

Cable added sugar to his coffee and took a sip. 'Do you think you're better than me? You do, don't you? You think you're cleverer. A better killer.'

'Better is a relative term. It doesn't mean anything.'

'You say you need my help getting to Harrington. But you forget one real important detail. Tommy's dead. No more work coming in for you. This Harrington guy is still active. If you piss him off, you risk losing the only source of work in the foreseeable future.'

'I'm not bothered.'

'Exactly. That's exactly my point. You're not. But you didn't think I'd think of that, did you? Harrington may offer me work. Especially when I tell him Tommy's clients will be looking for new companies.'

'Sure, you could risk that. Lose the five million. Get a bit of work every now and then. Or help me, become a millionaire. Maybe start your own company.'

'You're a talker, Jason Blaine. Yes, you are! A fucking talker.' Cable sat smiling, enjoying the banter. 'Tommy had it right. You could persuade anyone to do anything.'

'Just giving you options.'

'Yeah, options.' Cable took another sip of coffee. 'Okay, Blaine. I'll help you. But know this; if I get even the slightest niggle that you're double-crossing me, you're both dead.'

'The money will be all yours,' Blaine said. 'But we should hurry. I doubt they'll hang onto it for too long. The same with Jessica.'

Blaine took out a ten-pound note and left it on the table. The three of them exited and walked to their vehicles in the car park.

'So, where we headed?' Blaine said.

'Central,' Cable said.

'A lot of CCTV.'

'Buy a hat.'

Blaine's phone rang again. He didn't recognise the number. 'Yes?'

'This is Detective Sergeant Drake. I believe we met yesterday in Julie Jones' house.'

———

On Charlotte Street, Drake stood outside Tommy's office, phone against his ear. Police tape covered the front door, and people in white coveralls walked in and out carrying equipment.

'Look, don't hang up. I know you tried to help, but you must realise that things have gotten a little out of hand.'

'Mr Drake, how can I help you?'

'I'm at Tommy's office now. I assume this is your handy-work?'

'How did you get this number?'

'Nick Jones. He had it on him. Look, I'm trying to put the pieces together here, and since you're with Mrs Jones, I can only assume you're looking for her daughter. Did Tommy have something to do with it?'

'I'm hanging up now.'

'My only concern is for the girl. I want to help but I think you've seriously fucked things up here. Come in and let us help. Things can't get any worse now.' The phone beeped, indicating the man had hung up. Drake looked over to see Holly stood next to him.

'You phoned him?'

'We have his number. I figured we should at least ask them to give themselves up.'

'Is he coming in, then?'

'Didn't seem keen on the idea.'

'Who is this guy?'

'I don't know. At the house, he seemed professional. The guy you call when you need help. But, considering the wave of destruction he's left behind, I'm not so sure.'

'Think he's after the money?'

'Maybe. Get everyone on locating Thomas Carmine. We find Tommy, we find them.'

'And the girl? Shouldn't she be our first priority?'

'They're looking for her. It makes sense to follow their trail.'

Blaine and Julie followed Cable to an all-day car park. They left their vehicles, continued on foot to Bethnal Green tube station, and took the central line toward the centre of London. Blaine didn't feel too happy about heading back to the general vicinity of the double murder he'd committed earlier that morning, but needs must when the devil drives. Matt Cable led the way. He seemed uncomfortable having Julie around, and Blaine could understand that. This job was a solitary one, usually. The three of them riding the tube for half an hour in near silence felt awkward. Looks got exchanged. A few professional questions. They kept things low key. Julie had picked up a cap and sunglasses outside the station. She held her head low to avoid the gaze of any people watchers. Blaine hated the tube. People didn't talk. They looked. They watched. They imagined the life story of the people opposite. Blaine didn't. He didn't care. He also didn't enjoy the thought of others wondering about his life. He kept his eyes low. Glanced up every now and then to take in his surroundings. Kept an eye on Cable, who seemed more than happy to look at everyone else. He even started eye flirting with a girl who got on at Chancery Lane.

They exited the train at Tottenham Court Road and walked through the underground system to get on the Northern Line. They rode for one single stop and exited at Goodge Street. Blaine couldn't believe it. They stood just a two-minute walk from Tommy's office. He stopped himself from complaining, and Cable told them that the flat wasn't far. They followed him past a Tesco and walked up to a sex shop, where Cable stopped.

'A sex shop?' Blaine said.

'Above it. Top floor.' Cable walked to the door beside the shop and rang the top buzzer.

A reply came after a few seconds. 'Yeah?'

'Hey, I'm a friend of Richard Harrington. I think we met about a year ago.'

'Not me, buddy. I only moved in four months ago.'

Cable waited for a moment, then said, 'I don't suppose you have a forwarding address do you?'

'No, buddy, I don't, sorry.'

Blaine moved closer to the door and got Cable's attention. 'His name,' he said.

'You don't remember his name do you?' Cable said. A pause followed. Then a rustling of papers.

'Um ... yeah, I do have an old letter for him. John Davey.'

Cable smiled. 'Thanks.'

'What? So, we just Google him?' Julie asked.

'I have a better idea.' Blaine took out his phone, navigated to the last number that had called him, and touched the screen.

———

Drake's phone rang as he walked through the corridors of the police station. He pulled it out of his pocket. The name Tommy's guy came up on the screen. 'This is Drake.'

'Mr Drake. I need your help. I need an address for a John Davey. Previously at 23c Goodge Street.'

Drake walked at a brisk pace toward the room up ahead. 'Let me get into my office. One second.' He muted the call and burst into the room, where Holly sat at a computer. 'Holly, get a unit over to 23c Goodge Street.'

Holly picked up the phone on her desk.

Drake walked out of the office and into the adjacent one.

He un-muted the call. 'Okay, what was that name again?'

'John Davey.'

Drake sat at his desk and typed the name into his searchable database. 'If I do this, you need to do something for me.'

'What's that?'

'Julie needs to give herself up.'

'No way. Not until we have Jessica safe.'

The computer came up with a John Davey. Arrested twice in the past five years. Never convicted. 'That won't work. Looks like I've found your John Davey. Got his address right here. I can, easily, send officers over and see what he knows about multiple kidnappings.' A pause hung on the line. Drake waited.

'Okay. She'll do it. Just look up one more name for me. Richard Harrington. He's American.'

Drake typed the name into the database. 'I don't see anything here. Who is he?'

'What's the address for Davey?'

'You get that when Julie Jones comes into custody. I have officers on the way to Goodge Street. When I hear from them, I'll give you the address.'

Drake hung up. He wanted to leave the conversation with him on top. In control. He felt like he'd gotten somewhere now. With a grin, he pulled open his drawer, rummaged around in the back, and brought out a small tin cigar case. He opened it up. Inside lay three old thin cigars and a wrapped up piece of paper. Drake unfolded it, revealing the coke inside, and took the small cylindrical vial from his jacket pocket. Then he unscrewed the lid and poured the powder inside.

Holly burst in.

'They're on their way.'

Drake tried to hide the coke from her, spilling it over his crotch.

'Are you kidding?' she said. 'I thought you were done with that shit.'

'It's nothing. I didn't sleep well. It's just to keep me going.'

'It's not nothing.' Holly grabbed it from him. Drake stood, trying to snatch it.
'Give it back.'

'You don't need this.'

'I said, give it back.' Drake wrenched it from her hands.

'After everything I did for you,' she said. 'You're still fucking doing it.'

He could quit. It would be easy. Just not right now. Not in the middle of the afternoon. She wouldn't understand, though.

'Drake, you've made some bad decisions.'

'I know what I'm doing. After this case is done. I'm done. I promise.'

'You said the same thing when I first met you.'

'Julie Jones is giving herself up.'

'You're changing the subject,' Holly said.

Drake didn't reply.

'What about the guy she's with? And her daughter?'

'Like I said. I know what I'm doing.' Drake shoved the coke in his pocket and wrote down Davey's address from the computer screen.

23

DAVEY

Julie stepped toward Blaine. 'I'm not going anywhere. Not until Jessica is safe.'

'It's the only way we get Davey's address,' Blaine said. 'Drake's got officers on their way here as we speak.'

Cable looked on, rolling his eyes as though they were having a domestic.

'You knew this would happen eventually,' Blaine said. 'Let us finish it. Don't put yourself in danger.'

'This just isn't what I planned.'

'I know. A plan is just a list of things that don't happen.' Blaine saw her make the decision. She recognised that it made sense and had done more than any parent could have. Now, she had to step aside. Put her trust in him. It would be hard. He had watched her husband die the night before. This morning, he'd shot her father to death. Trust didn't come easy, but her choices were limited. She could tell the police everything. Let them handle it. But Julie knew just as well as Blaine did that this would, likely, end in bloodshed. And if that were the case, Blaine was her best option.

They left Julie on Goodge Street and made their way a few streets over. Blaine watched from a distance as a police unit arrived and picked her up.

'Just the two of us, then, eh,' Cable said.

'Just the two of us.' Blaine watched while the officers put Julie in a car and drove away. His phone vibrated not long after, indicating a text message. Drake had sent an address for John Davey.

'Hackney,' Blaine said.

'Fuck off. Not anywhere near Tommy's?'

'No. But close enough to make him uncomfortable.'

The address led to a house boat. The home looked as though it had sunk at least once and then drawn to the surface, and had a house number painted on the side. The canals leading off the Thames had thousands of these technically illegal dwellings. No running water. Usually waterlogged. Davey's place looked infested with insects. Graffiti covered the side from top to bottom. Cable stepped onto the deck and knocked on the makeshift door built into the boat. The vessel extended upward with little to no regard for any building regulations. Blaine joined him, treading carefully on the rotting wood panels beneath. The smell came pungent. Like rising damp and urine mixed together.

Davey opened the door and limped through. He held a crutch on his right side. His leg in plaster. His face swollen, unwashed. And it looked as though he had been attacked not too long ago. Maybe a week, judging by the bruises. His shaved hair didn't cover the array of scars and cuts on his head.

'Yeah?' Davey said.

'John Davey, right?' Cable said.

'Yeah.'

'Yeah, we met a while ago, with Richard Harrington. I'm looking for him now.'

'Harrington? You've come here, looking for Harrington?'

'Do you know where he might be?'

'Yeah, I got a pretty good idea where he might be. What do you want with him?'

Cable looked frustrated. He glanced at the man's feet and then back over his shoulder, looking for any passers by. Before Blaine could stop him, Cable pulled out his Glock and pushed Davey back through the doorway. His crutch fell to the ground, and Davey hopped backward for a few steps and collapsed onto the hard, wooden floor.

Cable shoved the gun in his face. 'Where's Harrington?'

'Yeah, fucking kill me. Get it over and done with, mate. Fucking go on.'

'Don't fucking test me. I'll fucking blow your brains all over that wall.'

'I don't give a shit. Look at me.' He laughed. 'You'd be doing me a favour.'

Cable looked even more frustrated than before. He cast his gaze around, searching for a way to make him talk. He pushed the gun against his knee cap. Blaine had used the same technique a few times. If you wanted information from someone, aim at their legs. Threatening them with death proved pointless. You wanted the information. You wanted them alive. A painful bullet wound in a kneecap would always loosen their vocal cords.

Blaine stepped through the door and leant against the wall. 'Where did you get the bruises?'

'A fucking fight, mate.'

'Looks like you lost.'

'Yeah. Ever the loser. That's me.'

Cable pulled the gun away from his knee. He could see Blaine had something up his sleeve.

'A lot of gang graffiti around here,' Blaine said.

'Yeah. Fucking pricks. No respect. If they only fucking knew the shit I've done in my life ... fuckin' hell. So, you want Harrington dead, or does he owe you money or what?'

'It's complicated,' Blaine said.

Davey sat up, holding his thigh. He took a few deep breaths and winced when he moved his leg with his hands. 'Look, if you're looking for Harrington, I've got a pretty fucking good idea where he is. Do what you want. I don't care. Me and him were like that, you know.' He crossed his fingers together.

Blaine could smell the alcohol seeping out of him with every word he spoke.

'We worked together for five years. I was a good soldier. He promised me a job when he'd put some of those plans of his into ... into ...' He drifted off, obviously going through his vocabulary until a word stuck. '... Motion. But he said he had no room for me. That I wasn't up to it. So, fuck it. Go do what you want.'

Blaine crouched next to him. 'Where is he? I can give you some cash.'

Davey waited for Blaine to pull notes from his jacket. He snatched them from him and held them close to his chest.

'I'll tell you. Yeah. If you do one thing.'

'What's that?'

'You kill the fuckers that did this to me.'

Cable joined Blaine at the corner of the street. They looked at the large estate in front of them. Music belted out of the windows. A mash up of different tracks all blended together from different floors of the four-storey building. Davey had given them detailed descriptions of the crew who'd harassed him. Seven of them. Multi-cultural, black and white, all under twenty. Vicious little punks, he had called them. Blaine recalled his run-in with the muggers in North London, two days ago when he and Cable had gone out for a drink. He'd had to show restraint that night. Now, he could let loose. It wouldn't be easy, though. The crew didn't run the estate. The big boys remained off-limits. Davey had explained how they'd paid him to carry their drugs to their dealers. He was reliable, and it provided his only source of income. But this young crew had no respect—wild and out of control. Whenever Davey had complained to the higher-ups on the estate, all he got was, *boys will be boys*. Then the crew would hear about his complaint and deliver another beating.

Blaine could see that Cable had grown hyped, ready to give these guys some pain, and would have been happy to walk straight in, guns blazing. But this wasn't a house clearance. They hadn't come there to lay waste to the place. If they were to get away with seven counts of murder, Blaine explained that it would be best to do it away from the estate.

They waited on the corner, watching the building, waiting for the crew to show themselves. Davey had said they would recognise them by one of their lackeys. Had described him as nearly as wide as he was tall. Their leader, a black guy called Dash, was nephew to one of the top dogs and a man that no-one dared mess with. Though only nineteen, the way Davey had described him made him sound like a force of nature. Blaine had watched the estate for nearly an hour. People had come and gone, but no Dash and no spherical gentleman.

'This is bullshit,' Cable said. 'Let's just head inside, pretend we're buying some weed, ask for Dash, and fucking do it.'

'Kill seven guys inside the estate? We'd never get out alive.'

'Oh, fuck that. I could walk in there and kill every single fucking chav piece of shit in under ten minutes. What, you scared?'

'I'm being practical.'

They continued to watch for another ten minutes. Blaine felt painfully aware that they stuck out. Two guys hanging out on a street corner, watching the estate for over an hour would look a little dodgy. They walked around and changed locations, keeping an eye on the front of the building. A group of guys walked past them and up toward the entrance. Big guy at the back. Six others ahead of him. Blaine watched them interact and singled out the tallest as Dash. They headed inside. Not ideal. Blaine had hoped that they would see them exit the building, so they could do it somewhere remote. Pull guns on them, force them against a wall, and just blast away. Quick, simple, efficient. Now they'd gone inside the building, it would make it harder to locate them.

'So, you wanna wait 'til they come back out?' Cable said.
'Ideally.'

'Fuck. I thought you were in a hurry. Isn't there a little girl you need to rescue or something?'

Blaine hated that he had it spot on. Time didn't lay on Jessica's side. The day had grown darker. It could be that these guys would settle in for the night. Better to wait, though.

'Let me ask you something,' Cable said. 'You're looking to split the money, right? I mean, you just told her what she wanted to hear, and you're gonna try and persuade me to give you half the cash.'

'If we get to Harrington, and it's still there, the cash is yours.'

'But why? Why are you helping her? Are you and her ...? You know?'

'No. A long time ago.'

'Well, you're not doing it out of any respect for Tommy. You still friends with her, then?'

'Not really. I hadn't spoken to her in over seven years.'

'Then, why help her? Fucking hell, Blaine. I thought you were the cautious one. You've been putting down bodies in your back garden. Shouldn't you be on a plane to Rio or something?'

He should be. And knew it. The longer he hung around London, the more likely that his face would get caught on CCTV. He couldn't afford that. Bad enough that Drake had seen him. It would only take a slight push for the detective to come after him. With a proper description, they would find his face in no time, and he would stay on record forevermore. Without the money from Tommy, the cash with Harrington offered his only option. He could live on five million quite happily. However, he wasn't about to tell Cable that.

'Maybe you're right,' Blaine said.

'About what?'

'Going in. It may be the only way.'

'Holy shit, Jason Blaine wants to walk into the building, guns blazing.'

'No guns.'

'No guns? What are you talking about? What do you want us to do? Strangle them to death? Poison them? Sneak up one-by-one video-game style and break their necks?'

'Even with suppressors, any shot will echo through the entire building. We'd have everyone on top of us within seconds.'

'Then, what do you suggest?'

'We do it quietly.'

'Video-game style.'

'This isn't a game.'

'We'll see. I bet you a grand you'll be smiling by the end of it.'

'I don't gamble.'

'Come on. A grand. If you enjoy yourself.'

Blaine, unused to working with others, tried to get his brain in the right frame of mind for what he needed to do. The last thing he needed was Cable betting him that he was about to get off on killing a whole lot of people.

'Fine,' Blaine said. He took off his black cashmere coat and ruffled his hair.

'What are you doing?'

'Fitting in.' He pulled out his shirt.

Cable looked at his clothes.

'What should I do?'

Blaine glanced at his leather jacket. His dark jeans. His brown boots. 'You'll be fine.' Then he placed his coat into his duffel bag and took out a pair of black leather gloves. He pulled them on and strapped the bag over his shoulder. 'Give me your gun.'

Cable shot a glance at Blaine. He looked insulted. 'I'll hang onto it.'

'Put it in the bag. You can't use it in there.'

'I'll keep hold of it. Thanks.'

Blaine could see there was no arguing with him.

The two men approached the front door of the tower block. The fragrant smell of marijuana reached them when they stepped inside. The hallway echoed with thumping music, and the smell of sweat and weed hung in the air, overpowering the slight scent of detergent. Blaine imagined council cleaners would come in and try their best to get rid of the lingering smells and wash the floors. But, every night, the smoky aroma would return. The cleaning pointless.

The building was large. Dash and his crew hung out somewhere inside, but to search the entire place would likely garner a lot of unwanted attention.

The small group of guys lounging in the hallway spoke among themselves. Blaine nudged Cable and pushed him toward the stairs. He figured it likely that Dash had his place at the top somewhere.

The group of guys in the hall got in their faces. 'Where ya goin', mate?'

'Here to see Dash, aren't we?' Blaine said.

'Dash knows that, does he?'

'He will do when we see him, yeah.'

'What's in the bag?'

'Dash's money. If he wants it.'

'What you talking about?'

'I'm told he's someone we should talk to. Got a business proposition.'

'Yeah? Well, how about you fuck him off and deal with us. What ya lookin' for?'

'I'm looking for Dash.' The guys seemed frustrated. They had managed to surround both of them. Cable tensed, looking for a fight. Blaine could see it in his eyes. He stared right at them. Ready to swing a punch. Adrenaline flowed through him, and he'd clenched his fists.

'Fuck off, you know Dash. You cops or what?' The guy snatched the bag around Blaine's shoulder and pulled. Blaine grabbed the other end, and it hung above the ground between them. The man's friends took a step closer, looking to give back-up. Blaine unzipped the bag and shoved his hand inside. The guy pulled the bag hard, and Blaine pulled out a wad of cash. All that remained of the grand that he had taken from his garage. A thick wad of twenty-pound notes. He shoved them in front of the guy's face.

'I'm here for business. We're not fucking pigs. I'm here to buy. I'm here to see Dash. That's all.'

The guy eased up and dropped the bag. Blaine pushed the cash back inside and zipped it shut. The man stepped closer to Blaine, looking him dead in the eye. 'Okay, we'll see if Dash knows you.' He barged past Blaine and walked up the stairs. Blaine and Cable followed him. The guy's friends stayed in the hallway.

While they walked up to the third floor, they passed several guys and girls, all of whom gave them odd looks. It seemed obvious that they weren't used to seeing strangers. If they had managed to get up the stairs alone, sooner or later, they would have had the same conversation with another group of guys. Better to have an escort leading them all the way to Dash's front door.

Their guide stepped out along the walkway of the third floor. Then someone stopped him. Blaine recognised him as part of Dash's crew. He had walked right next to Dash when they entered the building.

'Woah. Where the fuck are you goin?' he said.

'Hey, Ash, these guys say they have business with Dash.

I was gonna—'

'Gonna what?' Ash said. 'Deliver two fucking coppers to our front door? What the fuck's wrong with you?'

'We're not police,' Blaine said.

'Course you're not, officer.'

'Dash is expecting us.'

Ash looked at Blaine for a moment. 'He's not expecting anyone.'

'Ask him.'

'He's busy. And he's not expecting anyone.'

'They've got cash,' the guy said, and then grabbed the bag again.

Cable lashed out and gripped his hand, peeling it off the duffel bag. The guy went to swing a punch at Cable, but he telegraphed it. Even Blaine saw the punch coming. The guy scrunched up his face, leant back, brought his arm up, and swung his fist forward. Cable had plenty of time to jab out with his left fist and break the guy's nose. Cable let go of his hand, grabbed his shirt, and pushed him against the wall.

'Don't fucking touch it, sunshine,' he said.

Blaine turned back to Ash. 'Listen. He knows me. Come and hear us out.' Blaine pulled out the cash again and held it in the air. That kind of money opened a lot of doors. Even just the sight of it.

'Yeah, come in. We'll see what's goin' on.'

Cable let the other guy go, and they followed Ash to the noisy flat at the end of the row. Ash opened the door and showed them in. Blaine stepped inside. To their left stood a small kitchen with all sorts of crockery piled in the sink. In front of them lay a good-sized living area. Two other guys from Dash's crew sat on the sofa, rolling joints. The music that came from the laptop resting on the armchair sounded hideous. Drum and base or dub step. Whatever it was, its nonsensical beat thumped loud. Blaine hated to admit it to himself, but he so looked forward to taking down these guys. If only so he could turn off the music.

The two guys looked up at Ash. One of them said, 'What the fuck is this?'

'They say they know Dash. Got some business or something.'

'I ain't fucking seen 'em before.'

Ash stood beside the still-open door. Cable had a smile on his face. Blaine could see what would happen. Cable hoped the music would cover the shouting and destruction about to start. Blaine felt unsure it would. The last thing they needed was to get trapped in this flat with an army of guys trying to get in.

'Okay,' Cable said. 'Let's get this thing started, shall we?'

24

BODYCOUNT

Cable whipped out his leg and used it to slam closed the front door. Ash looked stunned when Cable brought his full weight toward him and punched him hard in the gut, winding him.

Blaine had no choice but to silence the two guys in the living room. While Cable held Ash in a choke hold, Blaine ran past the kitchen and headed for them. One of the men reached for something under the coffee table. Blaine leapt onto the first guy, letting his knees collide with his chest. He had to keep things as quiet as possible, which meant as little screaming as possible. The other one had pulled a machete from under the table. He swung it at Blaine, who lifted his duffel bag. The blade hit the bag in the centre. Blaine grabbed the man's wrist and pulled him close. The machete went past his body. Quickly, Blaine jabbed the guy in the nose, breaking it. His knees buckled, and he fell to the ground.

Blaine turned his attention back to the man on whom he'd landed. Though winded, he tried to get up, angry and shouting. An elbow to the throat silenced him. Blaine took hold of the man's head and brought it down as hard as he could onto his knee. Something gave in the man's face, and Blaine let him fall to the floor, spluttering blood over the filthy carpet.

The guy with the machete struggled to get to his feet. Somehow, he still grasped the blade in a tight grip. Blaine kicked him back onto the floor and took the machete from his hand. He plunged it into his throat and pushed his full weight down. The man coughed and lashed out with his hands while blood sprayed in plumes of jetted red liquid from his neck. Blaine watched the life in his eyes drain away and pulled the machete out of his body.

He looked over at Cable, who had suffocated Ash to death in the doorway. He dropped him on the floor.

'Didn't get a chance to ask him if he saw God, then?' Cable said.

Blaine didn't smile. He pushed the blade into the chest of the other guy and ignored the ungodly sounds that came from his mouth. The blade went between his rib cage and punctured his heart. The man convulsed but didn't fight back, in shock since the knee to the face. His eyes darted around, and Blaine watched them slow and face upward while the colour drained from his face. Then the man passed out and died.

'Nice,' Cable said. 'Come on; that was fun, right?'

'We need to move these bodies,' Blaine said.

'What are you talking about?'

'Put them in the bedroom. We need the place to look empty.' Cable, though arrogant, knew when to follow orders. Blaine dragged the bloody bodies into the bedroom at the far end of the flat, and Cable followed his cue. They shut the door to the bedroom and looked at the mess in the living room.

'You had to use the machete?' Cable said.

'Doesn't matter. As long as they don't see bodies. That's three. Four more to go.'

Blaine left the machete behind the sofa. Out of sight of anyone walking in. He rushed to the front door and looked out of the peephole. Guys gathered at the far end of the walkway. No sign of Dash or the others.

Cable pulled out a few drawers in the kitchen until he found the knives. 'They coming?'

'I don't see them.'

Cable discarded the huge chopping knife and held onto the smaller, easier to control one.

Blaine looked out again. The huge guy stood talking to the men outside. They pointed to the door. He made his way toward Blaine as quickly as his girth would allow.

'We've got incoming,' Blaine said. "The big guy.'

'Just him?'

'Just him. Let's let him come all the way in. Get behind him.' Blaine positioned himself in the living room, standing in front of the coffee table so that his body blocked the view of the blood on the floor.   Cable ducked down in the kitchen and waited. The door opened. The big guy walked in and saw Blaine standing there casually.

'Who're you?' he said.

Blaine looked up at him. 'Roger. Your guys are in the bedroom, testing the stuff.'

'What?' Confused and suspicious, he bolted past the kitchen and toward Blaine, who stepped back. The big guy stopped before he got to him. He looked down at the blood. Cable walked out of the kitchen and shut the front door. The big guy turned back and saw Cable. 'What the fuck is this?'

Cable advanced on him. The big guy yelled, 'Hey, Ash.' Cable jabbed his knife at him. He caught Cable's arm in his meaty hands and pulled him off his feet and over to the wall. Blaine leapt on his back and held his arm around his neck, trying to shut him up. The big guy reached over his head and hunched over. He grabbed Blaine's collar and pulled him over his shoulder and onto the glass coffee table. The centre smashed into pieces, and Blaine struggled to get out. The big guy grabbed his face. Blaine felt like his head was about to pull off. Cable got up and drove the knife into the big guy's back. Blaine didn't notice much change in expression in his face as he turned and backhanded Cable across the room. Blaine punched him hard in the face, but his fat, spongy features seemed to take the impact without much damage. He hit him again. The guy squeezed Blaine's head and lifted him. Blaine held onto his arms, trying to stop his neck from breaking. Cable had found the machete and swung it down hard onto the back of the guys head with a bone-crunching crack. It lodged in the back of his skull. The guy winced in pain. He let go of Blaine, who fell once again onto the broken table, tripping over it and into the laptop on the opposite armchair. It fell to the carpet, and Blaine came crashing down on top of it, breaking the screen. The music stopped.

Cable pulled the machete out of the guy's head, and blood streamed down the back of his neck and over his shoulders. He turned to Cable and lashed out with his right arm. Cable blocked it with the machete, cutting the man's wrist badly. He continued to punch at Cable, who fumbled backward, swinging the machete, blocking his punches, and slicing up his fists. Cable swatted the blade across the guy's face, cutting off half his nose. He screamed. Loudly. Then he held his face as blood poured.

Blaine got up while Cable swung the machete against the side of the guy's neck. It stuck in him with a squelch. Blaine reached around, locked his arms around the blunt side of the blade, and helped Cable push the machete into the swollen, red flesh. The screaming stopped when the man's throat filled up with blood. It sprayed over Cable's face when he pulled the machete across the neck, slicing it open. A spray of warm blood hit Blaine in the eyes. Instinctively, he closed them and felt Cable pull the machete away from the guy. Blaine's arms still gripped around his neck, but it no longer felt solid. Just a mass of torn skin and muscle. A gurgling sound reached him. The guy slumped, drowning in blood. He fell to the floor and hit what remained of the coffee table with an enormous crash, and blood poured out of his face.

Blaine wiped his eyes and looked up at Cable, blinking a few times. Red covered his face and soaked his hair. He looked back at Blaine and smiled. Blaine wiped the blood from around his nose and mouth and turned his attention to the door. He ran over and looked through the peephole. Though dark, Blaine could see the guys outside clearly. Everyone who'd hung around at the end of the walkway now walked toward the door.

'We can do this in here or out there,' Blaine said.

'It's a tight, thin walkway out there.'

Blaine nodded. He picked up his duffel bag and held onto the front door handle. Cable joined him, holding the machete. He threw Blaine the small knife that he'd pulled from the big guy's back. Blaine opened the door, and they ran out.

A small crowd of about seven guys stopped when they

witnessed two men covered in blood walk out of the flat. They gave mutterings of disbelief and swore. No-one seemed sure what to do. Blaine walked toward them, knife clutched in his hand. One of the men pulled a gun from his jeans. An old, black WW2 revolver. The men around him let him make his way to the front.

'Stay back,' he said. 'Drop those fucking things.'

Blaine continued forward. He grabbed the gun from the man's hand and stabbed him in the throat. His jugular rained red down his side, and he dropped to the ground. Blaine threw the gun over his shoulder. Cable caught it. He lunged forward, grabbed the next guy in front of him, and hauled him out of the crowd, then passed his body over to Cable, who hacked at him with the machete. Blaine carried on and fought a slew of incoming arms and fists, all trying to grab hold of him. Systematically, Blaine worked his way through each and every one of them. He slashed at their forearms to make them let go, and then went for their eyes to incapacitate them. The shouting brought more and more of the tenants to their doors. The smart ones stayed inside. Blaine waded through the bleeding mass of wannabe gangsters and let Cable finish them off behind him. Blaine reached the end of the walkway and waited for Cable to join him.

'Is that all of them?' Cable said.

'No Dash,' Blaine said. 'And two others we still need to get.' From the floor above, came yelling. Footsteps. He assumed they would have guns. 'I think we should head back down.'

'Fuck that, let's do the whole building.'

'We can't,' Blaine said.

Cable grabbed hold of him and pushed him against the wall. 'Don't think like that. Just let it go. Let it out.

Instinctive. Raw. Power. Just fucking let it out.' Cable released him and bolted up the stairs.

Blaine ran after him and watched while he ploughed into the small army heading down the stairs. Utterly vicious. Bones broke. Faces caved in. The shouting grew. Blaine looked back down the stairwell. More guys headed up. He waited for them to reach him. A quick look at their hands showed no sign of guns—just bats and knives. Blaine let them swing at him. He caught an arm and broke it. His knife sank into the man's temple. Then he kicked into the crowd, hard, causing half the men to tumble down the stairs. He had to finish this quickly before the police turned up. If it escalated into a gun fight, if any shots rang out, the place would end up crawling with armed units.

While the group of guys scrambled around on the stairs, Blaine caught a glimpse of Dash on the level below. His two pals stood by his side. Just this mass of screaming chavs between him and them. Blaine had the high ground and, methodically, worked his way through them. He buried his knife into each and every one of the men. Bodies flew over the railings and down to the ground floor. Others fell down the steps with stomach-churning crunches. Hands grabbed at his blood-stained clothes before he broke them and batted them away.

Dash and the two others ran downward, toward the ground floor. Blaine stepped over the bloody bodies in front of him and gave chase. As soon as they reached the bottom hallway, Dash turned and pulled out a semi-automatic. A Tokarev 9mm. Russian gun. Would have cost him about £300 to get a de-activated model. Maybe another £500 to get someone to bore the barrel and make it usable again. Blaine would never dare pull the trigger on a gun like that. It would, more than likely, blow your hand off. Dash didn't seem to mind. Blaine could see in his eyes that he'd grown desperate. Who would blame him? He'd just seen one man kill about eight people in front of him. For sure, he would fire. Blaine stood right in front of him. Nowhere to move to. No time to pull out his gun from the bag hung around his torso. All he could do was say something to stop him from shooting.

25

THE ADDRESS

'Your Uncle sent me,' Blaine said. Dash didn't shoot.

'What?' he said.

'They're coming for you. Right now. They're outside.
The door.' Blaine looked over his shoulder at the front door
and watched all three of them turn to look outside. Then he
stepped forward, pushed the gun aside, and delivered an
almighty blow to Dash's face when he turned back around.
He collapsed on the floor, gun still in his hand. Blaine kicked
the guy to his left in the stomach as hard as he could. The
other managed to punch Blaine in the side of the head.
Blaine spun around and elbowed him hard in the temple, and
then slammed the knife into the side of his assailant's head.

Dash crawled to the other side of the hallway and lifted
the gun. Blaine grabbed hold of Dash's friend, and threw him
at Dash, knocking the gun out of his grip. Quickly, Blaine
used the knife on Dash's neck, slashing it open, and then
turned back to the remaining guy, who had picked up the
gun and aimed it at Blaine. Cable grabbed him from behind
and took hold of the barrel. He pulled it back hard, breaking

the guy's trigger finger and sending him to his knees, screaming. Cable swung his machete down onto the man's face, who soon shut up. Another blow to the neck and it was all over. No screaming. No yelling. Just the thud, thud, thud of the constant music in the background. Blaine ran his fingers over his bloodied hair, slicking it back. It had been a long time since he had done anything like that. Adrenaline coursed through his body. He had the skills to fight a crowd but had never before had to put them to use. If at all possible, he preferred to dodge physical violence. A punch or a gunshot. Either one had to be used as a tool. As a way of getting something. He hadn't fought for survival like that in over ten years. It had left him exhilarated.

'You can pay me the grand later,' Cable said. 'I think we better get the fuck outta here.'

Each covered in blood, dripping in it, they strolled out of the front door and walked away from the building and its thumping music. Blaine hoped that all that the surrounding buildings would have heard was a harmless fight. A few commonplace shouts and screams. He didn't plan on hanging around to find out.

The state of their clothes made for their first concern. Though risky walking straight back to Davey's houseboat, it seemed the only place they could get to and wash the blood from their faces.

Blaine made sure that nobody followed, and stepped up onto Davey's boat. They pushed the door open and stepped inside. Blaine hoped Davey had some kind of running water and soap. By the smell of him, it would come as no surprise if he didn't.

'Davey?' Cable said. 'It's us. Look, we may have to borrow some clothes. But the job's done.' They walked to the back of the boat and into the kitchen area. Davey sat slumped to one side on the chair at the table. His face white and wrists slashed open.

'I don't fucking believe it,' Cable said. 'He's only gone and topped himself. Selfish fucking fucker.' He kicked Davey's leg.

Blaine looked at the table. Next to the half-empty bottle of vodka lay a scrap of paper and pen. He picked it up. It had one word written on it, all in capitals. ARDENT.

Drake sat in the interview room across the table from Julie. Next to him sat Holly. She hadn't said a word to him since they'd entered the room. Julie, happy to talk on the record, laid out the events of the last few days, starting with the kidnap of her daughter. Drake stayed quiet and let Holly oversee the questioning. When it came to the mysterious man that she'd hired, she kept quiet. Holly pushed her for details, and Julie simply declared that her husband had hired him. She said nothing more. Holly suspended the interview, turned off the digital recorder, and left the room.

Drake got up and stood by the door. He closed it. 'Mrs Jones. I want to help. I want to find your daughter. This man your husband hired, does he know what he's doing? Part of me wants to help him. Another part thinks he's going to get your daughter killed.'

'I'm not sure I understand the question,' Julie said.

'What I mean is, can you trust him?'

Julie looked down and rubbed a finger on her forehead. 'Honestly, I don't know. He'll do everything he can to find Jessica.'

'He'll keep the money,' Drake said. 'And that won't help your case. A jury will sympathise with your situation. Maybe they'll even understand the robbery. But without getting that cash back, the prosecution will find it too easy to paint you in a bad light. The fact is, you stole five-million pounds. If it doesn't turn up, it'll mean a lot of jail time.'

'I don't care about that,' Julie said. 'I did what I did to get Jessica back.'

'Your daughter won't want you in prison.'

'You want to know about this guy? He's a mercenary. Only cares about himself. He sees the world like a machine. His job was to retrieve the money, but he'll absolutely fuck me over if he sees the chance. Nothing else matters to him.'

Drake walked back to the table and sat opposite her. 'Why are you protecting this guy?'

———

Drake walked to the open-plan office. Constable Pritchard sat at his desk, tapping away at his computer. He'd asked him to do a nationwide search for Richard Harrington. Any details he could possibly get. Pritchard, a keen young officer, would do anything Drake told him. With Holly currently pissed off with him, it meant he couldn't rely on her to do things like that.

'I've got a Richard Harrington entering the UK two years ago on a work visa,' Pritchard said. 'He's been in and out of the country a few times since then. It doesn't specify anything else.'

'Any address?'

'No, Sir. Just a hotel near the airport.'

'For an outgoing flight?'

'No, the day he arrived two years ago. He gave the hotel as the place he'd be staying.'

'Okay, now we're rocking. Phone the hotel. Check that date and see if he gave them an address. I'll get on to Interpol and see if we can use their database. Someone's got to know where this guy's been living.'

Drake slapped his hand down on Pritchard's shoulder, and then left the room, buzzing. He felt good. Like he'd, finally, gotten somewhere. He just needed a fucking address. He could picture it, finding some house in the middle of nowhere, with this Harrington guy selling off kids to the highest bidder. He would swarm the place with armed police. Holly would apologise. Look at him as a hero instead of the fuck-up to which she'd grown used. Maybe, he would actually ask her out. No. She knew him too well. You can't get close to someone in that way when they've seen you at your lowest.

Drake walked through the busy police station corridors and up to DCI Miles' office. A quick okay from him would get the ball rolling with an Interpol search. He had to play it careful, though. Too much information sent their way and the whole investigation would get taken over, and he would get pushed aside. As far as anyone knew, this was just a simple kidnapping. He wanted it kept that way until the last moment.

Drake stopped outside the door but didn't knock. Holly stood inside. Through the window, he could just about make out her words. About him. Cocaine. Bad decisions. She wished she had seen the signs. She apologised for keeping it from the DCI. Miles didn't sound surprised. He muttered a few words that Drake couldn't make out. Holly then told Miles that Drake had helped one of the suspects. Said how he had let him go at the Jones' house. Miles went ballistic. Drake heard, loudly and clearly, that the DCI wanted him found, taken off the case, and brought to him.

Drake sped away from the office, keeping his head low. Miles' office door burst open with force, and he looked over his shoulder. Miles stormed his way through the corridor, back to where Pritchard sat working.

Drake hurried along the corridor and pushed open the emergency door, which revealed the concrete fire stairs. He ran up the echoey steps until he got three floors up and pushed open the door, which led to the roof.

He walked out and stepped over the air-conditioning pipes. The rooftops of London rarely got used to walk about on. Not a glamorous location. Every other footstep that Drake took, he stepped in pigeon shit. No lights up there. The sky at the horizon, a cool dark-blue, faded to pitch black above him. Drake pulled out his phone and dialled the extension for Pritchard's desk.

He answered quickly, 'Pritchard.'

'It's Drake.'

'Ah, look, Miles was asking about you. I wasn't sure what to do.'

'What were you doing?'

'Phoning the hotel. Miles made me hang up.'

'Did you manage to find out what address Harrington put?'

'I'm not sure I should talk to you. He ordered me to stop the investigation until they found you. The whole bloody floor is searching for you.'

'Pritchard, look, just tell me the address you found.'

'Miles is in the room. He's looking at me. He's walking over.'

'Pritchard, a little girl could well lose her life tonight. Do you understand? And you could, personally, save her life ... now, what did the hotel say?'

'Harrington didn't give an address. Didn't make the booking. Some company made it.'

'What company?'

'RTH Consulting. But they're an umbrella corporation. They have about ten companies all with different addresses.'

'What are the companies?'

'Drake, I have to go.'

Drake heard a scuffling noise, and then Miles' voice boomed out, 'Who is that? Is that Drake? Give me that.' More sounds of knocking and scuffling. 'Drake? Wherever you are, you need to come in. Right now.'

Drake hung up, ran to the edge of the building, and looked over.

'That's a long jump,' Holly said.

Drake turned around.

She stood at the emergency fire door, gun in hand.

26

NEEDS MUST

'You're gonna shoot me?' Drake shook his head.

Holly kept the gun held by her side. 'I'm trying to help you. You don't know what you're doing.'

'I've got a lead for where they're holding Jessica. I have to send it.' Drake raised his phone and typed.

'Leave it to us. We can do this. If you help that guy, and he gets Jessica killed, it'll rest on you.'

'That's just it; he's her best shot.'

Holly raised her gun. 'Put it down. Right now.'

'If you have to shoot me, then you shoot me. But I have to send this.'

The door to the roof burst open once more, and four uniformed officers, along with Miles, stepped out.

'Drake, what the hell are you doing?' Miles said.

Drake backed his way to the edge of the rooftop.

'Bring him back here.' On Miles' order, the officers rushed forward, past Holly. Drake stepped onto the fire-escape ladder. He looked at Holly and, for a moment, thought that she might fire. Maybe a warning shot, at least.

Holly lowered her gun. Drake descended the ladder and scaled his way to the bottom of the building. The officers gave chase. He could hear Miles' on his radio, telling people to cut him off at the ground floor. He just needed ten seconds to write a damn text message. That's all it would take. To find that ten seconds proved harder than he'd imagined.

Drake hit the ground running. More officers chased him from the back entrance. They shouted for someone to stop him. A marked car pulled into the station. With a slew of police officers chasing him, Drake looked like an escaped prisoner. The car wailed its siren and aimed straight for him. Drake leapt onto the bonnet and ran over the top of the car, feeling the roof dent with each step. He lost his footing around the light bar on top and collapsed onto the back window, cracking it.

Drake hit the ground on his back, knocking the wind out of him. His phone fell to the concrete. He shook off the pain and got to his feet. Then he picked up the phone and ran. The car behind him slowed his pursuers but not by much. A ten-second window where he could concentrate on his phone. It didn't seem like much. But ten seconds began to feel impossibly long.

Drake ran out into the street and raced down the pavement. It had grown dark. If he could lose his pursuers for just a moment at a corner, he could hide somewhere. Jump into a garden. Hop on a bus. While he ran, he saw no gardens. No buses. He needed to get inside somewhere. Frantic and frustrated, he ran across the busy street. Though way past rush-hour, traffic stayed permanent in London. Among the blaring horns of vehicles, he narrowly avoided getting hit and continued running. He glanced back to see officers halting traffic while others ran after him. Up ahead, he saw a Tesco Express. Small. Not large enough to hide for any good amount of time. But it had a toilet. With a lock. He ran inside and pushed his way past customers to the back of the shop. When he got to the toilets, he pushed the door for the Gents. Locked. Drake swore and looked around. The officers had come in. He ducked down and launched into the ladies. It held just a single cubicle. He stepped inside and locked the door just as the officers spotted him.

Drake held his phone in front of him. His heart beat so fast that he found it hard to hit the right keys. He typed out a simple and quick message while the officers pounded on the door. He pressed the send button. They kicked open the door. Drake put up his hands, and they grabbed him.

Blaine pulled on a black T-shirt and black jeans, which he'd found in Davey's wardrobe. He suspected they hadn't been washed in a while, despite getting put away. The unpleasant smell had Blaine looking around for something to spray on them. He found a roll-on deodorant and, with some trepidation, rolled the wet ball over his legs and chest. Then he found a plastic bag in a kitchen drawer and put his old, blood-stained clothes inside. He should burn them somehow. Just throwing them away wouldn't get rid of any DNA evidence. If it existed somewhere, someone would find it. The same for bodies. The same for clothes. He grabbed his shoulder bag, pulled out his cashmere coat, and shoved the plastic bag inside. Soon enough, he would find somewhere to get rid of it. He donned the coat and grabbed his phone from the kitchen counter. Just as he placed it in his coat pocket, it vibrated. Blaine unlocked the screen and read the text from Drake. *Check companies for RTH Consulting.*

Cable walked into the kitchen in his new clothes. Old jeans and a Parker coat. He looked like a junkie.

'I may have something,' Blaine said. 'RTH Consulting. Ever heard of it?'

'Nope,' Cable said.

Blaine opened an internet browser on his phone and searched for the corporation. He found it on a Ltd company database. It had associations with a number of other companies. One stuck out. Ardent International Solutions. He clicked on it and brought up its details. Harrington's name didn't show up anywhere, but the company did have an address.

'Looks as though Harrington's in Wales,' Blaine said.

'Well, then, looks like we'll need a car.'

'And guns.'

Cable grinned. 'That, I can help you with.'

'Car rental places open at eight tomorrow,' Blaine said. 'We should get some rest.'

'Here?'

'No. A hotel. Maybe somewhere near a rental shop.'

Cable snorted. 'You asking me to spend the night with you? We only just met properly two days ago.'

Blaine rolled his eyes.

They left Davey's boat and walked to the nearest 24-hour hotel. A twenty-minute walk took them to an upmarket establishment. They walked in and ordered a double room. Blaine paid cash. He didn't want Cable to leave his sight. Knew better than to trust him. The man helped him purely because of the money. If he managed to look up the address himself, he might just take off and try to take the money without him.

The large room had two double beds, a sofa, a writing desk, and a huge TV on the wall. The bathroom looked spacious too. The bar area remained open, but Blaine suggested they eat in the room instead, so as not to attract any attention. Cable agreed, and they ordered room service. A burger for Cable. Steak and chips for Blaine. Cable had a lager and Blaine ordered a Coke.

When they'd finished, they took turns in the bathroom. While Cable showered, Blaine took Tommy's laptop from his duffel bag. He powered it on. Another password window opened. Blaine tried a few words and names. Got nothing correct. He could call a few people who could hack the hard drive with ease. If Tommy had his client list and their details on here, Blaine would be laughing. He wouldn't need the cash and could spend the next few months preparing his own private company. A big if, though.

Harrington wanted the information himself. It had started this whole damn thing in the first place. Blaine figured it could give him some leverage if they did come face-to-face with the man. He turned off the computer and pushed it back into his bag, next to his handguns.

Cable walked out of the bathroom and headed over to his jacket, which lay on the desk, where he had placed his holster and gun.

Blaine, seated on the edge of his bed, reached down to his bag.

Cable picked up the holster, his back still to Blaine.

Blaine put his hand inside the bag and grasped the butt of his P229.

Cable turned around and saw Blaine with his hand in the bag. 'Relax. You think I'd shoot you in a hotel room?'

Cable pulled the gun out of the holster.

Blaine got to his feet and pulled his weapon out of the bag. He held it by his side but stayed ready to lift it at a moment's notice.

Cable said, 'I'd just feel a lot more comfortable having it within reach. That's all.' He walked to his bed and placed the gun under his pillow. 'Classic,' he said.

Blaine did the same.

Cable lay on his bed with both hands behind his head. 'What do you think Harrington is up to? Why does he need all those kids? You think he's trafficking?'

'It's strange. Usually, people-trafficking goes the other way. Young women brought in to work in dodgy brothels.'

'I get that Harrington is a businessman, but to be honest, he seemed more interested in the private sector. Private enforcement and all that.'

'Tommy said Harrington went after his contacts. For private security. Black ops. Maybe the kids give him a funding option. He makes cash from selling them. Puts it into his business.'

'Yeah, well, just seems risky.'

It was. Blaine churned it over in his mind. Something didn't sit right. He couldn't connect the two aspects of Harrington's dealings. It bothered him.

Cable said, 'All we know for sure is that Harrington is well armed, well funded, and has a lot of people working for him.'

'Your point being?'

'You hesitated. Back at the estate.'

'I got it done.'

'You held back. I saw it when we first met last week in that factory. You could've taken on those boys and me. You could've killed us all. But you opted for the safe route. Took out the target yourself.'

'It made the smart play. It wasn't worth the risk.'

'You keep it in check. That killer inside you. You know you do. You keep it buried deep down.'

'You have a psychology degree now?'

'Blaine, all I'm saying is that if you want to go up against Harrington, you're gonna need to unleash that fucking demon inside. Let it all out. You have to not give a fuck.'

'You don't have to worry about me.'

'Yeah, whatever. Just saying.'

They turned off the lights, and Cable watched online videos on his phone for a while. Blaine closed his eyes. He never slept soundly. Not like he used to. Not like any normal person. It was more like a deep rest. Always one eye open. He never felt comfortable enough to allow himself to fall into a deep slumber. The lack of rest had gotten to him. It formed a big part of the reason he needed that extended holiday. He just needed to get away. Just needed sleep. Real sleep. Not tonight, though. Tonight, he would rest. Tomorrow, he would find Jessica. He ran through in his mind all the possible outcomes. Too many factors. Cable was mostly chaotic. Blaine had promised him the money if they found Jessica. Even if they didn't, Blaine knew he would take the money. He needed him to get Jessica. That was a given. He couldn't do it alone. But the thought of losing all that money —everything he had worked for. Nope, he couldn't let it go. At some point, he would have to turn on Cable.

Cable's phone sounds stopped. Blaine opened his eyes. His companion shuffled to get comfy, one hand under his pillow. He had seen one too many movies. Blaine had never slept with a gun under his pillow before. It felt uncomfortable. Best to fit in, though. He closed his eyes again. And rested.

27

WHEN THE DEVIL DRIVES

Blaine opened his eyes when Cable got out of bed and walked past the curtains with the sun bursting through at the edges. He reached over to the bedside table and looked at his phone; 7:34 am.

The two of them went for breakfast in the hotel restaurant. Cable ordered tea and a full English. Blaine ordered coffee and bacon and eggs with toast.

'Who'll rent the car?' Cable said.

'I would say I will, but with the fiasco with the police yesterday, I think it may be safer if you do.'

'I didn't see much on the news about it. Your face didn't come up. If that's what you're worried about. Just a lot of stuff on Julie Jones. The news guys are pushing the heroic mum angle. She robbed a bank to get her daughter back. You know? Like she's a hero.'

'Maybe she is. Still, you never know what may have gotten circulated under the radar.'

'Yeah, yeah. I'll book the car. I've gotta drive it to my place anyway. Pick up the tools.'

Their food arrived quickly, and they ate. They had left their bags and jackets in the room, making sure the 'do not disturb' sign hung on the doorknob. When they finished, they went back to the room, packed up, and walked to reception. They dropped off the key and ambled to the car rental place they had found last night.

Blaine gave Cable cash to rent whatever car they had available and waited outside. Twenty minutes later, after signing a load of documents, Cable came out holding a set of keys. They'd hired a white Vauxhall Insignia, nothing too fancy, as it would blend in.

Blaine felt happy to get out of London. When anonymous, it felt fine. He disappeared into the crowd. But with the authorities searching for you, it turned the city into a maze-like trap. Within an hour, they reached the other side of the M25, headed west. Cable drove fast but kept his speed within reason. Even he realised that they couldn't afford to get caught speeding. Not even on camera. All his details had gotten put down on the hire car, after all. The vehicle had that new-car smell. The hire companies all seemed to use the same cleaning products, leaving every hire car with that distinct aroma.

'So, what's with you and the wife?' Cable said.

He had stayed quiet for a good ten minutes. A record for him. Perhaps, driving took a lot of concentration.

'We're old friends,' Blaine said.

'Yeah, real good friends, I bet.'

'It's not like that.'

'Oh, yeah? Like you're doing this for free? You promised me the money, remember?'

'I'll just take what got promised to me. You get all the rest.'

'I knew it.' Cable contorted his face into a wide smile. He looked over at Blaine, and then back at the road. 'I fucking knew it. Yeah, you're no different. You're just doing it for the money. Sure, you run around with her, act like you're the hero. What are you expecting? You turn up with the daughter, and she fucks your brains out?'

Blaine started to reply but then stopped. The conversation with Cable served no purpose. Not for him. Cable laughed and continued talking, moving on to the kind of porn he enjoyed and the immense manhood of adult star, Danny D. Blaine sat in silence and watched the road.

They pulled into an industrial estate and stopped in front of a large shutter door. Cable got out of the car and walked up to the front door next to the shutters and tried the handle. Locked. Blaine got out and looked around. It seemed quiet. The other units didn't have much going on. Not outside, at least. A few cars littered the parking area, but he couldn't see any people around.

'No keys,' Cable said.

Blaine reached into the car and opened his bag, from which he retrieved his small lock-picking kit, and then walked over to Cable, who stood looking around. His eyes darted from building to building.

Blaine placed the tension wrench in the lock and pushed in the pick. For expediency's sake, he chose the rake. He pushed it the full length inside and brought it out again. It took another two tries, but finally, the lock turned. The door opened. Cable moved inside with speed, and Blaine did likewise.

An alarm sounded. Cable pressed a code into the alarm box, and it stopped blaring. They walked through a small office that held a couple of computers.

'Weapons are through here,' Cable said. Blaine followed him into the main warehouse area and over to a combination-locked cupboard at the back. Cable grabbed the padlock and spun each dial until the lock opened. He pulled open the doors of the cupboard to reveal an array of weapons.

'What takes your fancy?' Cable said.

Immediately, Blaine's eyes fell on the M4 Carbine machine gun. Its compact size kept it light, but it still had stopping power. He picked it up from the rack and held it in his hands.

'Do you have a suppressor to go with this? Extra mags? Scope?'

Cable pulled open a drawer and revealed a slew of accessories. Blaine grabbed what he needed for the M4 and found a few extra magazines for his P229s, as well as several boxes of ammo for each.

'Can we get on those computers in the office?' Blaine said. 'We should look at the location again.'

'Yeah, go for it. I'll be a minute.'

Blaine woke up the computer and brought up the address in a browser window. A map of the area showed a large building with a lot of woodland and fields surrounding it. A single, winding road offered the only way to get to it by vehicle. Cable walked into the room, carrying a large bag full of weapons. He looked at the screen.

'That the place?'

'Yup. A few buildings. Lots of space. I have no idea how old this aerial photo is, though. A lot can change in a short time.'

'One road in?'

'One road.'

'They'll have outposts at the turn-off, here.'

'I'd have thought so.'

'So, we take them out and push through?'

'We go around. Use our phones' GPS to make our way to the buildings through the woodland areas. They're less likely to have men guarding such a large space.'

'Bloody Wales. How long's the drive?'

'About three and a half hours. We should get going.'

They left the building and loaded the back seat with the bags of weapons. Cable got in the driver's seat and, as soon as he closed the door, a dark-grey Land Rover screeched around the corner and drove straight for them.

'Get in.' Cable fired the engine in a panic.

'Why do I feel like we just robbed this place?' Blaine got in, and Cable peeled off in reverse. He backed out and kept his foot down, backing away from the incoming vehicle. It sped up toward them. Blaine looked out of the back window. They didn't have much more space to go.

'Are you thinking of backing through that wall?'

Cable pulled the steering wheel around to the right, and the car jolted to one side, skidding across its tyres. The Range Rover screeched to a halt, and the windows lowered. At least three men sat inside. They all carried handguns. Before they could fire, Cable put the car into gear and slammed down hard on the accelerator. With a squeal of wheel spin, the car jerked forward, and burning rubber soon replaced that new-car smell.

They sped out of the industrial estate and headed for the main road.

'What the fuck is going on, Cable?'

'Look ... that place isn't exactly mine.'

'You knew the codes.'

'Yeah. I know the guys who own it. Uh, I'm just not on

great standing with them right now.'

'We're trying to keep a low profile. This isn't helping.'

'I'll lose them on the motorway.'

'We'll get caught speeding on camera on the motorway. Get off this road. Get us somewhere remote.'

Gunfire erupted behind them, and the sound of bullets hitting the concrete road surface reached them. Cable pulled a quick left turn. The Range Rover came up fast behind them. Blaine reached into the back seat. The M4 Carbine lay on top of Cable's bag. Blaine picked it up, rifled through the assorted weaponry, and pulled out a box of 5.56mm rounds. He placed the M4 on his lap and pulled out the empty magazine. Cable took another corner, and Blaine ripped open the top of the cardboard box of ammunition. The shiny golden rounds came clipped. A metal clip held ten rounds in place, waiting to slide into the magazine. A small adapter fastened the two together. Blaine, however, hadn't picked up the adapter. He held the clip in his hands and unloaded the ammo into his lap so that they fell loose. He took two more ten-round clips and emptied them too.

Cable took a corner, and half the bullets on Blaine's legs rolled down the side of his seat. 'Keep it steady.' He reached down, looking for the bullets, but gave up. Instead, he grabbed another clip and unloaded it.

Blaine placed bullet after bullet into the magazine, pushing down on each casing and slotting each round into place until he had a fully loaded thirty-round magazine. He looked out the back window. The Range Rover still followed them, but now at a distance. Out of the front window, Blaine could see they travelled on a slim road. Grass and fields surrounded them. The engine revs increased when Cable sped up.

Blaine had to raise his voice,
'You know this road?'

'No. What about it?'

'Put your foot down. Get as much distance between us as you can.'

Cable pushed the car to its limit and bolted down the narrow byway. Blaine looked out of the back window once more. The Range Rover would catch up to them, for certain, but the quick burst of acceleration gave enough to put a good four-hundred-meters' distance between the vehicles.

Blaine pushed the magazine into the M4 and loaded the first round.

'Pull over now.'

The car screeched across the road surface, and within a few seconds, skidded to a halt. Blaine opened the door and stepped out. Calm, he walked to the middle of the road. The Range Rover accelerated toward him. It didn't slow. Surely, the driver had spotted him? It didn't look as if they planned on stopping just yet. The vehicle reached about two-hundred meters away. Blaine pulled the M4's stock out to its maximum length and raised the gun to his shoulder. He flicked the rate of fire to full-auto.

And stood there.

Motionless.

Waiting.

One-hundred meters.

Fifty.

Blaine pulled the trigger and fired a relentless stream of bullets into the windscreen, from right to left and back again. The windscreen became a mess of bullet holes and bright white spider webs of shattered glass. The Range Rover turned a sharp left, out of control, and darted off the road and into the green trees, which ran the length of the road. It smashed hard into the tree line and stopped. Smoke rose from the crumpled bonnet, and the engine spluttered and coughed until it died. Petrol trickled from underneath.

Blaine kept his gun raised for a moment, waiting for movement. Any kind of activity. But none came. Blaine lowered the gun and walked to the Insignia.

When he opened the back door, Cable stared at him in disbelief. 'Fuck me. I thought you liked to talk your way out of situations like that?'

Blaine released the magazine from his gun and placed the weapon on the back seat. 'You don't talk to a car full of armed men intent on killing you.'

'Hells, yeah, you don't! Fuck yes! That's what I'm talking about.'

Blaine pulled the plastic bag of bloodied clothes from his duffel bag. 'Grab your old stuff.'

'What are we doing?'

'Starting a fire.' Blaine walked back to the Range Rover and dipped the bag of garments in the spilled petrol. He opened the back door and threw it inside. Cable threw his old clothes over to Blaine, and he chucked them in too. Then he reached into the back seat and grabbed one of the guy's feet. He pulled off the man's shoe and stepped out again. Blaine held it under the trickling petrol until it filled and splashed some around the interior of the SUV. Satisfied, he stepped back and took out his lighter. After he'd ignited the flame, he threw it into the vehicle. It burst into flames, and Blaine walked back to their car. 'Let's get back on the main road.'

'Oh, we're going. Fuck. Now, I'm hyped. Bag full of guns. Building full of scumbags. We are gonna fucking do it.

A proper fucking gunfight.'

'Just drive the car.'

Blaine listened to Cable talk extensively about his weapons techniques and the art of the kill as they continued their journey west. The drive to Wales seemed longer than Danny D's penis.

28

SLICE

For a third time, Julie banged on the cell door. Footsteps headed in her direction. Large boots on the solid floor. The small metal hatch in the door opened, and the duty sergeant bent over to look inside.

'What?' he said.

'I want to talk to Detective Sergeant Drake.'

'He's unavailable.'

'It's important.'

'Well, that's a shame, 'cos he's unavailable.' He closed the window.

Julie banged on the door again.

'I want my phone call.'

The hatch opened once more. 'That's fine. I'll arrange it.'

'But I need to talk to Drake first.'

'Jesus, lady, you're like a bloody broken record. Look, he can't come and talk to you, okay? I'm serious.'

'Why? Don't tell me he's clocked off.'

'He got in trouble, okay. I don't know the details.' The duty sergeant waited a moment as though running options through his mind. He placed both hands on the door, either side of the hatch, and leant in closer. 'I'll talk to someone. See what's happening. Can't promise anything.'

'Thank you.' Julie managed a slight smile, and the duty sergeant closed the hatch. She sat back on her bunk and waited. The bed had a blue plastic-coated mattress. Julie had slept on worse, but slumber was the furthest thing from her mind.

About twenty minutes later, more footsteps walked toward her cell. Two pairs. The duty sergeant's and someone else's. These sounded lighter; faster-paced, too. A key clanked into place, and the door opened. DC Holly Barnes stood at the threshold, holding a large pizza box.

'Thanks, Terry,' she said. 'I won't be long.' Holly stepped inside, and the sergeant closed and locked the door behind her. She held out the pizza box to Julie. 'The food in this place is shocking.'

'Sure.' Julie took a slice and held it in her hand.

'You wanted to see Drake?'

'Where is he?'

'Suspended. Why do you want to see him?'

'He has a phone number I need.'

'The guy you were with? The man helping you get your daughter back, right?'

'I need to talk to him.'

'We can't let you do that. I know you think this guy is helping you, but he's left a trail of destruction in his wake. I understand you're desperate, Julie, I do. But you can't put the fate of your daughter in the hands of some gun for hire.'

'You don't understand.'

'Then, tell me. Make me understand.'

Julie took in a deep breath. She took a bite of the slice in her hand. It felt warm. Not hot enough to burn the roof of her mouth. The perfect temperature for pizza. 'How well do you know Drake?'

Holly sat on the mattress and placed the box between them. She took a slice herself and bit into it. 'I was nineteen when I joined. Drake had made a bit of a name for himself. He'd just come off an undercover gig. Huge bust. He seemed fearless. Always had a smile on his face. Bit of a legend around the station. We got partnered together, got close. Nothing romantic, just that we clicked, you know? He opened up. Told me he was using coke. Pretty much every day. Couldn't get through a day without it. Undercover, he had to blend in, you know? Did what he had to. I helped him. Got him off it. No-one else knew. Sure, he wasn't exactly his happy-go-lucky self anymore. But he got healthy. Now, I find he's using again. And look what's happened. He's giving information to your guy. Helping him.'

Holly put the pizza slice back in the box, half eaten. She gritted her teeth, holding back the anger.

'I know he's a good bloke,' Holly said. 'At heart, he means well. He does. He'd fight for the underdog any day of the week. But he just needs the right direction. Right now, he's unstable. Not thinking properly.'

'But, deep down, you trust him, right?' Julie said.

'Yeah. With my life.'

Julie leant back against the wall. 'I was in the Army ten years ago. My dad had been. His dad too. I don't think he expected me to join, but I was an only child and figured I had to. Met this guy. He seemed different from all the other pricks. Intelligent. Just seemed in control of his life. Attractive too. Well, we got together, and I saw this other side to him. Like he was a robot. All his emotions dulled. Or fake. By the time I saw what he was, I'd gotten into this heavy relationship with him. He had almost become best friends with my dad, too. And I found out about this other work that he did. Mercenary work. Dangerous stuff. I didn't want to know. So, I broke it off. Didn't look back. But it's never been the same with anyone else since. He wasn't bad to me. Never hurt me, not physically. He'll always be the one. I've known that for a long time. But I listened to my head.'

'Is that what you told Drake? Is that how you got him to trust this guy?'

'No. I didn't tell him that.'

'What did you say?'

29

SERMON

Cable stopped the car on the side of the Welsh country road. Blaine pulled out the charging cable for his phone, which he'd pushed into the cigarette lighter port. He looked at the map app on the screen. The address they headed toward lay about one-and-a-half miles north of them. They had passed the entrance to the long private road a mile back. A gated entrance. Sealed off to the public. From here on out, they would go on foot.

Blaine got out and opened a wooden gate in the corner of a field full of sheep. Cable pulled the car onto the field and stopped the engine.

'I'm sure we could have just left it on the side of the road,' Cable said. 'We haven't passed one car in ten minutes.'

'Best not to take the risk,' Blaine said. 'It only takes one police car—or one of Harrington's men to spot it.'

Cable opened the back door and pulled out the bag of weapons. North of the field ran a huge tree line. For five minutes, they would be out in the open for anyone on that road to see. They placed the bag on the ground and readied themselves.

They spent a good couple of minutes preparing everything they needed. Ammo. Extra magazines. Weapons. Blaine saw that Cable had picked up some body armour. Two ballistic-proof vests.

'Expecting a lot of resistance?' Blaine said.

'I know you wanna do this all sneaky,' Cable said. 'But there's a reason you're carrying two handguns and that rifle. I want a gun fight as much as I've wanted anything in life ... but I wanna come out on top.'

Blaine took off his coat and put on the vest over his black T-shirt. It weighed him down. With the one P229 on his hip and the other in a shoulder holster over the vest, his agility felt compromised. The vest had pockets for extra magazines for all his weapons. It made sense, but if you planned for something bad, it usually happened. He slung the M4 Carbine rifle over his shoulder and looked at Cable. He had stripped down to a white vest and placed his body armour over that. He'd gone full Rambo. A knife on his belt, a pump-action shotgun over his shoulder. Two Glocks in his leg holsters and a shit-load of extra ammo in his vest and on his belt. He expected close quarters combat. The very thing that Blaine looked to avoid.

The suppressor on his M4 would dull the sound of any gunfire. The subsonic ammo he'd managed to pick up meant there would be no crack of the sound barrier echoing for miles. If they could plant themselves a fair distance away, it would mean he could pick off a few assailants at a distance.

He left his duffel bag on the back seat. It still contained the laptop. The two men walked away from the car.

The forest was thick and dense. Anyone not using GPS would have soon found themselves walking in circles. After twenty minutes' walking, the woodland ended, and they found themselves stepping through a huge patch of grassland. The private road that led to the address snaked across their path up ahead. Blaine put away his phone and took hold of the M4. The entire area stayed disturbingly silent. Like nature had taken over. The sounds of any cars in the surrounding areas didn't reach them this side of the trees. Only the wind and birdsong.

Blaine crouched down and looked out at the road in front of them. Cable got down next to him.

'So?' Cable said. 'Doesn't seem like anyone's around. Let's keep going.'

Blaine said nothing. Slowly, he moved closer to the road and looked over to the right where the tarmac approached from the private entrance they had passed. Then he looked over to the left to where the blacktop led. A small building sat just off the road at the corner. No vehicles outside. It stood a fair way in the distance.

'It's nothing,' Cable said. 'There's no-one there.'

Blaine kept his eyes on the building. No cars. No vehicles of any kind. The sky grey and dull but still light. It would remain so for another couple of hours. No lights showed in the building. 'Okay,' Blaine said. 'Let's go.'

He got to his feet, staying low, and ran across the road with a glance across to his left. Birds flew out of the trees around where the tarmac curved. Then car headlights appeared. Blaine got to the other side and ducked into the tall grass.

'Stay down,' he said.

Cable had already reached the middle of the road. He looked and saw the car in the distance, and then ran back across and hid among the greenery, flat on his stomach.

Blaine lay flat on the ground too. He looked up to see the car drive past. Then, slowly, he raised his head and watched the car keep going and disappear around a bend. Blaine glanced over at Cable and waved him over. Cable got up and ran across to join him.

They trekked a further twenty minutes north and hit another thick forest. Blaine checked the map on his phone. The aerial photo displaying this area showed a thick forest with a clearing at the centre. They walked in, and after another twenty minutes of walking north, they heard talking. Like a speech. A man gave some kind of lecture up ahead. The two men reached the edge of the tree line and crouched, looking into the clearing. Several large buildings populated the area. Nothing like what the aerial photo online had shown. Up ahead to the left, large fields held assault courses. To the right seemed to be accommodation buildings. Around the field, just ahead of them, stood men in black tactical gear and armed with MP5 machine guns. Blaine found something odd about their clothing, though. Around the neck, they wore white clerical collars. The same with the man giving the speech. He hadn't armed himself. The man wore black trousers and a black shirt with a similar white collar as though a priest. Seated in front of him, Blaine counted around thirty children, all between the ages of seven and twelve. All of them wore small military uniforms. Black, adorned with Christian crosses. On the front row sat Jessica. She stared up at the tall man in front of her. Utterly captivated.

'Because God sees everything,' the man said. 'He watches you every second of every day and is always judging. Every one of us. We have all been chosen because we are special. Deep inside, you know you are special. God

Almighty has seen that. He knows that you know you are special. This mission he's given us—it is the single most important thing in our lives. We've spoken many times about the state of the world. The terrors. The villains. The people that want to hurt every one of you. The kind of people that destroyed your families. They are still out there—and they are only getting stronger. But we have been chosen to fight back. To show these evil people that we are not weak. We are strong. You are strong. Stronger than any others. And as we teach you—you will grow stronger still. The Lord has a plan, and that plan involves you.

'I know many of you are still getting used to your new home. Every one of us has been in that situation. Remember, you are not alone. It is okay to feel scared. Fear makes you faster. You will all learn that in time. Because we are here to teach you. You are here for an education. You are here for training. Everyone, stand.'

The children all rose. They tugged at their uniforms, making sure they hung straight with no creases, and looked onward at the man preaching to them.

'And now we must all thank the Lord,' he said. 'I want every one of you to let the Holy Spirit flow through you. We praise him in tongues. Oh Lord, we thank you.' He continued to pray by babbling his words. A spew of nonsense came out of his mouth as he looked up to the heavens and closed his eyes.

The children did the same. They raised their hands, as they must have done many times before, and let out a garbled prayer, each of them seemingly speaking in tongues.

The priest opened his eyes and wandered around the children. 'That's it; open your mouths and let it out. Let the Holy Spirit speak through you. Let it use your body. Let the

Lord God hear your words. Praise Him. Praise Him. Oh Lord, we praise and thank you.'

'What the fuck is this?' Cable said.

'A school,' Blaine said.

'What? For Jesus freaks? Why?'

'Training. Harrington takes these children as recruits. Brainwashes them. Turns them into servants of God. Christian extremists. In ten years, he'll have an army of assassins willing to do anything he tells them to as though it were the word of God. He wouldn't even have to pay them.'

Blaine watched as the sermon came to an end. The priest walked around every child, touching their heads as soon the wailing and jumbled words ceased. And silence descended.

'Do you see the kid?' Cable said.

'I see her.'

Cable lifted his shotgun and got into a ready stance. 'So, we head in?'

Blaine grabbed his vest and pulled him down. 'We wait.'

'For what? With all the kids there, they'll scream and scatter. We take down the guards, you grab the kid, and we find the money.'

'We can't just run in. Our way in isn't our way out. We can't run back carrying bags of cash and a kid. We'll need to take a vehicle. Take the road out of here. Which means we need keys. Which means we do this tactically.'

Guards led the children from the field and toward one of the buildings to the right. The priest headed to the left.

'The priest,' Cable said. 'If he's dishing out the orders, chances are, he's talking with Harrington, right?'

'I guess so,' Blaine said. 'We can make our way around the tree line to the left. Approach that building from behind. It won't be long before it's dark. We take that building.

Quietly.'

'Secure the cash,' Cable said.

'And a vehicle. Then we head to the children. Get Jessica.'

'You know, as soon as anyone hears a gunshot, all those guards are gonna come for us.'

'I know.'

'You're ready for this, right? It's gonna be a full on fucking bloodbath.'

'It doesn't need to be,' Blaine said.

'Just being realistic.'

Blaine got to his feet and walked around to the left, to the building that the priest had entered. Cable hadn't gotten it wrong. Contact with the enemy looked almost impossible to avoid. It was why Blaine needed him. Everything about the area appeared quantifiable and calculable. And getting to Jessica remained the only unknown factor. Blaine had no idea if the kids would even want to get rescued. Would they raise an alarm? Would they fight back? He saw it likely that they would have taught some of the older kids how to use a weapon, given that the guards openly carried them around the facility. Just what might he have to do if faced with a twelve-year-old boy with a machine gun pointed at him? Blaine had killed many people in his life. Most guilty of something. Never had he needed to kill a child, though. That switch in his head—the one he used to turn off his emotions —he had noticed that it hadn't worked so well lately. He hadn't felt sure if it meant a good or bad thing. The risk/reward ratio on this job kept getting worse with every problem. Without access to Tommy's accounts on his laptop, he needed the cash. If he didn't come back with Jessica, Julie would likely reveal his identity to the police.

Blaine squatted in the trees and looked out onto the surrounding buildings. He counted four guards walking the perimeter. All armed. He guessed another two would stay in the kids' accommodation. A few more with the priest and other higher-ups, which likely included Harrington. Silently securing that first building was the key. If they could clear it and get the cash without alerting any of the others outside, then they had a good chance of taking down the six remaining guards with ease. Even a small gunfight wouldn't be too painful against six.

A pair of headlights came into view. A large van pulled up to the facility. Cable squatted next to Blaine and watched while ten other men jumped out of the side of the vehicle and stood chatting to one another in front of the buildings. Every one of them wore body armour. Every one of them stood armed.

30

CLEARANCE

Cable let out a small chuckle. 'I like these odds.'

'This is no good,' Blaine said. 'With those guys right there—I just don't see this working.'

'You don't need to see it. We do what you said. Take the first building. Take those guys. Then the others. Element of surprise and all that.'

Blaine shook his head. His plan seemed shaky at best. Now, they'd become heavily outnumbered. Any kind of full frontal assault would be suicide.

'Just think of the money,' Cable said. 'Plus, we're better than these guys.'

'You want to wade into a gunfight so badly, be my guest. But I don't see any way that we come out on top in this situation.'

'You wanna head back? Give up?'

'I can't.' Blaine took his M4 from around his shoulder and placed it on the ground. He took a few steps forward and toward the first building. The one into which the priest had wandered.

'What are you doing?' Cable said.

'Stay behind me. Don't make a sound.' Blaine took another step toward the back of the building. Cable walked behind him, grasping his shotgun tightly. Blaine turned back to him. 'I mean it. You want the cash? No noise.'

'No problem.'

The lights glowed from inside. Upstairs and down. Stealthily, Blaine moved to the back door and braced himself against the wall. Voices came from inside. The laughter-filled conversation reached the door, which opened. A guard stepped out, still chuckling to himself about something. Good. That meant he'd come out distracted. The door opened toward Blaine, covering him from sight. It closed again, and the guard ambled away, making his rounds. Blaine pulled out a piece of garrotte wire and held it in his gloved hands. He crossed them over, making a loop. Then he timed his steps with the guard's, making longer paces. Quickly, Blaine caught up to the man, swung the wire over his head, and around his bare neck. Blaine pulled hard, cutting off his blood supply and crushing his windpipe. The guy tried to scream, but the more he fought, the harder Blaine pulled. The guard's knees gave way and buckled under his weight. He fell to the ground, fighting and clawing at his attacker. Blaine stood, looking stoic, above him and pushed his knee into the small of his back. Another thirty seconds passed, as the guard choked silently and spluttered until his arms dropped by his side and he passed out. Blaine held the wire tight. Not over yet. Just compressing his arteries and restricting blood flow to his brain would knock him out, but as soon as blood flow restored, he would wake up within a few seconds. Though the guard would be out of the fight, he could still raise the alarm.

Blaine acted quickly and let go of the wire. He turned the unconscious man over and unbuttoned his traditional clerical shirt. Then he pulled it off and threw it to one side.

Blaine pulled out the knife in his belt and, in one swift slash, slit the guard's throat and let him bleed out onto the earth.

Blaine wiped the knife on the grass and placed it back in his belt. He picked up the black shirt with its clerical collar and the guard's MP5 machine gun.

Cable stood watching a few feet behind him. Blaine couldn't tell if he felt impressed or impatient. He walked back to the door and unbuckled his tactical vest. Then he hauled it off and replaced his shirt with the guard's. Next, he placed the white clerical collar around his neck and pulled out his silenced P229.

'You just gonna walk in?'

'Even if they hesitate for a second—it's all I need.'

Cable looked down at Blaine's gun. 'That'll still make a lot of noise.'

'Just in case.' Blaine took a breath and placed his hand on the door handle. 'One room at a time. Follow my lead.'

Blaine turned the handle and opened the door, revealing a tiny kitchen area with a small living room behind it. The TV played some comedy quiz show. On the sofa, facing away from Blaine, sat another guard.

'You forget something?' he said.

Calmly, Blaine walked up to him as he got to his feet and turned to face him. A momentary look of confusion washed over the man's face. A moment was all it took for Blaine to lash out and strike him hard in the nose. A splash of blood and a crack of bone and the man fell to the ground. Blaine took out his knife and dealt with him swiftly; pushing the blade under his ribcage and into his heart. His body convulsed slightly but soon stopped.

Cable walked up behind him, still holding his shotgun. It made Blaine nervous. Just one errant yell would alert everyone to their presence. A shotgun blast would cause every guard outside to aim their weapons at the building.

Footsteps on stairs. Blaine pushed Cable back into the kitchen when the door to the living area opened, and the priest who had given the speech walked in. Blaine stood in front of the guard's body while it bled slowly around his feet.

'Can you tell those guys out there to keep it down?' the priest said. 'The kids need to know we're organised.' He turned his attention to the window when more laughter came. 'Oh, forget it, I'll tell them myself.' He walked out of the living area and opened the front door.

Blaine walked to the window and glanced out. The priest stood yelling at the armed guards, who proceeded to throw away their cigarettes and stand to attention. Blaine looked over at Cable, who had stayed in the corner. Sweat glistened on his face and forehead, and he stood gripping his shotgun tightly. Blaine held a hand up, indicating for him to stay in place. The priest finished telling off the guards and came back inside the house. He ignored Blaine and walked up the stairs. Blaine exhaled a sigh of relief and waved Cable over.

They walked into the dark hallway, and voices came from a room next to the bottom of the stairs. Another kitchen. This one bigger. Two distinct voices. Cable neared the doorway. He looked up to the top of the stairs and waited for Blaine to join him.

Blaine took out his P229. The suppressor would dampen the sound of the gunshot but not silence it totally. He pulled out the magazine from the butt of the gun and replaced it with one containing subsonic ammo. He didn't like using them. They contained less gunpowder, which meant less noise, but had no real stopping power. He would only have one single shot, too, as the lack of gunpowder reduced blowback, which was required to reload the next round.

He pushed the magazine inside and, gently, pulled back the slide, loading the first round into the chamber. Blaine inhaled deeply, held it for a while, and breathed out. He held the gun down behind him and walked through the door and into the kitchen, all casual and calm as if he belonged. Two guards sat snacking on some chicken from a plate. They turned to see Blaine, dressed as one of them. Blaine smiled. They nodded, unsure if they knew him or not. Blaine approached them with purpose, whipped out his hand, pushed the gun's barrel to the first guy's forehead, and pulled the trigger. A clunk of metal sliding against metal broke the silence that had fallen. The guard dropped to the floor. No spray of blood came from the back of his head. No brains blasted across the kitchen walls. The bullet remained inside him. The man behind reached for his pistol, still in its holster. Blaine slammed the weapon into his face, breaking his nose. Blood exploded over his cheeks and chin. A slight yelp of pain came from the guard, and he fell to his knees. Hurriedly, Blaine pulled back the slide of his gun, loaded the next round, and pushed the barrel of the suppressor against the man's head. He pulled the trigger. The guard fell on his back like a carelessly discarded rag doll.

Cable stood at the doorway, looking up the stairs, checking to see if anyone had heard the muffled thwacks of the shots. He looked at Blaine and nodded. Blaine joined him and reloaded his gun. They edged up the staircase with Cable leading. Every creak of the wood beneath their feet seemed louder than possible. Blaine stuck to the sides of the risers, hoping to make less noise.

Above, two people argued. One sounded like the priest. His voice distinctive. Loud, deep, and important. The other had an American accent. From what part of the US, Blaine had no clue. He'd put money on it belonging to Harrington, though.

'Where do you find these men?' The priest said. 'We're supposed to teach those children respect. How to obey orders. Now, they've likely overheard me telling off those men of yours.'

'Calm down,' the American said. 'These guys aren't the ever obedient soldiers you'd like to think they are. They're mercenaries. They work for money.'

'Well, I don't see why we need so many.'

'You don't need to see. You need to teach those kids the word of God. That's all. You don't need to concern yourself with soldiers. Or how I run this facility.' Yep, Harrington for definite.

'And the money? You asked for five million this time, and look at the shit-storm that's happened. There was a reason we all agreed on five hundred thousand. Jesus, I should have walked away from this project the moment I heard what you did. Let's not forget who the children listen to. Who they trust. You can't do this without me.'

'I don't plan to. Everything is under control. The money's a huge boost for us.'

The sound of a bag getting zipped open reached them.

'Just smell that,' Harrington said. 'That's power and control, and we'll both see a lot more in the future. Get a good night's sleep. I'll come back in a few days.'

The bag zipped up once more. Blaine looked at Cable,

who stood smiling. He knew just as well as Blaine did that the cash waited in that room. They hid only a few feet from it.

Adrenaline lit Cable's eyes. His grip on his shotgun increased, and his breathing got quicker.

Footsteps. The priest stepped out of the room and got confronted with the sight of Cable, stood at the top of the stairs. The priest's eyes widened, and Cable slammed the butt of the shotgun into his stomach. He stumbled back into the room, and Cable followed him, brandishing his shotgun, aiming it at Harrington.

'Don't fucking move,' Cable said.

Blaine launched himself up to the landing and looked around. What the fuck was he doing? They had no idea how many men occupied the upstairs. More guards could have populated that room for all they knew.

Sounds of the scraping of a chair on a wooden floor reached Blaine. The door to the room opposite opened, and another guard stepped out. His machine-gun held in his right hand casually. With haste, Blaine raised his gun and fired a round into the man's head. He dropped with a loud thump onto the wooden floorboards. His gun made an even louder impact. Blaine reloaded his gun once more and spun around to the right, covering all the other doors. He waited. He listened. He turned his attention downstairs. The only sound he could hear came from the drone of the television. That must be everyone in this building. He stepped into the doorway of Harrington's room and joined Cable. Then he trained his gun on the man's head.

'All those bloody soldiers made a *real* difference,' the priest said.

Cable shoved the end of his shotgun in his face. 'Get the

fuck back.'

'Matthew Cable,' Harrington said. 'It's been a while. Didn't realise you were still in the game. Still a loud-mouthed prick?' Harrington adjusted his glasses, pushing them up his nose. The suit he wore appeared tailored and fit him well. Designed to hide the minor bulge of the handgun in his shoulder holster.

'Shut the fuck up,' Cable said.

Harrington pointed at him. 'You shoot that thing, and you'll have every one of those men out there up your backside.'

'Blaine,' Cable said.

Blaine stepped forward and pointed his weapon at Harrington's face. 'Mine's a little more subtle. The keys to your car. Now.'

Slowly, the American put his hand in his pocket and pulled out the keys. He tossed them over, and Blaine caught them with his left hand and placed them in his pocket.

'You're Tommy's guy, right?' Harrington said.

'Don't let him talk,' Cable said. 'Just fucking do it, and let's go.'

'Which building is Jessica in?' Blaine said.

'Oh, I'm confused, did you come for the girl or the money? Or both? Jesus, you two fucks are gonna die either way. Sure, shoot us both. You think you can drag four bags of cash to my car without anyone seeing? You fucking morons.'

Blaine stepped past Cable and grabbed the priest. He pushed the gun against his head. 'The girl. Which building?'

'They're all in the building at the end,' the priest said. 'Green door.'

Harrington whipped the handgun from his shoulder

holster and fired at Blaine, who pushed the priest in front of him. Two bullets hit the man's chest. Blood sprayed Blaine's face and upper torso. The priest fell to the ground, and Blaine stumbled forward.

A shotgun blast from Cable sprayed the back wall and shattered the window behind Harrington. His arm splashed with blood, and he fell backward against the glass. Then he returned fire, as Cable cocked the pump-action shotgun, forcing him to step back and into the hallway.

The smoke alarm burst to life and rang out an impossibly loud, screeching sound.

Blaine raised his gun and fired. The bullet missed Harrington and flew out of the broken window. Harrington placed his hand on the shattered glass pane and launched himself out of the building. He dropped two stories, and Blaine heard him hit the grassy ground outside.

'Up there,' Harrington yelled. 'Get in, Goddammit. Take 'em out.'

Blaine backed out of the room and into the hallway. He ejected the magazine in his gun and replaced it with the original supersonic rounds. Then he holstered it and took hold of the MP5 he had around his shoulder. Tense, he pulled the magazine out and checked it remained full. Satisfied, he pushed it back in and loaded the first round.

Below, guards entered the building, urged onward by Harrington's increasingly frustrated voice. 'Go ... get in there,' he said. 'Destroy the place.' His voice changed as though he now spoke into a radio. 'Jackson, you there?' Blaine didn't hear the response; only Harrington's reply. 'I need everyone at the compound. Now ... everyone ... bring everyone!'

'Okay, Blaine,' Cable said. 'Here's where the fun starts.'

'Sure, you go first.'

'No problem.' Cable grabbed a flash-bang from his vest and pulled the pin. He threw it downstairs, into the hallway, and stepped back.

After the intensely bright explosion, Cable ran down the stairs. Shotgun blast after shotgun blast reached Blaine. Then machine-gun fire. More shotgun blasts. The man was fearless. Or stupid. Maybe a bit of both. Impressive, though. Blaine unbuttoned his bloody shirt at the top and pulled the white collar from around his neck. He gripped his machine gun tightly and ran down the stairs, leaving the white collar, stained with blood, next to the body of the priest.

31

THERE'S ALWAYS ROOM FOR A GUNFIGHT

The sound of constant gunfire covered the painful wail from the smoke alarms. The shotgun blast in the bedroom upstairs had left Blaine's ears ringing. The sound of machine-gun fire in the hallway downstairs rippled through his body. His internal organs shook with every shot. The reason gunfights never happened like they do in the movies. Too messy. Chaotic. No-one ever knew what was going on. An easy way to get yourself killed. Cable ignored all of that. He had unloaded all of his shotgun shells and thrown the weapon onto the ground. Out came his Glocks. One in each hand. He stood in the doorway to the living area, poking around the corner and blasting away. Smile on his face. How could shooting like this have any accuracy at all? Still, it kept the guards in the small kitchen.

The whiff of cordite filled Blaine's nostrils and became all he could smell. They had managed to push the guards back through the main door in the hallway and lock it. That didn't offer the only way in, however. Through the constant ringing in his ears and the downstairs smoke alarm, he heard the sound of another door opening. He spun back around and made his way to the bottom of the stairs. Multiple footsteps, incoming, thumped across the kitchen floor. He even heard them step over the two bodies on the ground.

Blaine crouched low and flicked the switch on his MP5 to three-round bursts. He leant out of the bottom of the doorway and fired quick successive blasts into the two men at the front. They fell backward. The two men behind them scrambled for cover.

Blaine leant back into the hallway when they returned fire, splintering the woodwork around the doorway. It ceased, and Blaine yelled, 'Frag out,' as though about to throw a grenade into the room. The men ran for the exit, a little less elegantly than they had entered. Blaine flicked the firing mode to full-auto, rushed into the kitchen, and sprayed the area. The two guards sprinted out of the house. Blaine bent down and picked up a spare magazine from one of the dead men on the ground. He hurried behind the island in the centre of the room and reloaded. Though he hated to admit it, exhilaration filled him. 'Cable?' He waited for a reply. The gunfire ceased.

Cable yelled from the hallway, 'Yeah?'

'Do we have a plan here?'

A single gunshot came from Cable, and the smoke alarm ceased. 'Kill them all. Good enough?'

Good enough. It offered the only option. Harrington remained alive and now knew that Blaine had come for Jessica. Even if they managed to kill all the guards, Blaine figured that the American would put a bullet in her just to spite him. It was why he had taken her in the first place. To spite Tommy. Blaine looked out around the corner to the rear of the kitchen. Bullet holes covered the back wall and peppered the wooden door, which hung ajar.

Blaine crept out from behind the island and stalked his way to the door. Outside, he could hear yelling. Orders. Running. Confusion. Still so many of them. He and Cable had gotten damn lucky so far, but luck never held out indefinitely. Gunshots started again. Cable fired into the crowd of guards. Sounded like the front. They shot back at him. Glass broke, and wood shattered, as the impact of bullets slammed into the house. Good. It meant all eyes stayed off him. Blaine moved outside and sprinted around the building to the back.

The body of the guard with the slit throat still lay on the ground. Next to it lay Blaine's M4 Carbine. Suppressor still attached to the barrel. Blaine grabbed it and pelted into the trees behind the house. In the shadows, he became invisible. With the suppressor and the amount of gunfire surrounding the building, he would be silent. He ran to the left of the house until the guards in front came into sight. Then he found a suitable tree branch and rested the rifle on top of it. No time to test the scope. It wasn't like his faithful one that he'd had to leave in Hitchin. He couldn't rely on it being set up perfectly.

His first shot would tell him exactly how far off the scope was, and how much he would have to compensate. Blaine aimed for the chest of one of the guards who stood firing small bursts into the house from behind the van parked in front. Blaine pulled the trigger. The bullet hit the van a good full meter to the right and slightly low. He altered the scope, turning the dials on the side a little. The man in his crosshairs had no idea from where the shot had come. Blaine aimed once more at his chest. Fired. The bullet hit the guard in the neck, and with a spurt of blood, he fell to the ground. The sights seemed set somewhat low. Blaine could deal with that. He aimed at another guard, who'd popped up his head to shoot back at the house. He pulled the trigger. The firing mechanism of the weapon sounded quiet compared to the MP5. Blaine hoped his ears would stop ringing soon but knew they wouldn't. It felt like he had just walked out of a 90's rave at 7:00 am.

The next few shots seemed like shooting babies in a pram. Simple. Effortless. No resistance. In under thirty seconds, he had thinned out the herd. Blaine took out his phone and looked at the time. He needed these guards dealt with now.

And still, he hadn't caught sight of Harrington. He glanced over to the building to the far left. The one with the green door that the priest had mentioned. Blaine took down one more guard, hitting him in the shoulder. This one, however, seemed to notice from exactly where the shot had come.

'In the trees,' he yelled. The others aimed at the tree line and fired. Blaine pulled his rifle from the branch and stood behind the thick trunk while bullets whipped past him. Some passed a good ten meters away. The guards fired blind. Time to end this.

Blaine marched out, gun held high. He switched to full auto and fired at the guards. Bullets ricocheted off the van while the men ducked behind it. His magazine emptied. He dropped the gun and ran to the building, taking cover against the wall. More shots rang out, and the sound of someone whooping and then shouting reached him, 'Come on, you fuckers! What's up?'

Cable had exited the house. Still alive. Still finding plenty of guns to shoot. Blaine pulled out his P229 with the suppressor attached and unscrewed it. Then he retrieved the other one too. Adrenaline coursed through his body. He smiled. Shook his head. Couldn't believe what he was doing. Crazy. Unprofessional. No-one held guns like this. Not one in each hand. Not if they wanted to hit anything. Yet there stood Cable, blasting away as if in a video game. And Blaine wanted to join in.

He bolted out from cover and raced toward the guards. Both guns firing. Surprised at how many of his rounds hit their targets. Cable raced in from the other side, as the final few guards ran from the van and fired back, blindly. Blaine hit the vehicle with his shoulder and crouched next to it, firing around the side. Cable approached but not running for cover. Instead, he scrambled up on top of the vehicle, stood on the roof, and rained down a hail of gunfire from above, pelting the men with a shower of lead. His guns emptied. He looked around, breathing fast. Blaine ran out of ammo too. Harrington remained out there somewhere. Blaine stood and holstered one gun. He pushed the magazine release of the other, and it dropped to the floor. Then he reloaded and clicked the slide back into place. Next, held it up at the other buildings, moving from one window to the other, watching for movement. Finally, he trained it on the building at the end. The one with the kids inside.

'Now, was that a rush or what?' Cable hopped off the roof of the van and threw his guns to the ground. He pulled a Beretta from one of the dead men at his feet and checked the ammo. 'That's what I was talking about. A real fucking gunfight. Blood, sweat, and mother-fucking tinnitus.' He picked up a spare magazine from the same body.

'We're not done yet,' Blaine said. The building at the end loomed large and intimidating. Darkness had fallen over the entire encampment, and only the light shining from the windows gave away its presence.

'Oh, you're right about that,' Cable said. He raised his gun and pointed it at Blaine. 'I'll give you a five-second head start.'

Blaine held his gun at his side. His finger moved from the trigger guard to the trigger. 'You think I didn't see this coming?'

'Come on, Blaine. One on one. You and me. A fight to the death. Winner takes all.'

Cable had gone crazy. Blaine could see that. A gunfight to the death? He would, happily, risk dying to take all the money for himself. But then, it wasn't about the money for him, but the thrill. He lived for it.

'Harrington has more men coming ... this is stupid.'

'I don't care. I just want the money ... and the keys to his car.'

Blaine took a deep breath. He needed to live. To survive. Cable hadn't shot him yet, and five seconds had elapsed already. He wanted this gunfight bad. The only way to live would be to give him what he wanted.

'Five-second head start, huh?' Blaine said.

'Ready?'

'Ready.' Blaine stepped back. Cable lowered his gun.

Blaine kept his eyes trained on him.

Cable's hand still gripped his weapon.

Blaine continued to increase the distance between them.

The corner of Cable's mouth formed a slight smirk. Blaine's five seconds were up.

Cable raised his gun as though drawing it from a holster strapped to his leg. Blaine fired from the hip, sending a bullet into the van next to Cable. He didn't need it to hit him. Just distract him enough so his first shot would come out of panic.

Cable fired. The bullet whizzed past the house and into the trees. Blaine gripped his gun with both hands, showing Cable that he aimed true. He fired multiple shots, causing Cable to duck behind the van.

Blaine ran for the house and made his way around the back, as the front door remained locked from the inside.

'That's the spirit, Blaine!' Cable shouted. 'Fucking bring it.'

Blaine stepped past the guard with the slit throat one more time. His bullet-proof vest still lay on the ground next to him. The sound of Cable running to the house was enough to make Blaine think twice. He left the vest and ran to the back door.

Cable waited outside the front, visible through the smashed window in the living area. When he saw Blaine, he fired multiple shots with both his handguns.

Blaine dived behind the small kitchen cabinets, and debris and crockery smashed and fell around him.

Silence. Then the sound of Cable reloading his guns. Blaine stood and fired at the window. Cable stayed out of sight, presumably ducked down below the window or to the side of it. Blaine aimed at the sharp shards of glass on the edges of the frame, hoping they would spray down on his adversary.

He stopped firing and ran through the living area and into the hallway.

The crunch of glass on carpet gave away Cable's entrance through the window. Blaine turned and unloaded the rest of his magazine toward him. Cable moved to the wall, taking cover, as splinters of wood flew past his face. He let out a whoop of excitement when Blaine ran to the stairs.

Cable moved out from cover and saw Blaine running. He fired. The impact of a bullet hit Blaine hard in the side. It felt like a wet slap. So solid that instead of pain there came numbness. The impact rippled through his body. Then came a tingle in his toes, somehow, as though his body shifted the pain elsewhere to try and get rid of it. He stumbled onto the stairs and attempted to return fire through the banister. Twice, he clicked the empty gun. Cable fired again. The wooden banister shattered in front of him, sending thousands of tiny splinters into his face. Instinctively, Blaine closed his eyes and dropped the gun. He climbed the stairs as fast as he could, eyes closed and galloping on all fours. Cable continued shooting, ploughing bullets into the wall behind him.

Blaine got to the top and rolled along the floor. He needed to get as much space between them as possible. The guard he had shot dead still lay on the ground. So did his gun. Blaine picked it up and aimed back at the top of the stairs. He pulled the trigger. Nothing. Just the sound of the trigger getting pulled back all the way. Damn safety. Cable ran up the stairs toward him. Blaine flicked the firing mode from safety to full auto and unleashed hell at the stairwell. The noise seemed deafening while he held the trigger back, struggling to keep the gun aimed straight. The wood of the walls and stairs splintered and shattered, and smoke filled the area. Cable fell back down to the bottom.

'Holy shit, Blaine,' he said. 'I thought you had me then!'

Blaine got to his feet, dropped the empty machine gun, and hauled himself into the room from which the guard had walked. The large room held two single beds, which protruded from the wall on the left. A window on the right. En suite bathroom at the far end. Blaine walked to the end of the room, and the pain hit him hard. His toes had turned numb. The wound on his side burst with agony. He felt as though on fire while he limped toward the bathroom at the end. The bullet wound in his leg had split open. Blood ran down his trouser leg, filling his shoe. He stepped forward, putting all his weight on the leg, and blacked out.

Blaine came to on the floor; his head must have hit the wall hard, as it throbbed with pain. He was still alive. Which meant he'd only passed out for a second or two. He turned over and pulled his second gun out of his holster. Had he reloaded? He wasn't sure. To check, he pulled out the magazine. Empty.

Footsteps. Creaks of splintered wood echoed up through the house, which now lay silent except for the constant ringing in his ears. Cable didn't shout. Didn't give any of his usual banter. He meant to kill. No more playing.

Blaine just needed more time. Extra seconds would sort everything out. He searched his belt for more ammo. Nothing. He'd run out. Out of ammo. Out of options. He threw the gun away. He wanted to look defeated. He wanted to look like no competition at all. He wanted Cable to talk.

Cable shoved open the door with a brutal kick and flew into the room, aiming his gun at Blaine, who lay half-hidden behind the second bed. Cable stepped forward and saw Blaine on the ground, bleeding, helpless.

'That's the way to go out,' he said. 'Guns blazing. You're good at your job. I'll give you that. You're smart. Methodical and all that. But when it comes to straight out killing, you can't beat me. You never could.'

Blaine placed his hand on the ground slowly and propped himself up against the wall. 'It was that important to know?'

'Now Tommy's gone, there'll be a lot of opportunities

for people like us. A lot of work going. A lot of money. And to be honest, I just needed to know who was the best out of us.' He smiled, satisfied. Proud. Fulfilled. 'Ready?'

Cable's hands shook.

Blaine said, 'Ready when you are.'

Sweat dripped from Cable's forehead. Pools of it gathered on his brow and upper lip. The gun seemed to get heavier and heavier for him, as though he struggled to hold it out straight. He eyes darted about the place. And he tried to pull the trigger but had no control over his fingers. The gun lowered slowly, still shaking in his now feeble hands.

'Feeling a little under the weather, Matthew?'

Cable dropped to his knees, still fighting it. 'What the fuck is this? Poison? You fucking poisoned me? When?'

Blaine winced and got to his feet, standing over him. 'The bar.'

Cable started to convulse, dropped his gun, and fell backward onto the ground. He looked up at Blaine, who stepped forward, looking down at him. 'The bar?—That was ... three days ago. How did ... you know ... I wanted ... to kill you?'

Blaine crouched, picked up the Glock, and checked the magazine. He looked into Cable's dazed, confused eyes. 'Like I told you that night, no-one can ever know who I am. And no-one ever will.'

Cable managed a smirk one last time, as though amused with himself that he could have possibly thought himself better than Jason Blaine. His smirk turned to pain, and he scowled while he went into his death throes.

Blaine moved closer. 'What do you see?' he said. 'What do you see?'

Cable's body became still as though a calm breezed over

him. 'I see ... nothing.' He managed a small smile and chuckled, spluttering blood with every laugh. Blaine took his hand and held it. The grip didn't last long. Cable breathed out one last time, and then stilled.

Blaine let go of his hand and sat on the ground next to him. He leant against the single bed and closed his eyes. He felt a mess. A confrontation with Harrington would end with him or Jessica dead. Likely both. He had the money. It waited right there in the other room.

Blaine reached into his pocket and pulled out the keys for Harrington's car. The extra men he had called still hadn't arrived; he had time. He could throw the bags out of the window right now and load up the vehicle. Get out of the compound before any other hired guns turned up. He could do that. He knew he could. That switch in his head. The one that turns off all those pesky emotions. He flicked it. The girl didn't matter. Not in the grand scheme of things. Julie didn't matter. She despised him anyhow. The money. All about the money. And rescuing Jessica was only about seeing that grateful look on Julie's face. No such thing as a selfless act.

The first bag landed with a thump on the ground below. Blaine looked over at the building at the end. The one with the green door. Movement came from inside. Figures walked around. It seemed that something was about to happen in that place. Blaine ignored it and threw the other bags down to the grass. He took out Harrington's keys and pressed the unlock button. A beep and a flash of lights came from a vehicle parked about ten meters away from the van outside. He only hoped that it hadn't caught many stray bullets.

32
JESSICA

The black van smelled of sweaty men. Two of them sat in the back with her. Leant against the side of the vehicle. From the back, she couldn't see the front. There were no windows either. Jessica could not stop crying. A throbbing pain came from her arms and legs where the men had pulled her from the car. Even her wrists hurt where her mummy had held onto her tightly, trying to keep her safe.

The men didn't tie her up. Didn't hurt her. Just placed her in the back seat of the van and put on her seatbelt. She didn't have a booster seat. Not like the one in Mummy's car. It meant that she ended up too low, and the seatbelt dug into her cheek. She had to hold onto it and pull it down. Though shivering, she didn't feel cold. Her underwear felt damp, but she didn't want to say anything. The men stayed mostly silent, but occasionally, chatted to each other quietly.

After an hour or so of driving, the van stopped. She heard the front doors open, and the men in the front get out. The two men in the back looked at her. They told her that if she stayed quiet, they would bring her food and water.

However, if she screamed or cried, they would have to tape her mouth, and she wouldn't get anything. Jessica nodded. She didn't think she could scream out for help if she tried.

After a few minutes, the side door opened a few inches, and a plastic bag got handed to the men. As the van set off once again, the two men handed her a sandwich and a bottle of water. Jessica didn't feel hungry. She drank some water, though, as her throat hurt. Only then did she take a few bites of the sandwich, and then left the rest.

Her eyes felt sore, and she closed them, leaning against the seatbelt. Maybe this was all a dream. Maybe if she were to fall asleep, she would wake up back at home with Mummy and Daddy. She closed her eyes tightly. She needed to fall asleep. She had to. But she couldn't. So, she just sat there, eyes closed, listening to everything around her. The rumble of the engine. The drone of the road beneath.

It felt like they had travelled for hours. Jessica needed the toilet. She'd tried to hold it for ages but couldn't anymore. Nope, she would have to tell the men she needed to go. It took her a long time to work up the courage. When she finally did, her voice came out all wobbly. Then men looked over. They didn't seem mean. They didn't look angry. They simply asked what she wanted. She made her request, and one of them undid his seatbelt and walked to the back. It worried Jessica that they might hurt her. But the man didn't. He pulled out a white portable toilet from behind the seats and told her to use it. Then he sat back down.

Jessica didn't want to go to the toilet in front of them but couldn't keep holding it. She undid her seatbelt and used the toilet. Tears formed in her eyes again.

When the van stopped at last, and the door opened, she saw that it had grown dark outside. Lots of trees surrounded several buildings. They led her to a building with a green door, where a man—a priest—greeted her, 'My name is Father Cullen. You'll be safe here.' He showed her to a bathroom where she could shower and put on some new clothes. She did so. They seemed like a uniform of sorts. Like her school one but darker.

Father Cullen showed her to a bedroom, where she met two other children, nine-year-old Billy and seven-year-old Samantha. The priest left them alone and told them that dinner would be in half an hour and that Billy and Samantha should help her fit in.

The two of them asked where Jessica came from. They seemed friendly, but still, she just wanted to go home. Then they said they'd both felt the same when they first arrived, but everything would get explained. And then they told her that God had chosen all of them and that they should be happy.

At dinner time, one of the older boys, Jack, led everyone out of the building, and they walked over to the dining hall. Jack looked about fourteen, and Jessica could see that they had put him in charge of all the children. She counted about thirty of them. They all sat along several large wooden tables, and the smell of cooked food filled the air. Everyone sat smiling and looked forward to dinner time. The children joked and laughed while they found their seats. Some argued about who should sit next to who, and it came down to Jack to sort them out. And not in a nice way either. He would shout and grab at the younger children. They always listened to him.

Before the food got brought out, Father Cullen stood and told everyone to pray. He thanked God for the food they were about to eat and for helping them all become stronger as people. He said they should all try hard to work together and always do what God wanted. Then he said Amen, which everyone repeated.

The food tasted good. Beef stew with rice and potatoes. Pots of it sat on each table, and the diners allowed to take as much as they wanted. Always, it seemed, they had more left over. Pudding, a custard tart, had chocolate sprinkles on.

Billy said, 'My favourite.'

He liked to lick off the custard and then eat the pastry. Samantha thought him silly for doing it, especially when he ended up with custard all over his face. It got a good few laughs from everyone around them, but Jack soon got up and told Billy off, saying that he would have punishment that night. Billy didn't say anything else for the rest of the evening.

After dinner, Father Cullen talked a little about their new addition and that everyone should make her feel welcome. Then he told Jessica that this was a special place full of God's chosen few. He made her feel special indeed. Even Billy managed a smile.

That night when they lay in their beds, Jessica told Samantha how she missed her mummy and that she wanted to go home. Samantha told her that none of them could go home. They'd all become orphans now, and God looked after them. This confused Jessica, but Samantha told her that Father Cullen would explain it better tomorrow.

Just when Jessica had managed to fall asleep, she heard the noise of the door opening. She opened her eyes and peered into the gloom. Jack stepped in, walked over to Billy's bed, and yanked off the covers. With a start, Billy sat up. Jack held a gun, which he pointed at Billy's stomach and fired. The gun popped loudly, and Billy grabbed his tummy in

pain, crying and blubbering. The sound of the small plastic
BB pellet bounced around the room. Jessica could see that it
was a plastic, pretend gun, like the one her daddy had. Jack
told the three of them they had ten seconds to run and hide
and that he would come after them. He started counting in
loud, booming tones.

Billy jumped off the bed, and Samantha and Jessica
followed with haste when Jack fired more BB pellets at them.
The three children ran through the long corridor at the top of
the house, and Billy pelted down the stairs until they stood in
the living room. A large room, it had plenty of seating. No
television, just lots of books on shelves and a giant fireplace.

Jessica suggested that they get Father Cullen, but Billy
told her that Jack was allowed to do what he wanted. And he
remained intent on terrorising them. The front door stood
locked, and they could hear Jack coming down the stairs,
taunting them. All the other children would hear too. Most
likely, they all stood and listened at their doors, waiting to see
what would happen and just how bad the new kid would get
it.

Billy pointed to the cupboard in the corner and
suggested that they hide there. Jessica didn't like that idea. It
meant they had nowhere to run to if they got caught. She
and Samantha got in the cupboard with Billy, regardless, and
waited while they heard Jack creeping around, looking for
them. Jessica said, 'We should split up. That way, at least if
he finds one of us, the others would get away.'

Samantha didn't like that idea, but Jessica had a plan.
Jack wasn't that much older; only a few years, but still a boy.
If she and Billy could sneak up behind him, she felt sure they
could get that gun of his off him. The prospect of angering
Jack more terrified Billy, but for definite, he didn't want to

get shot again.

As soon as they heard Jack searching for them in another room, she and Billy got out of the cupboard. Samantha waited behind and made some noise to lure Jack back into the living room. Jessica and Billy waited behind the door, as Jack ran in and listened. He heard the noise in the cupboard and walked over. Billy and Jessica ran at him and pushed him into the cupboard door. His head hit the wood, hard. He turned around and shoved Billy backward and onto the ground. Jessica remembered what her mummy had taught her. If a boy ever tried to hurt her, she should kick him as hard as she could between his legs. At the time, she had laughed at her mummy for saying so, but she put that advice to good use now. Swiftly, she brought her leg into Jack's groin and kicked him hard. He dropped to the floor almost immediately. Jessica took hold of the gun that he still gripped and yanked it hard out of his hand. He lashed out, grabbing hold of the barrel, and Jessica moved her finger to the trigger and fired. The pop banged louder than she'd expected. The plastic pellet hit Jack in the throat, and he let go and shielded his face. Jessica fired again, hitting him in the arm. Jack got up and ran as fast as he could out of the living room. Jessica followed.

Jack ran to the stairs, and Jessica fired again and again while he screamed out in pain. Children watched from the landing above and laughed. Jack yelled out for her to stop, but she didn't want to. She wanted to keep shooting him. Keep dishing out the pain. Jessica hated him. The front door unlocked, and in stepped Father Cullen, who placed his hand on Jessica's, and she stopped shooting.

While Jack sobbed at the bottom of the stairs, Father Cullen crouched next to her.

'You're not in trouble,' he said. 'There are bullies like Jack all over the world and of all ages. God needs people like you to stand up to them. You want to stand up to bullies, don't you, Jessica?'

She nodded.

'We'll teach you how you can. Teach you the best way you can help. We can make it so you will never have to feel afraid of anyone, ever. Would you like that?'

She nodded.

33

UNLOCKED

Holly held her phone up to her ear. The ringing on the other end went on for a while. Just what kind of state would Drake be in? Would he even be at home? Chances were that he'd have gone out to a pub, drowning his sorrows for getting suspended.

She had found a quiet corner of the cafeteria in the station. Closed at this time, it made a useful place for a private call.

Drake picked up.

'Yeah?'

'It's Holly.'

'What do you want?'

'To apologise. I think you had it right.'

'Oh yeah? Well, a bit late now, isn't it? You drew your fucking gun on me.'

'I know. I didn't have all the facts. Why didn't you tell me?'

'Oh, so it's my fault you suddenly chose not to trust me?'

'No, it's just with the coke—'

'I thought this was an apology?'

'I'm sorry, Danny. I am. I need your help. Julie needs your help.'

'I'm not sure what I can do from here.'

'She wants to call the guy. You know? Tommy's guy. She said you had the number.'

'Um ... not on me. My phone ...'

'The one currently in evidence?'

'That's the one.'

'I could get it.'

'Holly, if you get caught removing evidence, you'll get suspended too.'

'I can get it. What's your pin code?'

'No pin.'

'Great.'

'Thumb scanner.'

'For fuck's sake.'

'You could sneak me in?'

'No. I'll get the phone and meet you outside the station. The back of the pub on the corner.'

'Okay. I'll be there.'

'Okay. Okay, see you in a bit.' Holly ended the call.

The evidence lock-up lived on the ground floor. A signed slip from Miles gave the only way to retrieve something, which he wouldn't give her. Not for the phone. Evidence held something else that she could get, though.

Miles seemed about to head off when Holly knocked on his office door, grasping the printed evidence form in her hand. She walked in and saw him tidying his desk.

'You're not still at it, are you, Barnes?'

'I wanted to interview Julie Jones.'

'Now? Leave it until tomorrow. A night in the cells will get her talking.'

'I just think time is of the essence. If you don't mind?'

'What do you need from me?' He pushed in his chair and walked out from behind his desk, turning off his lamp.

'I'd like to take a look at her phone. Read some texts. Show her some family pictures. You know.'

'Yeah ... tug at the heart strings a bit. Sure, okay.' He waved her over, and she handed him the form. The DCI glanced over it, filled it in, and signed. 'Don't work too late, okay.'

'I won't.' She looked at the form, hoping she could alter it somehow. Change the name of who owned the phone. But Miles had stated definitively that the slip was for Julie's phone.

Aaron sat at the desk in evidence. The man had always fancied her. He would always make terrible puns when she was around because she laughed at a joke he'd told one night. She hated herself for it, but she figured playing it flirty offered her only option.

'Hey,' she said.

'Hey, yourself,' Aaron said.

'Had a good day?'

'Yeah, not bad. And I see plenty of *evidence* of a good day tomorrow too!'

Holly laughed and shook her head. 'Oh, Aaron, you are always so sharp.'

'Thank you. So, what can I do for you, m'lady?'

'I need to go grab a phone.'

'Oh, I'll get that for you.'

'It's fine. I know exactly what I'm looking for.'

'Well, there are still kinda rules about it.' Though being

friendly, she could see he wouldn't budge. She hadn't realised he could be such a stickler for the rules.

'Why don't we both go? I wouldn't mind a little late night tour of your kingdom.'

'Yeah?' He smiled but looked surprised.

Holly played it cool, looking like she felt tired of work. 'Yeah.'

Aaron picked up his keys and opened the door for her. They walked into the back, and a smaller version of the ending of Raiders of The Lost Ark met her. On each of the metal shelving units sat sickly-coloured cardboard boxes. Rows upon rows of them. Each with a bright-yellow sticker on them, showing a unique number.

'Well, here we are,' Aaron said. 'Enough boxes to last you a lifetime. Although, I'm not sure what you'd actually use them for at home. Too small to move house with. You know.'

He stood babbling. Nerves. Holly smiled at him. It made him chuckle and look around the room. 'It's like Raiders of the Lost Ark in here, isn't it?' he said.

'I just thought that exact same thing.' Holly looked at the evidence slip, which prompted Aaron to look too and help her.

'Yep. Over here,' he said. 'End of the row.' They walked over to the shelf and found the specific box that contained Julie's belongings. Two cartons away from it sat the newest arrival in the evidence room. No others near it. The container had to have Drake's phone in there.

'It's just the phone I need,' Holly said.

'Sure.' Aaron smiled and opened the box, revealing everything that Julie'd had on her at the time of her arrest. Aaron handed her the phone. 'So, what do you think of my world of never ending evidence?'

'It's great, Aaron. Can I tell you something?'

He gulped. 'Yeah. Yeah, of course.'

'I've been meaning to ask you for a drink but ...'

'But what?'

'Oh, this is silly ...'

'What?'

'Can you make sure no-one else will come in?'

'No-one else will come in. I promise.'

'But ... could you just check?'

'Okay.' He smiled again and licked his lips as he took a few steps toward the door. He must have beamed with delight inside. It looked like he could hardly contain himself. Eventually, he turned away and headed for the door.

Holly grabbed the evidence box at the end and opened it up. No phone. Just a small bag of what looked like cocaine and some cash. That couldn't be right. That shelf held no other boxes. Drake's phone should have come in. It should be right there. She put the lid back on the box and opened another. And another. She started to panic. Aaron would have looked around the corridor by now. He would be on his way back. She opened another. Nothing. No phone. Aaron stepped back into the room at the far corner. She had seconds before he would see her. Holly had to calm down. She looked at the numbers on the labels. They weren't sequential. Aaron had some crazy filing system. The shelf she stood looking at contained all criminal evidence for people here in the cells. One of the others had to contain other new evidence. She had five shelves to choose from. Five rows on each. If Drake's phone proved the last thing to come in, it would have to occupy the end of a row. Aaron made his way toward her.

'No-one out there,' he said. 'Think we're all alone.'

The top shelf. Further down. Not many boxes on that level. She walked down the aisle and reached up, grabbing the box on the end. Opened it. A single phone sat inside. Quickly, she swapped phones and put the box back. Aaron practically skipped around the corner to see her.

'So, you thought maybe getting a drink sometime?'

'Yeah,' said Holly. 'I'm just not sure it's professional though, is it?'

Aaron's face dropped. 'We could be ... very ... professional about it.'

'It's probably not a good idea, Aaron. I'd better go. Thanks for this.' She held up the phone, tightly gripping it in her hand so as not to reveal the completely different brand.

'Well,' Aaron said. 'I'll be here. If you change your mind. Trying not to get ... bored.' He laughed to himself. 'Cardboard ... bored. No? Aah.'

With a chuckle, she walked out, leaving Aaron alone with his boxes.

———

Drake waited at the back of the police station's local pub for her. Rain had begun to fall. He smiled. Though he didn't look drunk, Holly couldn't tell for sure.

'Hi,' she said.

'Did you get it?'

'I got it.'

'You are good, Miss Barnes. I'll give you that.'

'Are we doing the right thing?'

'If it saves that kid. Yeah. Sometimes, you have to do something wrong when it's for the right reasons.'

'I guess so.' She pulled out the phone and handed it to

Drake. He turned it on and placed his thumb on the scanner. 'I'm sorry I didn't trust you, Drake,' she said.

'You called me Danny on the phone.'

'You want me to call you Danny?'

'Yes, call me Danny!'

'Okay, I'll call you Danny.'

'Except for if we end up in bed ... then call me Drake. Sounds official.'

Holly laughed. She couldn't help but picture it, and not a bad picture either. Just how much of a joke had he intended? 'Do you think it's a possibility?'

'Who knows,' he said, trying to look confident. He navigated the phone to his contacts and held out the screen toward her. She snapped a photo of the number and took Drake's phone back.

The rain came down harder and made Holly squint her eyes as it splashed off her face. 'Okay, I'd better get back.'

'Yeah,' Drake said. 'Me too. Look, keep me updated, okay?'

'I will,' she said. They waited for a moment; standing in the rain together.

Drake reached into his pocket. 'Holly. I wanted you to see this.' He pulled out the small vial of coke she had caught him with. He ran it over his fingers for a while and then launched it as hard as he could over the back wall.

'What are you doing?' Holly said. 'Some kid could find that!'

'I was trying to do something meaningful ... throwing it away, you know?'

'You could have tipped it out. Or stepped on it?'

'Jesus, Holly, I'm trying to do the right thing here.'

Holly sighed and lunged forward, kissing Drake on the

lips. He kissed her back, placing his hands on her face, caressing her damp skin.

Slowly, Holly pulled back and smiled. She didn't say anything else. Didn't feel like she needed to. She liked seeing a surprised look on his face.

———

Back at the station, Holly walked into Julie's cell, and the woman looked relieved to see her. The detective handed Julie a note with the number written on it and told her that she had arranged her phone call. She passed her the phone and waited by the door.

Julie punched the number into the keypad and held the phone to her ear. She waited for several rings before someone answered. 'It's Julie,' she said. 'No, I'm still here. They let me have a phone call, so I called. Do you have her?'

Julie listened. Her face dropped. Tears welled in her eyes. 'Stop,' she said. 'Just stop talking and listen. Are you listening? You have to go back. Right now. You have to. I don't care how hard it'll be. I don't care what you have to do. But you *will* go back and you *will* pick Jessica up and you *will* drive her back to me, right now, and I'll tell you why you'll do it, Jason.' She paused for a moment, as though gathering her thoughts. 'You'll do it because I know you only look out for yourself. I know you don't care about anyone but your own flesh and blood. But, Jason, she's your daughter.'

34

KIDS WITH MACHINE GUNS

Blaine hauled the final bag of cash into the back of Harrington's car. His whole body ached, and blood continued to trickle down his leg. It wouldn't make the first time he would have to stop in the middle of nowhere to sort himself out; stop the bleeding—change his clothes. He needed to get out of the area fast. Movement in the building with the green door caught his eye. Blaine closed the back of the vehicle, and suddenly, an onslaught of machine gun fire met him. Short bursts fired from the open windows of the building. Nothing hit close. All the shots went too high and hit the building behind him. Blaine got into the car and started the engine. A couple of bullets hit the roof, but the angle caused them to ping off with a whizzing sound. The side window at the back shattered, as he pushed down on the accelerator and drove away. The firing stopped. He didn't want to think about who handled those guns.

The road ahead lay completely dark. No streetlights. Only the headlights on the car illuminated the winding path to the exit. It gave the only way in or out by vehicle. Blaine had gotten a hundred meters away from the encampment when his phone vibrated in his pocket. He let it ring, wanting to concentrate on getting out first. But only a few people had the number. And three of them now lay dead somewhere. He pulled out the phone and answered.

'Yes?'

Julie spoke.

'Did they let you out already?' he said. Drake listened to her ask if he had Jessica. He pulled over and cut the engine, so at least he could hear if people were coming. 'Julie ... I'm in a bad way. Cable's dead. More soldiers are coming. It's just impossible. I'm sorry.'

She cut him off. Her voice sounded grating and angry.

'I know this isn't what you want to hear, Julie—' She cut him off again. Her words filled with such incredible passion and love with a biting edge that Blaine had never experienced from anyone before. It made him listen. And then she said it. Blaine's heart raced. He didn't want it to be true. More than anything, he wanted her to be lying, trying to manipulate him. But she wasn't. Deep down, he knew. Always had.

Blaine pulled the phone away from his ear and hung up. He looked at the black screen for a moment, his dark reflection staring back, and put the phone back in his pocket. Tonight, he would die.

Resigned, he placed his hand on the gear stick and put the vehicle in reverse. After a messy three-point turn, he headed back to the encampment.

At terrific speed, he drove the car back to the building with the green door. He wanted to catch Harrington unawares. Once there, he skidded to a halt and climbed out, holding Cable's Glock in his right hand. He marched up to the front door and fired at the lock, shattering the wood to pieces. Then he kicked the door wide open and walked in. Footsteps ran around upstairs. Muffled talking reached him.

Then a loud, booming American voice sounded, 'Okay, kids ... this is what you've trained for. He's here to kill you all. Sent by the devil. But he's just a man. So, pick up your guns, and you don't stop firing until he's lying on the ground.'

The voice came from upstairs, and Blaine stepped toward them. A kid moved out from the end of the hallway. Only about twelve. In his hands, he held an MP5K machine gun. Slightly smaller than the MP5 with an added grip at the front. The perfect automatic weapon for a child to handle, and he'd aimed it at Blaine. The boy didn't fire, but Blaine could see him building up the nerve to do so. Likely, another fifteen children occupied the building, who would do the same. A gunshot would only scare them more.

'Son, put down the gun,' Blaine said. 'I'm not here to hurt you.'

The boy said nothing. His hands shook.

Blaine took a step away from the stairs and looked into the boy's eyes with his most sincere expression. 'Put down the gun,' he said.

The boy closed his eyes. He would pull the trigger. He wouldn't listen. He wouldn't drop the gun.

A loud bang sounded, and the boy's right shoulder exploded with blood. He fell to the ground, screaming, and dropped the weapon. Immediately, Blaine raised his weapon to the top of the stairs, where two more boys had appeared, also holding MP5Ks. Blaine fired up at the wall next to them, showering them with debris. They backed off.

Machine gun fire came from his left. Three kids at the doorway of the living room. They shot blind. Best to clear the ground floor before moving up. Speedily, Blaine limped his way to the living room and waited at the door. A gun, once again, poked around the frame, but before it could fire, Blaine grabbed it and yanked it hard out of the kid's hands. He walked around the corner and saw three children—a boy and two girls. Only the boy had fired.

The girls looked utterly terrified and raised their weapons. Blaine swung the MP5K he had in his left hand onto their faces. One dropped her gun. The other pulled the trigger. It sprayed a blast of three bullets into the wall behind him. Blaine dropped both guns he had and grabbed hers. He yanked it from her grip and pulled out the magazine. The boy grabbed at him, trying to get the weapon back. Blaine picked him up and threw him hard against the wall. Not enough to seriously injure, just bruise enough not to get up.

He took the guns and, one-by-one, quickly stripped them down to their separate parts. He kept the locking pins too, so even if the kids had been shown how to field strip and assemble them, they would now prove useless. He left the two other kids huddled together, bleeding from their noses, and crying. Blaine walked through the living room and out through another door, stepping over the first kid, who now lay on the ground bleeding, still wailing in pain. The smoke alarms set off, and Blaine fired at the white disc on the ceiling, stopping the screeching sound. The ground floor cleared, he moved back to the stairs and fired a couple of rounds up, letting the kids know to get out of his way.

Blaine ignored the pains in his leg and side and ran up the steps. A long corridor lay beside him with a good few doors. The stairs continued up in a spiral next to him. He could hear voices both in the rooms and on the second floor.

Harrington's huge, pissed-off voice boomed out, 'I'm

not hearing anyone firing.'

A door opened outward, and another frightened boy stepped out, holding his gun. Blaine sprinted toward him and kicked the door back onto his face. Then he took his gun from him and left it in pieces. A few more tried their luck, but Blaine walked through them as though they were made of paper, leaving them bruised and bloodied. He walked up to the second floor, which appeared more open plan. A few closed doors led off, but mainly one large space with lots of seating greeted him. More kids scattered around. Only three armed.

Harrington pounced out of the doorway to his right, gun in hand. Blaine grabbed his wrists, as he fired a shot, which went past Blaine's body. He brought his elbow up at speed and clocked Harrington hard in the chin. He winced and had bitten his tongue. Blood trickled out of his mouth, and he brought a knee up into Blaine's leg.

The sharp pain of his wound ricocheted through his body and, for a moment, his legs gave way. He held onto Harrington, as he didn't want to put any space between them. Not with the gun still in Harrington's hand. The American took advantage and delivered a devastating few blows to Blaine's face. Jason shrugged off the assault and concentrated on aiming the gun downward. He fired, blowing a couple of toes off Harrington's right foot. The guy screamed out in pain and let go of his gun, which thumped onto the wooden floorboards. Blaine pushed him back onto the ground and held his gun up at his chest.

'Stop.'

The yell came from a boy, older than the others; about fourteen. He held a handgun to Jessica's head, hiding behind her.

'Drop the gun,' he said. 'Do it.'

'Good boy, Jack,' Harrington said.

Blaine looked at Jessica, who stood sobbing quietly. Her eyes red. Her cheeks stained with dried tears.

Harrington winced and smiled at Blaine. 'Put down the gun. Or I tell him to do it. And, believe me, he will do it. Won't you, Jack?'

'Yes, Sir,' he said.

Blaine believed him. He could see it in the boy's eyes. Like a mirror. He had a thirst for blood. Enjoyed the power.

'What was the plan, Harrington?' Blaine said. 'Train them to become assassins? You have some patience.'

'It took time and planning but it'll be worth it. They do the Lord's work. Without question. They won't backstab. They won't ask for more money. They'll die getting the job done.'

'And you'll hire them out. An army of devout killers all at your control. And all funded by their own kidnappings.'

'Oh, we have more funding. You have no idea. I mean, who the fuck are you?'

'I'm the guy shutting you down.' Blaine stepped on his foot, and Harrington screamed some more.

'Hey!' Jack said.

Blaine turned his attention to him and stepped forward.

'Don't fucking move,' Jack said. He put his arm around Jessica and lifted her up slightly, still holding the gun to her head. Then he moved backward.

'Jack. These people kidnapped you,' Blaine said. 'They took you from your parents. And they've filled your head with bullshit. There is no God here. Just death ... and money.'

'I'm not an idiot.' He screamed the words out of his

mouth. 'I know what this is. And I don't care. I don't want it to end. So, put your fucking gun down.'

The boy was losing it. Blaine had a chance to end this quickly. Though risky, that was his job. To make the tough decisions. He took another step forward and tightened his grip on his gun.

Jack's face grew angrier. 'Stop. Moving. Forward.'

'You little prick. You wanna play with guns, do you? Come on, then. Shoot me. That's all you have to do to stop this. Don't hide behind a girl like a fucking pansy. Are you a killer or not? Eh? Jack? Or is it Jill? What are you gonna do? Huh? What the fuck is a little lost boy like you gonna do, you pathetic piece of shit. Go on, have a cry. Go on.'

'Shut the fuck up.' Jack removed the weapon from Jessica's head and pointed it at Blaine.

Blaine lifted his gun fast and fired at Jack's exposed shins. Along with the bang of the gunshot came a crack of bone, and both Jack and Jessica fell to the ground. Jack proved tougher than he'd thought, though. While screaming in pain, he raised the gun to Jessica's head. Blaine raised his weapon once more and held his breath. He couldn't miss. He fired. The bullet whipped through Jack's skull, making a contorted mess of his face. The boy fell limp to the ground. Jessica held back the tears.

Another gunshot rang out, and Blaine felt the bullet hit him in the lower back, on his left-hand side. He fell to one knee and turned to see Harrington. Gun in hand. Blaine returned fire. Two rounds. Both hit Harrington square in the face.

Blaine held up his gun at the other children. He waved it from one to the other. 'This is over,' he said. 'I don't want to hurt you. Put down your guns. Now.' They did. He got to his feet, staggered over to Jessica—who still lay on the ground —and knelt next to her. 'Jessica?'

She looked up at him.

'I'm a friend of your mummy. She asked me to come and take you home. Shall we go see her?'

Jessica nodded and burst into tears. Blaine held out a hand, which she took hold of.

'What about the others?' Jessica said.

'What?'

'The others. Are you taking the others home too?'

Blaine glanced around the room. The children all looked hopeful.

'I'll see what I can do.'

They made their way downstairs, and Jessica told everyone that he'd come here to take them home. It seemed like a light bulb switched on in their minds. All that brainwashing suddenly disappeared at the thought of seeing their parents again. Blaine didn't have the heart to tell them that, most likely, they'd all become orphans.

They got to the ground floor and stepped outside. Vehicle lights approached. More than one. At least three vehicles made their way up the road to the compound. Harrington's backup. The men he had called earlier. They had arrived, and Blaine didn't have long until he bled to death.

35
FLESH AND BLOOD

'Get back inside,' Blaine said. 'Get upstairs.' The children rushed back up the stairs. Outside, the armed men exited the three large SUVs. It looked like four men in each. Twelve in total. All coming for him. He pushed the door closed. The broken lock meant it would never stay shut without help. With a grunt, he grabbed the wooden table next to it and knocked it on its side in front of the door. Though not heavy enough to keep them out, it would keep it shut. 'Jessica,' Blaine said, seeing her panicking near him. 'Bring me that gun. And any magazines you can find.'

Jessica retrieved an MP5K from the floor and handed it to Blaine, who checked the ammo—full. He would need it. The men outside circled the building. They would soon have every entrance covered. Blaine moved into the living room. Immediately, the men outside the front spotted him. They opened fire, shattering the large window. Blaine moved back to the hallway and returned fire. One of the men took a hit in the chest and stumbled backward. He didn't go down. They all wore heavy-grade body armour. Blaine moved as fast as he could toward the back. Gunfire at the front would make a perfect distraction for others to enter through the back door.

And, right on cue, he heard a door opening. The other side of the kitchen. They'd entered the house. Pain lanced and throbbed throughout his whole body, and doubly so with every step he made. Blaine put his back to the wall with the entrance to the kitchen next to him. With the strap of the MP5K over his shoulder, he pulled out the Glock. The 9mm bullets it contained had more stopping power. He waited while the sounds of creeping footsteps grew closer. Slowly, the barrel of a gun protruded from the doorway. Blaine grabbed hold of it, shoved his Glock into the man's face, and fired. It sprayed an explosion of blood and bone over the men behind him. Then Blaine grabbed hold of the man without a face and held him close to his body. The two other men in the kitchen fired. Their shots slammed into the body armour of their colleague. Blaine shoved the Glock under the dead man's arm and fired from his armpit. Another headshot. The other man stopped firing and moved for cover further inside the kitchen.

Blaine pushed the body he held into the room and dived along with it. The soldier fired his gun, hitting the dead body again, and sending plumes of red over Blaine's face. They hit the ground with a splash of blood, and Blaine fired repeatedly into the man's legs, tearing them to pieces. He yelled out in pain and collapsed to his knees, which gave way on impact with a stomach-churning crunch. Blaine fired once more into the man's face, putting him out of his misery.

He pushed the body from him and dropped the empty Glock. On each of the men's vests hung three grenades. Blaine grabbed one.

Feet crunched on broken glass. The men had climbed in through the broken window at the front. Blaine grabbed hold of the machine gun and walked back to the hallway. Jessica lay curled on the ground with her hands over her ears. The soldiers stood in the living room. One wall away.

'Get upstairs,' Blaine said. 'Go.' He fired at the living-room doorway, and the girl ran up the stairs. The men returned fire, through the wall. Dust and plaster flew around Blaine, and he hit the ground fast. The hallway filled with smoke and dust, and Blaine moved as close to the wall as possible. The doors of the large cupboard in the hall splintered apart when hot metal flew through them. The top hinge of the left door pinged off and hit the opposite wall. The door flew open wide to reveal several small coats, now shredded. Light shone through the bullet holes in the wall at the back. It looked thin. Breakable.

The gunfire died down. Soldiers walked into the hallway from both sides. Blaine dropped his MP5K and pulled the pin on the grenade. He stood and ran for the cupboard, dropping the grenade behind him. The men held their guns up at Blaine and shot. Through a hail of gunfire, Blaine slammed into the cupboard, through the tattered coats, and smashed through the broken drywall. The men collected at the cupboard and fired at Blaine, who rolled out of sight. The grenade exploded behind, ripping their limbs from their bodies and sending a dense cloud of red through the wall and into the living room. Blaine's ears had grown used to the gunfire, but that explosion left him almost entirely deaf. His head thumped with pain. He found it hard to breathe and had no gun. More gunfire came from outside. He estimated four more men to go. Blaine crawled back through the smoking hole in the wall and picked up one of the men's machine guns and another grenade. Every step left a puddle of blood. His right foot felt soaking wet. He didn't want to pass out again but could feel it coming. With a shake of his head to clear it, he stepped toward the front door. The unmistakable sound of two grenades hitting the living room floor reached him. He had seconds before they blew. Frustrated and fighting to remain conscious, he wrenched the table away from the door and stepped outside.

The living room exploded, sending glass and debris out of the window. Blaine stood still while smoke surrounded him. He could see two men behind the SUVs, taking cover. Quickly, he threw the two grenades under the vehicle and yelled, 'Frag out!' Blaine aimed the machine gun, holding it steady in his bleeding hands. The men ran from behind the vehicle and directly into Blaine's gunfire. He didn't stop until they both lay dead.

More shots rang out behind him. One hit him in the left arm. Blaine turned and fired back, holding the machine gun with his right hand. His aim went all over the place while he tried to spot his attackers. One guy on the left-hand corner of the building. Another on the right. He took out the man on the left, but his gun had emptied. And he had no way to reload. Also, no time. The guy on the right stepped out. Blaine staggered and fell to one knee. He couldn't stay upright. The man took his time to aim his gun. Directly at Blaine's head. A burst of gunfire screamed out. The man's side ripped apart when two of the children, one of them Jessica, fired their weapons. The soldier turned toward them, but the barrage of bullets kept coming, tearing the body armour on his chest and making a mess of his face. He fell to the ground, and the kids stopped. They looked around, covering the area like experts.

'Clear,' Jessica said.

Blaine took in a deep breath and collapsed to the grass.

He awoke to find Jessica and a few of the other children tending to his wounds. Someone had taught them a lot. A tight bandage wrapped his leg, and tape covered his arm and side, stopping the bleeding from his many wounds. He still lay on the ground outside.

'He's awake,' a girl said.

Jessica looked over at him with a serious expression. 'Are we still going home?'

Blaine put his hands on the earth and lifted himself to a seated position. He looked at the thirty or so children, and then over at Harrington's car. 'Yeah.' He nodded. 'We're still going home.' It took some effort, but he managed to get to his feet with the help of the kids and looked over at the SUVs. Still not enough space. Only the black van that had arrived a while ago would suit their needs. It sat full of bullet holes, and the windows had smashed and shattered, but the tyres seemed fine. If the engine would start, it would provide their only way home.

He limped over to the van and opened the driver's door. No keys in the ignition. 'Okay, kids, I need you to find the keys. They're probably in the trouser pocket of one of these guys. Check around here and then in the house. Search everyone.'

Without hesitation, they reached inside the mens' blood-soaked pockets. Blaine pointed to Harrington's vehicle. 'I need the four bags from that car taken out and brought over.'

The children obeyed without question and dragged over the huge bags of money. 'Okay,' Blaine said. 'Put them in the back of the van, and then get everyone inside too.' They did as instructed and pushed in the bags.

'We found a few keys.' Jessica ran over and showed them to Blaine. He picked out one set.

'These are the ones,' he said, and then moved to the driver's seat and put the keys in the ignition. The engine roared to life. He couldn't believe it. Even with all those holes, it started.

'I don't think we'll all fit,' Jessica said.

Blaine stepped out and looked into the back of the vehicle. The four huge bags of cash took up so much space. And about ten kids still stood waiting to squash themselves in somehow. 'Just move up,' Blaine said. 'Squash up. Some of you can ride in the front too.'

'There's not enough room with the bags,' Jessica said.

'Okay.' Blaine frowned in thought. 'I can call the police; they can come collect you.'

'No,' one girl said. 'Don't leave us.'

Blaine said nothing. He looked at the children, all huddled close together in the van. If they were all a few years younger, they would have fit. 'Get out,' he said. 'Everyone out.'

He pulled out his phone and dialled the last number to call him. He didn't have to wait long before someone answered. 'I want to talk to Julie Jones,' he said. 'You know who it is. Put her on.'

He waited.

'Julie. I've got her. She's coming home.'

He waited for one more moment.

'Can you put the officer back on. I have a few

conditions.'

36

I'M NOT HERE, I NEVER WAS

Blaine kept his demands simple. He wanted Julie to meet him at the Banbury Cricket Club off the M40, a place he had noticed when checking the map before he and Cable had headed off. A large open car park that offered plenty of space. It even had a Premier Inn with a Toby Carvery next to it. The officer he had spoken to, Holly, told him that it might take some doing to get that signed off, but she would do everything she could. Blaine's second demand had to remain secret. He wanted Drake to meet him also, but the authorities couldn't know this. Holly gave him her private number and said she would get back to him.

Blaine drove the van out of the compound and back to the stashed rented car in which he and Cable had arrived. He reclaimed his duffel bag and continued to drive out of Wales, only staying awake through sheer pain. Jessica fell asleep next to him in no time. They didn't speak. He caught himself glancing over at her. A tough little thing. He liked that. Part of him wanted to tell her he was her father, but he knew it would only make life that much harder for her. Instead, he put it out of his mind.

Two-and-a-half hours later, and the van ran on fumes. Blaine had considered it lucky that the van had a nearly full tank. The last thing he needed was to pull up to a petrol station looking the way he did. He wouldn't have been able to use the self-pay service either, as he only had cash. At Banbury, he pulled off the M40 and drove past the Premier Inn to the car park of the cricket club behind. Two cars waited for him.

Blaine came to a stop. Drake stepped out of one car and Holly and Julie out of the other. Blaine opened his door and climbed out. The two police officers stood waiting. Julie didn't manage as much calm. She rushed over to the van while Blaine opened the passenger door and lifted a still sleeping Jessica into his arms. He could see the panic on Julie's face while he held the limp body of their daughter. The cold night air woke her up, and Blaine lowered her to the ground.

Jessica saw Julie running toward her and shouted, 'Mummy.' Julie wrapped her arms around her and lifted her off the ground, holding her tightly.

Drake and Holly walked over, and Blaine opened the side door of the van, and one by one, the missing children all stepped out.

'Jesus fucking Christ,' Drake said. Holly nudged him with her elbow as though telling him not to swear in front of kids.

None of them had any idea what the youngsters had gone through. For sure, hearing a few swear words seemed like nothing when compared to taking a man's life.

Julie put Jessica down and held her hand as the children walked past them and over to Holly and Drake. She looked at Blaine and walked straight up to him, still holding Jessica's hand. Once near, she hugged him. It hurt. And felt good. The three of them stood there for a moment, close to each other.

'Thank you,' Julie said. She turned her attention back to Jessica and told her to go and wait with her friend Holly, and the girl did so.

'Is she okay?' Julie said.

'She's tough,' Blaine said.

'Really?' Julie had tears in her eyes. 'I couldn't stop thinking how she would scream and cry whenever I brushed her hair. I couldn't even imagine how she felt, getting taken like that.'

Blaine smiled. 'I think she'll surprise you.'

Julie's face turned serious. 'Don't think this makes up for the damage you've done. For the decision you made me make. I'll never forgive you for that, no matter how grateful I am that Jessica is safe. Okay?'

Blaine nodded. Julie walked back over to Jessica, and they got back in Holly's car.

Drake stepped over. 'You wanted me here?'

'Yes,' Blaine said. 'You got a call from me this afternoon, telling you to meet me at that location in Wales. Together, we stormed a compound filled with armed men and rescued the kidnapped children. I got shot and killed. The police will find the body of a man on the first floor of one of the buildings. In a bedroom. Along with the five-million pounds that Julie took.'

'And you?'

'I'm not here. I never was.'

'They'll never believe that I managed to do this.'

'Doesn't matter. It looks better than the truth. So, they'll go for it.'

'But the children ... they'll take statements from them. We can't ask them to lie.'

'Kids,' Blaine said. They looked over at him. 'If anyone asks ... this is the man who rescued you. Okay?'

They all responded with a 'Yes, Sir,' and Blaine looked back at Drake with a sly smirk.

'What were they doing up there?' Drake said.

'I don't know.'

Drake nodded, unsure whether to believe him. He looked Blaine up and down, noticing the state of him. 'We should get you to a hospital.'

'No hospital.'

'You have multiple gunshot wounds. You need help.'

'I know a guy. Not far from here. He's good with repairs. Bullet wounds and laptops.' Blaine looked over at the kids, as Holly herded them toward the warmth of the Premier Inn.

'You need a lift?' Drake said.

'I need your car. I'll let you know where to find it tomorrow.'

Drake held up his keys. 'What choice do I have?'

Blaine took them, pulled his bag out of the van, and walked over to Drake's car.

'Is all the money still there?' Drake said. 'The whole lot?'

Blaine placed his overfilled duffel bag in the passenger seat and looked back at Drake. 'Pretty much.'

'It's probably not a good idea to leave the country just yet. Not looking like that.'

Blaine looked over at Holly's car, which held Julie hugging Jessica in the back. 'Who said I planned to leave?'

Blaine got in the car and started the engine. Julie looked

over at him. Maybe she would smile. She didn't. Jessica's head popped up from her mother's shoulder and looked over. She did smile; waved as well.

Blaine returned the smile and wave. He put the car into gear, placed a hand on the duffel bag next to him, and drove out of the car park. As he pulled out onto the motorway, Blaine reached into his pocket and retrieved his phone. He scrolled down to the contact named *Repairs* and dialled. His contact answered in a couple of rings.

'Yeah?'

'I need a repair job.'

'Body or tech?'

'Both.'